Old Ground

Dominic Kearney

Old Ground

Copyright © 2025 Dominic Kearney

All Rights Reserved

All rights reserved. No portion of this book may be reproduced, stored in a retrieval system or transmitted at any time or by any means mechanical, electronic, photocopying, recording or otherwise without the prior written permission of the publisher.

The authors of the respective chapters within are reproduced here with permission, and with their individual rights asserted in accordance with the Copyright, Design and Patents Act 1988.

ISBN: 978-1-0369-2460-7

DisclaimerThe views, thoughts, and opinions expressed in each chapter are those of the respective author and do not necessarily reflect those of the host, curator, or publisher. While every effort has been made to ensure accuracy and appropriateness, the responsibility for all content lies solely with the contributing author. The author and TAUK Publishing accept no liability for any errors, omissions, or statements that may be construed as defamatory, libellous, or otherwise actionable.

Published in the United Kingdom

For Fionnuala and Sorcha.

Acknowledgements

Thank you to Steve and Ella for their comments and advice, and to Brendan for taking the time to read through the drafts.

Contents

Chapter One	1
Chapter Two	4
Chapter Three	6
Chapter Four	22
Chapter Five	25
Chapter Six	28
Chapter Seven	38
Chapter Eight	41
Chapter Nine	47
Chapter Ten	52
Chapter Eleven	61
Chapter Twelve	65
Chapter Thirteen	68
Chapter Fourteen	74
Chapter Fifteen	91

Chapter Sixteen	100
Chapter Seventeen	115
Chapter Eighteen	138
Chapter Nineteen	144
Chapter Twenty	150
Chapter Twenty-one	159
Chapter Twenty-two	174
Chapter Twenty-three	179
Chapter Twenty-four	181
Chapter Twenty-five	185
Chapter Twenty-six	200
Chapter Twenty-seven	209
Chapter Twenty-eight	218
Chapter Twenty-nine	222
Chapter Thirty	235
About the author	239
Past Titles	241

Chapter One

Now

Rosalind looked at her watch without seeing the time and then looked again and saw it was just coming up to 10.30am. She had no idea how long the train had been standing there. She hadn't noticed it stopping in the first place.

Not long, she guessed, given that none of the other passengers was showing signs of impatience or restlessness. Maybe there'd been an announcement she hadn't heard, giving the reason and duration. Maybe there hadn't, and they'd just shrugged and accepted it. That was certainly how Rosalind felt. There was nothing she could do, so she did nothing.

There were whispered conversations in the carriage, the kind people have when all around is silence. The man sitting opposite Rosalind was staring out of the window. Rosalind did the same. She looked at fields of hard soil and blades of grass still held by frost beneath a sky that was blue with spatters of cloud and a dazzling sun that filled the carriage with light and no heat. The sunlight scorched her mind, filled it with blazing white that threatened pain. The light would fade soon, she thought.

She had no idea where the train was and couldn't recall what time it had left or when it was due at its destination.

When Jack was a boy, he and Rosalind used to play a game. It was whispered on buses or trains so as not to be overheard.

They would pick out other passengers and make up stories about them: where they were going, why they were making the journey, who they would meet.

She briefly asked herself about the man sitting opposite. Maybe thirty years old, dressed neatly and casually in a crew neck sweater and shirt. He was slim, had short hair and was clean-shaven. On the seat next to him was a laptop bag; on the table that divided them he had placed his phone and a novel, the title and author of which she didn't recognise.

Why is he making this journey? she wondered. *Why is he travelling all the way from Exeter to Manchester? Maybe he isn't, of course. Maybe he'll get off at one of the stops along the way, to attend a meeting or address a conference. Not to shop, though, and it's too early in December for him to be travelling for Christmas. And what if he is playing the same game? What would he see? He'd think me old: an old woman, pale, her skin lined and dull. A battered shoulder bag stuffed with underwear and a change of clothes. Her hair grey and brittle, in need of attention, in need of a cut that would cost more than she could afford. She hasn't yet taken off that thin, drab, navy raincoat, underneath which was an old sweater, worn at the elbows, underneath which was a thin and tired body in need of food and coffee.*

He would never guess the reason for my journey, she thought. *He could never look at me and think I am travelling to keep vigil at the side of my son Jack's hospital bed, to watch helpless while he recovers or dies. Dies.*

The train moved off; a sense of relief and return to normality swept through the carriage. Normal volume was restored.

Rosalind had felt no impatience, and now she felt no ease despite the urgency of her mission. She had laid down her arms and surrendered the moment she opened the door to find a police officer, anxious, uncertain, unused to the task facing her.

The surrender was due. There was no point in pretending to fight on. Jack was the final blow.

And so she did nothing and felt nothing. Just yielded, yielded all semblance of control and power. No need, then, to question her feelings or actions, no need, no desire. No self-recrimination. No guilt. If she had no control, if she was litter caught in the wind, then how could she have blame? She understood that and welcomed it, a release, a blessed release. No obligation now to halt the slow slide, to arrest the deterioration, to pretend things could be better if only she tried harder. She would just do. No requirement to think any longer.

Chapter Two

Now

She picked up her phone and scrolled down to Gerard's number. How long had it been since they saw each other last? 1990? Maybe '91, '92? Call it thirty years, a nice round number. Thirty years since they split up. A couple of phone calls since then, no more than that, and only in the weeks following the break-up, to sort the odds and ends that remained when all else had gone, following a relationship that lasted two years and had seemed set to last for many more at one point. A toothbrush, some clothes, books, always more than you think, boxed or bagged and retrieved during polite, brief visits.

"I think I got everything," Gerard said. "But have a look for yourself."

He was in Manchester, where Rosalind would have to change for Liverpool. She had no reason to call him. She had given him little thought since the break-up and didn't think he'd have given her much thought either. They exchanged Christmas cards for a few years. When she and Mark and Jack moved house, she sent Gerard her new address and included her mobile number. He gave her his mobile in a card: 'Wishing you every happiness in your new home'. And they remembered each other's birthdays for a while. But such contact was sporadic, and the messages inside the cards never suggested regret for either of them, went barely any further than the printed messages the cards already contained.

She pressed 'Dial' and then immediately ended the call, pressed 'Dial' again and then immediately ended the call again. She called a third time and let it ring until Gerard answered.

"It's me." He didn't recognise her voice, she could tell. "Ros," she said. She could tell that even then, he wasn't sure, couldn't immediately find the name in his files, couldn't make it fit anywhere. It had been thirty years. She sensed him floundering. "Rosalind," she said. "We used to…"

"Ros," he said. "Yes, sorry. Of course. Rosalind. Sorry, I was just…I wasn't…"

Thirty years.

"I shouldn't have called," she said. "Are you busy?"

"Yes," he said. She liked that, liked the directness of the response. He didn't use to be like that. And then he breathed, recovered himself, recalled social convention. "I mean, it's okay." He forced brightness. "What can I do for you?"

"It doesn't matter," she said. "I'll call later." She hung up before Gerard could say, "No, wait," or in case he didn't.

She pictured him thinking about calling back, deciding against it. She wondered where he was. He sounded indoors. At his desk at work? Stressed? Preoccupied with meeting a deadline? Strange how you can go from knowing someone so intimately, knowing everything about them, to knowing nothing.

If he wants to call back, he will, she told herself.

Chapter Three

Then

"Ah, Miss Duncan!"

Mr Grayson, the headteacher of Queensmead High School, always greeted her like this whenever he met her in the corridor, hailing her, a wide grin spread across his features. He was a big man, solid rather than fat, with a beard and a thick head of curly, unruly hair. As ever, his tie was twisted, and his jacket was in need of a dry clean. He would say often that his wife was always nagging him to smarten up and get some new suits, but he wasn't the corporate type and, besides, there was plenty of wear left in this jacket.

He had a loud voice and a big presence and could be intimidating to staff and pupils alike, but Rosalind knew he respected her and admired the way she went about her work. She knew he had a soft spot for her — avuncular, not at all inappropriate. Slight, elfin, small, she felt dwarfed by him and thought of him as a giant teddy bear.

She stopped and waited for him to reach her. Feigning indignation, she said, as she always did, "Headteacher, it's Ms Duncan, not Miss!"

And as he always did, the headteacher said, "Forgive me, my dear." He added, "I suppose I'm not allowed to say that, either." And he smiled his broad smile, and she smiled her lopsided smile, and her eyes danced. In so many other men, this would have been tiresome, but she enjoyed the routine with the head, liking him and knowing he liked her and knowing, too, that he was a good man who would do anything for his pupils and those members of staff who deserved it.

"Actually, I'm glad I caught you," he said, his voice now soft and quiet, gently conspiratorial. "Have you seen the Careers post is up for grabs?"

"Err, oh, I saw it, yes," said Rosalind.

At times — when excited or anticipating something good — her speech became full of hesitations, the delivery deliberate, slow, and cautious, but with a comical bounce. Her eyes could sparkle and appear unconvinced at the same time.

"And?" the head said.

"And, er, well...I..." she responded. She shifted the books in her arms. "I don't know what to say. I haven't thought..."

"Well, you should," he said. "Think." And then he marched off, leaving Rosalind standing still before she remembered she had a lesson to teach. She felt a tingle of expectation, felt part of the head's conspiracy, and went off to her lesson much happier than before.

There were some grumblings when she got the job, mainly from the only other applicant, Trevor Jervis, a science teacher in his late 40s.

"Don't know why I bothered applying," he said to Rosalind. "It was always going to be you, wasn't it?"

"Thanks, Trevor," Rosalind said, thrilled and relieved to have been offered the post. It was only later, back in the house she shared with Naomi, that she reflected on what he said. It struck her it wasn't a generous comment at all, but one seeking to undermine her confidence, to deflate her, make her doubt herself.

Jervis was a tall, lean, powerful man, capable of both charm and threat. He had never taught anywhere but Queensmead.

His sourness and resentment were relatively recent developments. He had once loved teaching, loved being in the classroom, and shown no interest in either moving school to gain experience or seeking any of the internal posts that came up regularly. Any sort of promotion would have meant less time in the classroom and more time on administration, paperwork, and management.

"I didn't come into teaching to fill in forms," he used to say.

But his love of teaching faded as he entered his 40s, and he looked around and saw younger – and, in his view, always less able – colleagues overtake him, earning more than him, telling him what to do. If the colleague was a woman, he felt the resentment more keenly. Women were there to flirt with and, if possible, sleep with. Too late, he started applying for the internal posts that came up. Failure fed his resentment to the point where failure was preferable to success. He needed the bitterness more than the extra responsibility.

He was pleased with his comment to Rosalind and tickled that she had taken it as praise. Further comments were blunter, unambiguous, made in her hearing to the small group of equally bitter teachers, resentful of the time they had yet to serve before retirement, contemptuous of anyone outside their little group, convinced of their ability to do everything better, who gathered in a particular corner of the staffroom to bitch and await their retirement.

"Of course, the head likes to have his stable of fillies."

"Pretty young thing, though. I certainly would."

"Of course, if I had legs like that..."

He said nothing directly to Rosalind, gave no indication he was talking about her. But Rosalind knew exactly what he was doing.

"Oh, that's just Trevor," they said.

"You've just got to ignore him," they said.

"If you show him you're bothered, he's won," they said.

"Are you sure he was talking about you?" they said.

He was friendly when she first joined the school and made a point of asking her how she was getting on, even though they were in different departments. She looked back on some of his comments and realised he was coming on to her, that he was being suggestive but with plausible deniability.

The best thing about the new job was that it came with an office. In a corner of the school away from the main arteries, no bigger than a store cupboard and without windows, it was, nevertheless, a sign of a form of status. She had a phone with an extension number, and a filing cabinet, and she could lock the door. The evening she got the job, Rosalind stopped at a shopping centre and bought a pot plant and a small radio.

The previous incumbent hadn't strained himself, content to distribute leaflets and invite guest speakers to address assemblies now and then. Rosalind, however, was determined that she would raise the profile of the careers office and set about her new post with gusto, considering, for a while at least, that this could be the direction her own career would take.

The flagship policy which she brought up at the interview was a basic form of psychometric testing. Prior to the interview, she received some useful advice from her landlady, Naomi.

"Everyone talks rubbish in interviews," she said. "Everyone gabbles and hesitates and panics. What you have to do is this: whoever asks you a question, look them in the eye while you're answering, but include the rest of the panel, too. Smile, lean forward, and sound enthusiastic. Leave them in no doubt that you want the job." At this point, Naomi turned Rosalind to face her squarely. She put her hands on her shoulders. "Make them know that you want it! Right?"

"Right," said Rosalind. Naomi, older than Rosalind and divorced, thought herself worldly-wise. From the day she moved in, she'd decided that Rosalind was to be taken under her wing. She came into her room most evenings. What you have to do is this... was something she said a lot.

It was good advice. Rosalind got the job anyway. As usual for jobs in teaching, candidates were asked to wait while the panel discussed their relative merits, with the successful applicant called into the room once the decision was reached.

Naomi was home when Rosalind got back. She came dashing downstairs when she heard the front door.

"Well?" she said.

"I got it," Rosalind told her, and Naomi hugged her tightly.

"I told you, didn't I?" said Naomi. "Leave them in no doubt you want the job!" Naomi just assumed that Rosalind had followed her advice, and it was this that swung things in her favour. "Now, you sit yourself down." She pointed to the couch as if Rosalind needed help deciding where to sit. "I'll go and put the kettle on."

"Actually, Naomi," said Rosalind, "I'm a bit done in. I might just go and lie down upstairs."

"What you need is a nice cup of camomile tea," Naomi called from the kitchen. "Just the thing to give you a gentle lift." She popped her head around the door. "Sit yourself down and then you can tell me all about it."

Rosalind did as she was told. The debrief lasted longer than the interview. Just as Rosalind thought it had finished, Naomi said, "And what about this Derek Jervis? He couldn't have been happy."

"He was fine about it, actually," said Rosalind. "Congratulated me. Said he knew it was always going to be me."

"Did he now?" Naomi said.

Her tone troubled Rosalind. She went upstairs to change and lie down, but the sudden concern that Jervis's words might have had another meaning kept her from relaxing and enjoying her moment.

The headteacher announced Rosalind's appointment at the morning staff briefing the following day, also mentioning that she would be presenting her proposals on psychometric testing at the training day next week.

This was news to Rosalind, and she sought out the head when the briefing finished.

"You'll have to walk with me," he said. "I've a parent waiting."

Rosalind kept pace with his quick stride. She wasn't quite sure of what to say now that she had his attention. Or had his attention up to a point. The head seemed to speak to every pupil he passed, greeting each one cheerfully, interrupting Rosalind as she spoke.

"Erm, that was a bit of a surprise," she said. She spoke in the way she always did to the head — coy, familiar, a half-smile in her words.

"What was?" Mr Grayson's tone was different today, formal, business-like, severe, not at all his usual manner with her.

"The, er, erm, what you said about the presentation," Rosalind said.

"It will need to last an hour," Mr Grayson said. "Keep it clear, detailed. Show how the pupils will benefit. None of that blabbering like in the interview." A pupil approached, a fifth-year boy, a habitual latecomer. "Ah, good afternoon, young Michael. So nice of you to drop in." Michael grinned and apologised.

Rosalind stopped walking. Mr Grayson continued to his office, paying no attention to the fact she was no longer alongside him.

She did not know what had changed with the head. His words and manner kept her awake. If she managed to put them out of her mind, they were quickly replaced by Jervis's comment following the interview. Soon the two merged, the head's manner and Jervis's false congratulations. She didn't consider that the head might have been busy or had something else on his mind. No, Jervis had said something to him, made some assertion at his debrief about the reason for her appointment, and turned Grayson against her. She didn't give Grayson a chance to convince her otherwise. Her mind was made up, and nothing would convince her otherwise.

Between the announcement of her presentation and the presentation itself, she slept little and did little else but prepare for it. She arrived at school as the caretaker was opening up and had to be told to leave hours after everyone else had gone.

The presentation went well. She spoke clearly and fluently, like a grown-up, she thought, and not like the little girl she felt herself to be. Only when the questioning began did she start to crumble, stuttering in answer to objections and criticisms of the very notion of psychometric testing. Jervis didn't ask a single question but his sidekicks all did, and Rosalind grew hot and red, aware of his smirk even though she didn't once look at him.

The testing went ahead, but on a much smaller scale than she had originally proposed, limited to sixth form volunteers rather than the top four years of the school, as she had intended, her idea being that such a process would help focus minds and drive achievement.

She tried one more big project, a careers day when all lessons would be suspended for the entire sixth form, as the students experienced in practice the work done by a variety of professionals Rosalind had persuaded to come in. Not quite a failure; still, it didn't go anywhere near as well as she had hoped. Some teachers, Jervis among them, refused to release their students from what they insisted were vital lessons. Some teachers, Jervis among them again, insisted on using the special catering brought in to feed the visitors from outside.

It took just a term for Rosalind to surrender, after which she did the job the way her predecessor had done it, giving out leaflets and bringing in the occasional guest speaker to address assemblies. The plant she bought for her office died, overwatered.

The office came into its own, although it became a refuge, a hideaway, rather than the buzzing hive of activity and progress she had envisaged. And it became a meeting place for a handful of sixth form girls from Rosalind's History class. Breaks and lunchtimes, free periods, after school, a small group of girls would gather at Miss Duncan's door. Only a few, and not always the same ones. They would knock and enter, put the kettle on, enjoy the biscuits Rosalind provided but never ate. They would talk about music and boys and schoolwork and the prospect of university. Rosalind was only five or six years older than them and could remember kissing Barry on the train at Derby as if it were yesterday and easily allowed herself to imagine she was embarking on the same journey as the girls.

They, on the other hand, thought of Rosalind as a mature, successful woman. When she talked about her A levels and her visits to various universities, they listened intently. They could not hear the longing in her voice, the yearning to be in the same position again. Flattered though she was by their admiration, she knew she wasn't the woman they thought her to be. And she didn't want to be. She just wanted to be one of them.

There were some lunchtimes when no one came to her office. Rosalind felt slighted by the no-shows, didn't see that, to them, as fond as they were of her, she was still a teacher. On these occasions, however, Rosalind would quickly overcome her sense of grievance and find an excuse to wander into the sixth form common room, to put up a notice, contrive an excuse to have a word with one of the students, pass on some information that could have waited, in search of warmth and belonging.

On one of these sorties, Rosalind brought a leaflet that she might otherwise have simply thrown away. She held it in her hand at the entrance to the common room, surveying the space for the group she was looking for. She spotted them sitting around a coffee table, eating their lunch. Dismissing the question of why they'd chosen to stay here rather than come to her office, she made her way over, business-like, busy.

"Hi, girls," she said. "Sorry to interrupt your lunch, but I was thinking you'd be interested in this." She handed the leaflet to the girl closest to her. "You, especially, Jenny, after what you were saying the other day."

Jenny took the leaflet, only remembering what she'd said when she began reading it.

"Oh, yeah," said Jenny. "Women in engineering. Cool." She passed the leaflet to the girl next to her.

"If you're interested," said Rosalind, "and I would guess you are, I can book us in today."

"No rush, though, Miss," said the girl who'd taken the information from Jenny. "It's not until the month after next."

Rosalind felt herself blushing; it felt like she'd been caught out. "No time like the present, though," she said, hoping she sounded convincing. "Besides, these things book up fast." She didn't wait for approval. "I'll get right on it," she said. "Looks good, I must say."

The trip would have appealed to Rosalind at any time. Now, though, with her confidence shaken, feeling her roots in Queensmead starting to shrivel, and worried that she was a target in the staffroom, it was especially attractive. It was a day out of school, a blessed relief. Organising it gave her the chance to make lists, set deadlines, tick off tasks completed, and lose herself in mindless activity with different coloured pens and ruled lines and arrows, just as she had done when she was a schoolgirl.

The only black cloud was the need to get the head's permission to take a group out, and she had to do this before anything else. It nearly put her off the whole enterprise, and she spent a late night going over how she would approach it.

She had kept out of Mr Grayson's way as much as possible since the day after her appointment. It was unavoidable at times, of course. Like her, he taught History, and so attended the regular departmental meetings, always insisting he be treated as just another member of the team, effusive with his apologies when arriving late or leaving early, for which the head of department always excused him even though he wouldn't have done it for anyone else. At these meetings he was jovial and affable, self-deprecating. He was especially cheerful with Rosalind, often looking to catch her eye when he mock-shamefully admitted he hadn't sorted the coursework as promised.

At other times, away from these meetings, he was distant, cold, and – in Rosalind's eyes, at least – went out of his way to make her feel bad. He sought her out in her office following the shambolic Jobs Experience Day she had organised. It was a lunchtime, and a few sixth-form girls had gathered there.

"I was going to suggest we discussed how it went," he said. "Suffice it to say we won't be doing such an event again." He looked at the girls sitting on the floor and then, with what she saw as contempt, at Rosalind. She burned with shame and embarrassment. The girls left, and Rosalind cried alone.

In need of his permission for the day out of school, she went down to his office, hoping he wouldn't be there. She had photocopied the leaflet and written a proposal to accompany it, stressing the value of the trip, justifying it as thoroughly as possible, anticipating objections, intending to leave the material with his secretary and get his approval or otherwise from her the following day. But Mr Grayson was in his secretary's office when Rosalind got there, and she had no choice but to speak to him.

"I'll look at it now," he said, taking the papers from her. "Come into my office." He barely read anything Rosalind gave to him. "Yes," he said. "Go ahead. Any objections, just tell them I okayed the thing." His tone was neutral. He didn't look at her. As she was leaving his office, he said, "Ros. Before you go." Whatever he was going to say, he changed his mind about saying it. "It doesn't matter."

Once the head's permission was granted and all the details were sorted, the day at the fair was one Rosalind looked forward to, time away from the usual grind, with a group of sixth form girls who were clever and fun, girls who were nearly her friends. Rosalind took her teaching duties seriously, but sometimes the responsibility, the need to be a grown-up, weighed heavily on her, and she wished people could see she was still just a young woman with no clear idea of who she was and what she wanted. The job demanded certainty. Time away from the school with these girls — free to display a worldliness they didn't actually have — released her, let her be someone it was easier being.

Most of the girls had a clear idea of what they were going to do on leaving school, so there was no sense of urgency or purpose in their presence. It was just a day out, really. Once off the coach and in the conference centre, they split into groups and wandered away, leaving Rosalind alone. She mooched from stand to stand, picking up leaflets that she put in her handbag to throw away later. Something aroused her curiosity at one presentation stand, staffed by a man who looked happily undisturbed.

Rosalind decided to disturb him.

"What exactly is an actuary?" Rosalind asked.

"That's a good question," the man answered. "And if you ever find out, you must let me know."

It was only then that Rosalind looked properly at the man at the jobs fair stand. There was something about him, something that attracted her. He wasn't her usual type, even though she would have struggled to say what that was. Taller than her, for sure, which this man wasn't. In fact, he was barely even the same height as her. His features were small, and his face looked slightly squashed, somehow, but he had eyes which suggested laughter, and soft blond hair, and he wasn't pushy at all, or even remotely business-like. His poorly knotted tie and creased shirt were in stark contrast to the crisply presented staff at the other stalls, and his reply to her didn't seem to indicate a hard sales drive.

"It's quite an old-sounding word, isn't it?" Rosalind said. "Like…"

"Alchemist," said the man. "Or apothecary."

"Is it something to do with engineering?" she asked.

"Not even remotely," said the man. "That much I do know."

Rosalind knew he was only feigning ignorance, but she was enjoying herself for the first time since she'd arrived at the jobs fair. Nice though it was to be away from school, she found the whole thing dreary. The girls were enjoying themselves, though, or they seemed to be, at least. She'd not seen any of them for a little while.

"Then why are you here?" Rosalind said. "This is all meant to be about jobs for women in engineering."

The man shrugged his shoulders and sighed. Rosalind could see fun in his blue eyes.

"I'm here," he said, "because the company's HR manager was owed a favour by my manager. And my manager, Miss Duncan, believed I was the best man to do that favour."

Rosalind looked down at the name badge she wore, as if to check he'd got it right. She hadn't noticed him looking and was impressed.

"That doesn't seem at all fair, Mr..." Rosalind leaned across the table to get a closer look at his name badge, dangling on the end of a lanyard around his neck, although she could read it easily enough without doing so. "...Clark. Or may I call you Terence?"

"You may indeed," he replied. "Although it's not my name."

Rosalind said, "But..." and pointed to the badge.

"Terence Clark is the HR manager responsible for recruitment, the one my manager owed a favour. His badge came with all this material." He gestured across the length of the table, his hand sweeping over pencil sharpeners, booklets, bookmarks, pencils, biros, and erasers, all bearing the company name and logo. "My name is Gerard Murphy. I'm just being Terence Clark for the day."

"And how is that working out for you?" She hoped he'd take this opportunity to compliment her. Without realising she was doing so, she tipped her head to one side and smiled.

"Not bad," said Gerard. "Terry's a lot taller than me, so that makes a nice change."

Rosalind giggled. She preferred this answer to the one she was hoping for.

A group of three serious-looking girls arrived at the display stand. Unlike the girls Rosalind had brought from her school, they were impeccably dressed in their school uniform. They questioned Gerard sternly. Rosalind stayed where she was, pretending to study the company literature while listening to him answer the girls' questions, matching their gravity with his own.

When the girls moved away, Rosalind put down the brochure. "So you do know what you're talking about, then? You analyse statistics to assess risk for insurance purposes."

"A shot in the dark," said Gerard. "And it's not as exciting as it sounds." He nodded in the direction the girls had taken. "They were very earnest, weren't they? Wouldn't even take a pencil sharpener." He took a pen from a pot on the table. "Talking of which, could I press you to a biro?"

Rosalind smiled and took one. This is where he asks for my number, she thought. Bit cheesy, but that's okay. He didn't, however, and Rosalind, who was convinced there was a spark they'd both felt, was disappointed and confused. Her nose out of joint, she told Gerard she had to find the girls she'd brought and wandered around the fair, put out, surprised, and preoccupied.

Twenty minutes later, she was back at Gerard's display stand, keen to show him she wasn't interested in him, only in the careers for women his company could offer. He was sitting behind his table, doing a crossword.

"Oh, hello," he said, looking up. "I don't suppose you know any Burmese dances, do you?"

Rosalind had made up her mind to be direct and business-like, and the question threw her.

"What?" she said. "I...no...what? Burmese dances?"

"Five letters," said Gerard. He tapped the paper with the pen. "Crossword. I never do these things. Just found the paper in the box there. Thought it might pass the time. Dances from Burma, it says. I don't know any."

"Rumba," said Rosalind. When Gerard looked puzzled, she added, "It's an anagram of Burma."

"Of course!" Gerard said. "Anagram of Burma." He wrote the answer in and put down the pen and paper. "Now," he said, standing up, "how can I help you?"

Rosalind did her best to recover.

"I just..." She tried to recall the speech she'd prepared. "I'm here with...I'm the careers officer at..."

"Queensmead School," Gerard interrupted. He pointed at the name badge and smiled a warm smile. "I'm glad you came back. I was going to see if you wanted someone to come to your school to talk about careers for women in actuarial work." Rosalind was nonplussed. "It's quite dry," Gerard continued. "But fascinating. In its own way."

"That'd be great," Rosalind said, her speech forgotten. "Are you sure?"

"Sure. Unless you'd rather I get Terence Clark?"

"No," Rosalind said, smiling. "No. You'll do."

Rosalind got back to the minibus late and found the girls waiting for her.

"Sorry, girls," she said. "Was it okay for you? Get any ideas?"

"Not as many ideas as you got, Miss," one of the girls said.

Rosalind blushed. "I don't know what on earth you mean, Jenny."

"Fancy a career in actuarial work, do you, Miss?" another girl said.

"I was just arranging for Mr Murphy to come and speak at school." Rosalind loved this, being one of the girls in a way she had never been when she was a girl herself. "Anyway, how was it?"

"I got loads of pens and pencils," said a girl. "All free!"

"How about you, Miss?" said Jenny. "Did Mr Murphy have any rubbers?"

Gerard never came to speak at Rosalind's school. When he called, he suggested a drink instead, and Rosalind agreed. They went out together for nearly two years. "You'll do," she said to him, and, for a while at least, she genuinely thought he would.

Rosalind stayed at Queensmead until the end of that academic year. Once it was known she was leaving, Trevor Jervis openly propositioned her, coming into her classroom when she was alone, stroking her back and telling her he was sorry she was going.

The head remained distant for the most part. Rosalind came to see that if he was a teddy bear, he was a ruthless one who could turn cold with ease. She hoped he might say something when she told him she was leaving, but all he said was, "Yes, it hasn't turned out the way I expected." To someone else, his meaning would have been clear, but Rosalind had started to hold on to more and more things and to pull at them and watch them fray. She simply added the head's remark to the list. She could never stop wishing she'd confronted him about the change in his manner. She couldn't let it go.

Chapter Four

Now

Gerard was sometimes called upon to write reports – summaries, assessments, recommendations — as part of his consultancy work. Now and then, he toyed with the idea of writing a report on himself. It would be easy enough, so long as he kept limits on its scope. He wouldn't want to venture into making observations or recommending action to be taken. He didn't want an audit of his accounts. That might force him to confront aspects that would cause unease.

Born: Gerard Francis Murphy; 1 July 1963; Altrincham, Trafford, Greater Manchester
Education: Manchester Grammar School; Exeter University
Occupation: Actuary (ret'd); freelance actuarial consultant
Marital status: single
Children: none
Siblings: none
Parents: Mary Murphy, née Price, deceased; Michael Joseph Murphy, deceased

And it wouldn't need to stretch much beyond those basics. In the spy novels he read, the agents always varied their routines, never repeated routes, never established patterns of behaviour. Or, if they did, it was their downfall. Gerard would be easy to tail, easy to predict. From day to day and week to week, his routine never changed. Diet, work, exercise, hobbies, sleep, entertainment, the order in which he did things – all unvarying.

It wasn't quite rigid. There'd be a few minutes difference here and there. He wasn't quite a robot. But he didn't need to think, or to wonder. It was all laid out for him. All under control. No requirement to engage.

He hadn't arranged things this way deliberately. He didn't sit down one day and plan how his minutes would be filled. This was just the way things evolved. Waking at seven, walking for his daily paper at eight, getting coffee after leaving the newsagents, working from nine to 11.30, reading until lunch, and so on. Always the same paper, the same coffee, the same lunch. Nothing intruded. Not because he didn't let them, but because, through circumstance – along with a little bit of careful planning – there was nothing that might intrude. He had no family to worry about, no wayward children that might cause him concern, no ageing parents to demand his time and attention. No money worries, either. He'd long since paid for his flat. He had a good private pension, a tidy lump sum following his early retirement, and a decent income arising from the consultancy work he was asked to do.

Things suited him. Things didn't have to suit anyone else. There was no one else to suit. It was the way he got things done. Meticulous, precise, orderly. It was the way he managed.

Of course, not everything was under his control. As he got older, ill health might become a factor. But that wasn't something he needed to worry about just yet. He was in fine fettle, and he was able to convince himself he always would be. Life could be kept at arm's length. Not that he ignored the world, mind. He read the paper; he followed the news. He read books and went to the cinema and the theatre and to concerts. He listened to music. He enjoyed casual conversations with the woman in the newsagent's and the man in the deli. He took holidays and visited galleries and museums. He went to Mass, where he nodded and smiled at fellow worshippers. He just wasn't part of things, but that was okay for the most part.

So, a report would be easy. There was nothing to change. He could leave the section on future actions blank.

Chapter Five

Now

Gerard stared at his phone until the screen went blank and then put it down on the edge of his desk. He looked at his watch: coming up to twenty-five to eleven. Just under an hour before he finished work for the morning, before he made coffee, before he sat drinking his coffee, reading or looking at the crossword. Then lunch. Then a return to his desk to continue working until 3.30pm.

He picked up his pen, turned his attention back to the papers in front of him, and found the words and numbers no longer made any sense. He continued to stare at them, determined to extract meaning from the patterns in front of him, but, even when he could recognise the words and figures, any meaning he found stayed only momentarily before slipping away like water down a drain.

Thirty years since they'd spoken. And then she'd hung up, aggrieved, he imagined, that he hadn't instantly recognised her name. Couldn't she consider for a moment that he might have been concentrating on something else? That a call from her was the last thing he was expecting? That it had been years since she was anything more than the next name on his Christmas card list?

If she wants to call back, she will.

Still no meaning from the papers before him. Reluctantly, Gerard went to the kitchen to make his coffee. He checked the time again so he'd know when to get back to his desk, to make up the hour he was losing now.

He regarded it as a ritual, coffee making, and he enjoyed every step. Not for Gerard Murphy the filling of the kettle and a spoonful of instant from a glass jar into the first mug that came to hand. It was coffee beans from a specialist shop in town, and the grinder acquired after careful research in consumer magazines.

Each weekday morning at 11.30 he would take the airtight canister from the fridge and tip the required amount of coffee beans (imported from Japan–rich, clean, complex, balanced, with hazelnut and strawberry notes) into the grinder. The clattering of the blades hurled the beans furiously against the sides of the grinder, delighted him, as did the spluttering of the boiling water through the grounds in the stovetop espresso maker. The noises spoke to him of sophistication and insistence on quality, of careful consideration and knowledge.

He didn't like to admit to himself that he couldn't always taste the hazelnut notes or tell the difference between this coffee and instant. So he didn't admit it to himself. He simply relished the process and enjoyed using the particular cups and saucers he'd bought in the Design Museum. And making his coffee this way took up more time, too, which was always a bonus.

After turning off the hob, he went back into his study to get his phone. He would have heard it ring, but he checked for a missed call anyway. There wasn't one.

Taking the coffee pot, cup and saucer, and milk to the table in the living room, he flicked through his phone to Calls Received. He hadn't looked at the screen when she rang, had answered it with his mind elsewhere. But he saw the name now: Rosalind Duncan. Her maiden name, he thought. Not Rosalind Jones, which she'd been when she gave him her number.

What did she want?

Her call annoyed him because it had broken his stride, intruded upon his routine. And because it reminded him of things he didn't like about her—especially her refusal to see others had needs and preferences that might not match her own but were just as valid as hers. So he didn't recognise her voice? Couldn't immediately place her name? So what? Thirty years it had been. Thirty years during which she'd married and had a child, and he'd stayed single and childless.

And she took umbrage at him?

Chapter Six

Then

She didn't need to say anything. He could tell everything he needed to know from the way she hugged him. Too tightly. For too long. Her head down, forehead crushed against his chest.

It was just the same with Jessica.

Still, he waited for her to speak, just in case he was wrong. He didn't want to get his hopes up. She eventually released her hold and stepped back, taking his left hand in both of hers. She couldn't look at him and kept her head down. This was it. He was sure of it.

"I'm sorry, Gerry," Rosalind said. *I'm right,* he thought. *She never calls me Gerry.* "I...it's just that..." She hadn't planned the words. She only knew they needed to be said. "I won't be going to Manchester. I'm staying here. I think we should..."

Gerard felt he ought to leap in here. He didn't want some sort of diluted arrangement, some uncertain compromise that might leave an opening.

"It's okay," he said. He squeezed her hand. It was easy to feel tenderness again now. He wondered if he should suggest going to bed together, one last time, to feel again that abandonment they'd not enjoyed for so long. Or not enjoyed together. He wasn't sure if she'd slept with Mark yet. He dismissed the idea, although he knew she would have agreed. "I'll call Gary. Tell him we won't be over."

"Gary?" Rosalind said. She looked puzzled. Her attention momentarily shifted from the pain at hand.

"Gary," said Gerard. "We're meant to be going to his tonight. For something to eat. His new flat." Gerard thought this was typical of her, that she was so wrapped up in herself and her concerns that she forgot others. But just as he'd done in the past, he said nothing.

"Oh, God, Gary," she said. "I completely forgot. Would you mind?"

"No," Gerard said. "I'll call him now." *Though it should really be you making the call. You're the one making it necessary.* He thought the words but said nothing. No need for confrontation. He didn't want to spoil things.

"Do you have to call him right now?" said Rosalind. "I mean, we've got things..."

"We're due there in less than an hour," said Gerard. "It's not fair on him."

"I suppose you're right."

Gerard went up the hall and made the call. Rosalind went through into the kitchen and lit a cigarette, playing with it until Gerard came back.

"He was okay about it," Gerard said. "You could tell he was a bit thrown, but..."

"You didn't tell him why?"

"No. I'll give him a ring tomorrow. Explain."

He sat down opposite Rosalind. The table was folded down to its two-seater position, tucked into the corner of the kitchen. Gerard watched the smoke curling up from her cigarette. She smoked like a girl trying it for the first time, tentatively, the cigarette held right at the ends of her fingers, and when she put it to her mouth, she narrowed her eyes and puckered her lips to meet the filter. She inhaled knowing she wouldn't like it.

"Packing's going well, I see," said Rosalind. There were cardboard boxes against the wall of the kitchen and in the hall.

"No point leaving it to the last minute."

Rosalind nodded. "What do you want to do now?" she asked. "Drink?"

"Yes," Gerard said. "Friday night, after all." He was keen. He had something to celebrate, although he was careful not to show it. He didn't want Rosalind to see how relieved he was.

It wasn't just the same with Jessica.

They went to the Sergeant-at-Arms, his local – their local – a couple of hundred yards from Gerard's flat. It was still early, around 6.30, and they found a table easily enough. Gerard bought the first round.

"He's here again," he said, putting the drinks down on the table.

"Who?" said Rosalind.

"That man at the bar." He nodded over towards a man in a suit and tie, in his 40s most likely, slightly florid, balding, with a pint of Guinness in front of him and a carrier bag at his feet. "What do you reckon's in that bag? He always has one with him." Rosalind shrugged. "His dinner, probably," said Gerard. "A ready meal from Marks and Spencer. Three pints on his way back from work and then home. Regular as clockwork."

The man had started a conversation with a customer waiting to be served. When the customer had got his drinks and his change, he moved away to the table where his friends were sitting. The man left alone at the bar took a drink and pulled a face to try and suggest to anyone watching he didn't mind not having anyone to talk to.

Gerard looked around and saw another face he recognised, that girl he liked, with the deep, copper-coloured hair arranged in a half beehive. She lived nearby, although Gerard didn't know where. He saw her or tried to see her most mornings when she walked past his flat on the way to the bus stop. He tried to time it so he would leave for work as she was passing. When he had the chance, he always said hello, and she always replied and never gave him a second thought. He looked at her now, in her short jacket and calf-length jeans, and was glad he no longer needed to pretend with Rosalind.

"So," said Rosalind. "All set for the move?"

Gerard took a drink. "Pretty much," he said. "All the packing's done, or as much as possible, anyway. I'll move some up next week and then come back for the rest soon after. The flat's paid up until the end of the month, so there's no rush. Couple of trips should do it."

"And you'll stay with your mum until you're settled?"

"Not for long," said Gerard. "I've got an appointment with an estate agent. They've got a couple of flats that should suit, so I shouldn't be with Mum long. Soon as I can, I'll buy somewhere."

"Got it all sorted out, then?" said Rosalind.

Gerard was tempted to spoil things, to introduce a note of bitterness, recrimination. To give the impression he was hurt, to gain sympathy he didn't deserve or need. He took the opportunity.

"You know I have," he said. "We've talked about it."

It worked.

"I'm sorry," said Rosalind. "I'm so sorry." She reached across the table and put her hand on his.

And now to be magnanimous, understanding. Princely, even! He patted her hand.

"It's okay," he said. "Can't be helped." He became more buoyant. He felt good, and while he was always ready to grab a chance for sympathy, he didn't want to go too far. He didn't want to spoil the evening. "Anyway, what about you? Will it be tricky, you staying here? Now you've resigned?"

They'd never actually discussed things properly. They'd never planned anything, never talked thoroughly about what they'd do. They'd just hoped it would never actually happen. If they avoided the subject, it might not. It was all loose. Gerard said he was tired of Exeter. He wanted to move back north and get a fresh start at the company's Manchester office, where there'd be more opportunities.

Rosalind had encouraged him enthusiastically, prompted him to chase things up. About her own intentions, she was more vague. She said she would talk to one of the senior managers, talk to the headteacher. She gave the impression she had resigned – "I've spoken to the head, and it's all sorted" – and threw words like "sabbatical" and "supply work" into the conversation. Both she and Gerard knew it was impractical, but they never said. Just like they never spoke about the engagement. Not that they were ever engaged, not really. Nothing went beyond that night they had the argument, and Gerard said, "We're getting on so badly we should get married." Rosalind stopped shouting and laughed and said, "Yes, let's!" and the argument was forgotten instantly.

Rosalind took a drink, lit a cigarette and smoked it like it was her first again. She shifted the burning tip around in the ashtray. She didn't look at Gerard.

"I didn't resign," she said. She looked up at him then, shrugged her shoulders slowly and gave him an apologetic look.

Gerard turned away and saw again the girl he liked. She was smoking, too. She sat with her legs crossed, one arm across her body, the cigarette held in front of her mouth. She looked…poised. *That's the word,* Gerard thought. *Confident, elegant, sitting between two men around her own age, trying to impress her, but she doesn't really fancy either of them. And why would she fancy me?*

He turned back to Rosalind. He could justifiably be angry, but the truth was he didn't care. He had known things between them were over for months now but had been too scared to say anything. He told himself he didn't want to hurt her, that he was worried she might take it badly, even to the point of doing something stupid. After all, she had struggled with things at times, worked herself into a state over work, reacted badly when he mentioned he'd had lunch with Sarah from work. And then there was the time she heard him say hello to the girl who was in the pub now. She mocked him then, with that tone in her voice, the smile that said she saw right through him.

But all that concern was simply a mask for his fear, his cowardice. He was just too scared to say the words to bring the relationship to a close. So now? Now the relationship was over, and it was Rosalind who'd ended it? He could enjoy the relief and indulge in some counterfeit self-pity because he was at least as dishonest with himself as he was with others.

"Oh," he said, and looked first hurt and then brave. "Well, I guess it doesn't matter now."

Rosalind nodded slowly. "No," she said. "I guess not."

Another drink. Gerard said he'd get this one, too. When he came back, smiling, trying to catch that girl's eye and somehow communicate that Rosalind wasn't his girlfriend, that she was just a friend, that he was available, Rosalind said, "I thought you'd be angry."

"About what? The job thing?"

Rosalind nodded. "You'd have every right to be."

"Well, I suppose so." He wasn't angry, not in the least, but he didn't want Rosalind to know that or to know why he wasn't. "I guess it's just, well, like I said, it doesn't matter now. It's bigger than the details." No point telling her he didn't care, that he was relieved, that he felt off the hook. But equally, no reason to dismiss it that easily. "So you never even came close to resigning?"

"No," she said.

"You picked your words carefully, didn't you? Got it all sorted, you said."

"I didn't lie."

"No, no. You didn't lie." He said the words with enough emphasis to make Rosalind feel guilty but not so much as to ruin the evening. "Jesuitical," he added. She knew what he meant. She'd teased him about his Catholicism plenty of times, and argued with him about it, and become exasperated by it.

And then they moved on. They talked about Gerard's move, his excitement at the prospect of being back up north, about his determination not to spend any longer than he had to living with his mother again. About the moving allowance and the discount he was getting at a gym near his new office. ("Good way to meet girls," Rosalind said when he mentioned this, and Gerard had thought the same thing more than once but didn't say that to her.) Rosalind kept the conversation content about Gerard. She knew he preferred it that way, and she didn't want to say too much about her plans and intentions.

They laughed a lot. They talked as they had done early in the relationship, two years and light years ago.

Another round. Rosalind insisting on paying and going to the bar, joking about Gerard's habit in the early days of going to the bar for her.

"He's still there," she said, putting the drinks on the table. "The man with the ready meal. Talks very grandly, doesn't he? Called me my dear young lady." She sat down. "Cheers." She was enjoying the sensation of the drinks after the weeks of tension she'd gone through knowing what she had to say to Gerard.

"Cheers," he replied.

"To the good times we had," she said. That pushed them into silent reflection. When she felt in need of a response, a sudden anxiety about the past, a need for reassurance, Rosalind said, "We did have good times, didn't we?"

"Oh, yes."

"I mean," said Rosalind, "at one point, I even thought..." It was safe for her to broach the subject now after so many months of avoiding it.

"Yes," said Gerard, closing the subject.

In the time they had to wait for the atmosphere to return to its earlier jollity, Gerard looked at Rosalind closely. She wasn't Jessica. That was the problem. It had always been the problem. Not her fault, of course. Still, there was a time he had thought her perfect. Funny, a bit of sparkle about her, something a little out of the normal run of things, a clanging coming-together of independence and need. And how he had desired her, how he loved the way she looked – slight, a lovely coyness that hid an eagerness, that revealed a lack of inhibition he hadn't anticipated. That also hid a darkness, too, of course, a worm that nagged away inside her, destabilised her.

His mother called her a pixie and said she was elfin after that one time she met Rosalind. She didn't mean it as praise.

"She's weak and shallow," his mother said. "That's the opposite of what you need." Gerard heard the words his mother left unsaid. "She'll break," she threw in, for good measure.

Rosalind and Gerard silently agreed to relax and enjoy themselves for the rest of the evening. They left the pub after their fifth drink, both a little drunker than they realised, happier in each other's company than they'd been for over a year. It was nearly nine. The road was busy, summer drinkers in short sleeves and short skirts heading into town.

They stood outside the Sergeant-at-Arms as they had done many times before, but with a hesitancy that was unfamiliar. Gerard wondered if he wanted her to come back to his flat. Rosalind wondered if she wanted to. But the time for sex had passed. If they were going to make love for the last time, it should have been before they left the flat. So they stood awkwardly until Rosalind said she'd better look for a taxi.

"Back to Mark's?" said Gerard. He instantly regretted it. He didn't care if they'd slept together or not, and this lost him the advantage and gave Rosalind the chance to be exasperated with him. She took it.

"Back to mine," she said. Firm, cross. "We aren't even...We haven't...if that's what you think."

Not like with Jessica. They had, Gerard remembered.

"I'm sorry," he said. "I didn't mean it. I'll wait until you find a cab."

"No need," she said. But a taxi came straight away, and Gerard watched as she got in. She turned halfway through the door. "I'm sorry." No anger now. "I'll call you." She waited until the door was closed before giving the driver the address.

Gerard watched the taxi as it waited for the lights to turn green. He wondered if Rosalind would turn around to look at him. She didn't, and the taxi moved away when the lights changed. He stayed where he was. In his own relief that the relationship was over, he acknowledged the relief he sensed in her that it was over, too. And she was the one who'd had the courage to end it. He would have drifted on, resentful, frustrated, convincing himself that it would hurt her too much if he ended things, but really too much of a coward to speak up.

Gerard finished the packing the next morning. There wasn't much left to do. There hadn't been much to start with. He had guarded against accumulating too many possessions, not out of meanness or lack of interest but because he hadn't felt settled or ready to settle and didn't want to gather things around him until he did. The move to Manchester, where he'd buy somewhere of his own, would be the time to settle and accumulate.

Although he told Rosalind he'd need two trips, when he looked around the flat at the boxes and cases he had packed, he rightly estimated one would suffice. There was the box of Rosalind's things, of course, things she had left for when she stayed at his. Toothbrush, hairbrush, shampoo and conditioner, that expensive soap she liked. Some clothes. A couple of books and CDs. Two bras. Four pairs of pants.

He remembered the times when he longed to undress her or to watch her undress, when the sight of her stripped down to her underwear filled him with desire. He thought of Rosalind's own passion, unchecked, unleashed, her initiation of sex, her enjoyment of sex, her response to his touch and his to hers. They were just pieces of cloth now, and he felt nothing as he took them out of the drawers and put them into the box.

On Monday morning, he rang work and said he was taking the leave due to him and made the move a week sooner than planned. He called at Rosalind's house and put the box by the front door. He rang the bell and walked away quickly before anyone answered the door.

Chapter Seven

Now

Gerard's coffee was cold. He'd not looked at the paper. It was the wrong time. That was the problem.

He looked around the room and saw everything perfectly positioned, everything so carefully selected for function, purpose, style, aesthetics. That table for his chess set, that sofa and chair from that contemporary furniture store. Expensive, yes, but so what? He didn't spend money he didn't have. He spent wisely, always had. And it was perfect for what he wanted. Nothing out of place. Nothing over-elaborate. Clean. Clean lines. Exactly what and where he wanted. Same with the books and the records and the pictures on the wall.

Why shouldn't he arrange things the way he wanted? He lived alone. He wasn't in a relationship. He had no one to answer to but himself. So why shouldn't he order things to suit himself? And if he was going to be productive, to work well, he had to follow a schedule. Everyone did. Everyone had to be somewhere at a particular time, take their breaks when a schedule allowed. So why should it be different for him? This was the life he had constructed, that he maintained carefully each day.

He was happy that way. What was it to do with anyone else?

The phone call from Rosalind. That was what had stirred him up, made him feel this resentment, this need to defend himself, explain his lifestyle. Explain it to an empty room in an empty flat, where everything was carefully selected for its look, function and fit. If anyone asked, he could tell them exactly where and when he'd bought that sofa or that table or that turntable and say where he'd done the research, the lengths he'd gone to to get exactly what he wanted. He could name the designer, explain why it suited him, why the quality mattered.

This was his life, constructed just the way he wanted it. Nothing could interfere. And yet something had. Rosalind had. Rosalind, a woman he went out with for two years three decades ago. Rosalind, who wasn't even the woman he would have changed everything for, who never had been and still wasn't Jessica, had called, and something had changed. The call had made cracks in the plaster, threatening to expose what the plaster covered. He couldn't say why, but it had.

He took the coffee pot, cup and saucer, and milk jug on the tray back to the kitchen, where he washed and rinsed them and left them to drain. Feeling cold, he went to his wardrobe and selected a cardigan, buttoning it up in front of the full-length mirror and smoothing his tie.

He never thought about Rosalind. He sent her a card at Christmas, but she was just another name on his list, and when he opened hers, he gave it no more than a quick glance before putting it up on the shelf and throwing the envelope into the recycling.

Rosalind wasn't the woman he loved most, or even one of the women from his past whose memory sometimes squeezed through his defences, and he wished he could see again, do things differently. She wasn't the great 'if only'.

Her voice had unsettled him though. Hearing her say the words, "It's Ros." That had done it. Greetings cards make no sound. A voice calls to you, makes you look. It was the return — the unexpected, unhoped-for return — of a past he had closed his face towards. That was what Gerard had done with the past, closed his face towards it. He hadn't done anything wrong. There was no great sin or crime that he wished to forget. He didn't want the past because it disappointed him and because he would never get it back, never reclaim the chances that he'd had.

His routine sustained him and kept him present, and so he returned to his desk and tried to concentrate on his work. Realising the pointlessness of it all, he called Rosalind.

Chapter Eight

Now

He gave it some thought before he made the call, carefully considering what to say and how to say it.

He tried out. "So, what can I do for you?" He emphasised the last word to make her feel special after forgetting who she was but thought it sounded maybe a bit too much like a game show host.

"So, why the call?" would come across as possibly too direct. "What do you want?" was exactly what he wanted to say, but was far too blunt and aggressive for him, altogether not his style.

In the end, Gerard selected a cheery, positive tone. He didn't feel it but managed it convincingly enough for him. It was the right choice—arm's length.

"Ros, hi! It's Gerard... Great to hear from you... Sorry about earlier. Miles away... So, to what do I owe this pleasure?"

Hollowness came easily to Gerard. Faking it had become second nature. Often, he wanted people to see behind the mask or to try to look beyond it, but not this time. Besides, it was thirty years since they'd last spoken. Thirty years since they'd seen each other. Maybe a couple of dozen Christmas and birthday cards in total exchanged.

Rosalind didn't mention Jack being in hospital, said nothing about the attack, just that she was on her way to Liverpool and changing trains at Piccadilly and did he want to meet her and have coffee while she waited for her connection.

This made Gerard pause. It threw him, and he struggled for a moment to maintain the façade of bonhomie but recovered quickly and hoped she didn't notice.

"Let me see, let me see... this afternoon..." He went through the motions of looking at his diary, as if she was there in front of him, as if he didn't know precisely what was written there, as if acting it out would somehow give his words authenticity.

"If it's too much bother," said Rosalind. And there, Gerard felt the advantage slip away.

"No, no, not at all," he said. "What time does your train get in?"

"I don't know," said Rosalind. "You could look it up."

It was silently decided then. He did look it up and was now sitting at a concourse café with a coffee he didn't want, looking at the display board, which told him that the delayed 10.42 train from Exeter was now arriving at Platform Three.

He looked at his watch — 3.30. He thought about going to the gate to meet Rosalind as she came off the train, but he didn't. It would look wrong and feel wrong. Lovers reuniting at journey's end. It would be the wrong woman coming through the gate, and it would be too much of a lie, and the lie of it kept him away. Not that he minded lying; he lied every day, but he would have liked it to be true. Just not with Rosalind.

So he stayed where he was, at one of the tables that had been put outside the café onto the concourse, aping pavement society, with another untouched coffee and the newspaper unopened, his phone in his hand in case she called.

And suddenly, there she was. She hadn't seen him, and Gerard, instead of calling to her, just sat and watched her, waiting until she did see him.

Thirty years. Everyone changes. But still. She looked worn out, as if she had walked from the south coast rather than caught the train. She shuffled at her own singular pace, oblivious to the Friday commuters surging around her. Her narrowed, unseeing eyes searched for Gerard. She was lost, grey, weary. Drab. Gerard saw no clue to the quirky, funny, confident, wary woman with her own uncertain, distinctive sense of style that he once knew.

A flicker of the eyes, the merest raise of the brow, told him she had spotted him. Beyond that, there was no reaction, not of pleasure or surprise or relief or exasperation–barely of recognition, even. She just walked over, and people walked around her.

Gerard stood and smiled, ready to resume the act he had started earlier on the phone.

"Ros!" he said, spreading his arms open in case she expected a hug. "So good to see you."

"You're very smart," she said, her voice flat. She ignored his open arms.

Gerard suddenly felt self-conscious. Even though he had retired and now only worked from home, he always wore a suit and tie each day. He told himself it was to put himself in the right frame of mind to work, and it was, but it was a uniform for the benefit of others, too, so they got the right message. He touched his tie and said, "Oh, this old thing? I just threw something on." He smiled.

Rosalind just said, "Oh."

Her face. Paper-thin skin, dry enough to crack and crumble in the hand like a dead leaf. And her eyes. Gerard remembered a twinkle, part-doubt, part-mischief. But now? It wasn't that she looked beaten. It was worse than surrender. It was more that she looked accustomed. She was so used to pain that it no longer registered. It was a companion.

He thought about those times she begged him never to leave her, when she seemed so fragile, dipping beneath the surface for so long that he wondered if she'd ever come back up for air, some internal anxieties that she couldn't control spilling out and infecting all aspects of her life – work, friendships, their relationship. Those times when she could barely breathe, and he didn't know what to do or how to react, careering between helpless concern and mute rage.

"So, first things first." Gerard kept things bright and false. He stood up and clapped his hands together. "Coffee? No. I know just the thing."

He didn't wait for a response. Waiting to be served, he vented his frustration to himself. *What's the matter with her? Can barely be bothered to speak, having dragged me out here in the middle of the day.* But she didn't drag him, of course. She had just suggested it, and Gerard, who could have made an excuse and didn't know why he hadn't, complied.

He returned to the table, his annoyance suppressed, with another coffee for himself and a hot chocolate for Rosalind. It was in a tall glass, the drink topped with a swirl of cream dotted with marshmallows. A long spoon poked out from the side of the glass. Rosalind took hold of it and began joylessly spooning cream and marshmallow into her mouth.

"There's meant to be cinnamon in there, too," said Gerard. "For Christmas." Rosalind sipped her drink, leaving a cream moustache on her upper lip. "So," said Gerard. "Good trip?"

"Have you come from work?" said Rosalind. "Do you work round here?"

"No," said Gerard. *Why doesn't she wipe the cream from her lip?* It was annoying him; she was annoying him, just leaving it there. *She must know it's there.* He waited for her to ask him more, but she didn't.

Rosalind nodded. She had drunk her hot chocolate quickly and was now spooning the dregs from the bottom of the glass. Some of the drink spilled from the spoon onto her lap. She ignored it.

"Here." Gerard gave her a tissue. Rosalind took it but didn't use it. She just kept it scrunched in her hand. "Are you going to...?" Gerard pointed to the spill on her coat and then gestured to his own face, trying to make Rosalind wipe the cream from her mouth. Exasperation flashed across his face. Memories of their time together poured through his head, of her listlessness, her refusal at times to act, to take charge of her situation. And then he went back to faking cheeriness. "Yes," he said, answering a question she hadn't asked. "I retired. Feels strange saying that. You always think of old people when you say retired. I still work, though. Freelance consultant. For my sins. For the same company. And others, too. From home. Keeps me occupied." He was babbling.

"Jack," said Rosalind.

"Jack?" Gerard didn't know who she was talking about.

"Jack," repeated Rosalind. And then, firmly, a touch of indignation, "My son. Jack."

How am I supposed to know who Jack is? Gerard, thinking, not saying.

"He's in hospital," said Rosalind. "That's why I'm here."

"Oh, God, Ros," he said. "I'm so...what's the matter?"

"He was attacked. Stabbed. I'm going to see him." She looked up at the departure board. "That's my train now. Platform 13. Senseless and unprovoked, the police said."

Rosalind stood up. Gerard noticed for the first time that she was carrying a bag — battered, old, the leather scratched and cracked — crosswise from one shoulder to the opposite hip. She walked away from him without looking back.

"But, Ros," said Gerard. "What..."

He stayed where he was, watching her shuffle again through the rushing commuters.

Gerard always imagined he was being observed. It wasn't paranoia or conceit. He was just self-conscious to the point where he thought of himself — without actually thinking it — of being in a film and so being watched by others. He wasn't deluded enough to regard himself as being at the centre of anyone's attention, but he was too much at the centre of his own attention. So, while everyone else in the café or walking through the station ignored him, he acted as if all eyes were on him. He must not be caught out; he must not give the impression of a misstep or lack of control. So he checked his watch without seeing the time, peered up at the departures board, and acted the role of a man whose train would be leaving shortly. Not the role of someone in danger of missing his train, but, nevertheless, a character with little time to dawdle. He picked up his paper, took the coffee he didn't want to the counter to get it poured into a takeaway cup, and headed out into the flow of people. His overcoat was open. He loosened his tie. He was a man weary of the week's work, heading home early on a Friday, a well-deserved early dart, maybe stopping for a drink in his local before getting back to the house.

Even if he'd looked properly at the departure board, it could have told him nothing he needed to know. He was heading for the Metro, for the local tram that would take him back to Burton Road, where a short walk would take him back to his empty flat.

Chapter Nine

Now

Gerard could have caught a tram at Piccadilly, but he walked down to Victoria instead, so he wouldn't have to change.

He was agitated, disgruntled, concerned, shocked. He felt guilty. He felt resentful. His schedule had been thrown off completely. This was the time for his daily swim. He should be at his fitness club, working his way through his hour of lengths, looking forward to his Friday wine.

He considered going to the cinema to take his mind off things, or to a bookshop, but they were Saturday activities. He felt momentarily stupid for following such a strict regime, but he had shackled himself with it. Now, he was content with the shackles and was indignant that Rosalind had scuppered things, caused him to feel this discontent.

The Metro emptied at Victoria, and he had his pick of seats. It would fill up again at St Peter's Square, but he had the window seat he wanted so he could watch the stations go by—Trafford Bar, Firswood, Chorlton, St Werburgh's Road. He liked to look at the flats that stood on either side of the tramline, to glimpse movement within them, a view into the routines of people grown used to fleeting examinations from the passing trams. The view changed as the tram drew away from the city centre. Banks of untended grass and weeds, flat, industrial drabness, and then into the suburbs, and more windows into lives in the redbrick semis backing onto the line. It was more or less dark now, lights coming on, curtains being drawn.

Rosalind wasn't Jessica, and she never had been. If Jessica had called... If Jessica had wanted to see him... He would have dropped everything and anyone at any time between their last meeting and now. He would have rushed to wherever she was. Wouldn't he? He'd clung to Jessica, and she'd had to shake him free. She said that she needed time. He waited and waited until he gave up waiting.

He thought about that hug, the hug that confirmed things. Looking back now—nearly forty years—he could still feel it. Jessica's arms around his back, pressing him to her as hard as she could. Her head bowed against his chest. He thought he sensed her crying.

They'd gone in different directions after university. She went north, and he went south, but the aim was always to stay together, to find work in the same place. They saw each other as often as possible, exchanged passionate, funny, intimate, loving letters. There was no phone in the rented house he was sharing, so he would go to the phone box and call her four or five times a week, pockets full of change. Hard to believe now.

He knew before the hug, of course, or had his suspicions, at least. He told himself he was wrong and knew he was right. It was that letter. She hadn't responded to his questions or suggestion of a weekend away together. No mention. Just a list of things she'd done, the casual mention of that name, and then an apology because she was too tired to write any more. It was different, like the way the air pressure changes when a storm is imminent. It closed in on him.

He knew but still clung on.

When she hugged him, he said, "It's okay. It'll be all right." And then he said, "We'll be fine."

But Jessica didn't want them to be fine. She would be fine with someone else, and Gerard would try and fail to be fine with a succession of women until he gave up and settled for being single and self-pitying and pretending to be okay and hoping people would see he wasn't.

Looking out at the backs of houses, he thought about Jessica so deeply he missed his stop and had to pretend to no one watching that the next stop was his. All it meant was a slightly longer walk.

Jessica was his first girlfriend, a girl he met at university who teased him and taught him. Life was so easy then. He was complacent with Jessica. Loving and tender and kind and thoughtful, but he took it for granted they would be together or, at least, that it wouldn't be her who ended things. He knew, or assumed, she thought he was the one. The realisation that he wasn't changed him. It frightened him, drained him of confidence and gave him the fear that infected every subsequent relationship. Frightened to speak up. Frightened to say he was unhappy, that this wasn't what he wanted, that he was angry.

He should have left it there. He should have taken her arms from around him, said something, or maybe said nothing at all, and walked out of her house and got into his car and driven away. Not called or written. This was Jessica. This was how it ended. But he didn't leave it there. He'd seen to it that it dragged on.

You can always tell with a hug, can't you? What it means. Affection, passion, desire, friendship, sympathy. Or finality.

The thing was, he already knew. And knew, too, that there was someone else. He should have left the letter unanswered. Instead, he drove up the following weekend to see her. And he summoned up the courage to ask her the question he knew the answer to. That was when she hugged him. Arms tight around his neck, head pressed into his shoulder.

"Bye, Jess. Hope things go well for you."

But no. Instead: "It's okay. It'll be okay. We'll be fine."

And he stayed the rest of the weekend, sharing the bed she wanted to share with another man. And then he persisted in trying to make the relationship work, relentless in his attempts to remind her of the happiness they once shared, the fun they'd had, simultaneously unable to dismiss from his mind the thought of this man inside her. He dragged things on until she sent him another letter, asking for space, saying she'd be in touch once she'd thought things through. Months passed, then years passed too.

What would he do if Jessica called him now, this minute? If by some miracle she found his number, rang him, told him she'd made a mistake all those years ago? Would he go to her? Would he go home, pack, leave his flat, his life, the routine that protected him, that sustained and suffocated him? Would he? Jessica was the first one his thoughts always returned to when a weakness in his fortress was found, an unguarded, overlooked opening through which those thoughts could crawl in single file, before the breach was discovered and the invaders repelled.

He didn't want to think about Rosalind. He couldn't work out why hearing from her, hearing her voice, meeting her, seeing her, had had such an effect on him. She was a woman he once loved but now didn't. A woman he rarely thought of. A name on his Christmas card list he sometimes didn't bother to send a card to.

And yet, he felt things crumbling in the architecture he had so carefully constructed.

Oh, but the way they finished, though, how he'd been, that was it. That was what seeing her brought back. When Rosalind told him it was over, he put on an act. He played the role of a brave man accepting his lover no longer had feelings for him, when, had he been honest, he would have said, "Yes, that is what I want also. I no longer have feelings for you." He would have done it himself, sooner than Rosalind, but he waited for her, lying to himself that to finish things would have broken her, compounding the lies by telling himself he kept his own counsel because there was no need to hurt her.

And so more ingredients were added to every subsequent relationship. Fear, dishonesty, cowardice, pretence. Every subsequent relationship and, indeed, his work, his whole life. He didn't say what he felt. He didn't act on the truth of what he felt. He lacked pride.

Chapter Ten

Then

Gerard was thirty-one. While TV shows, films, magazines and newspaper features told him the world was full of single women looking for a good man, Gerard's experience told him the opposite was the case. Everyone was in a relationship. Everyone. And not only were they in a relationship, but they were all happy, too, content with their partners. They were getting married, having children, settling down. Wherever he looked, he saw couples or couples with young children.

He began turning down wedding invitations, developing the habit of doing things early and alone. An early drink. The early showing at the cinema. He would eat lunch out by himself, with a newspaper or magazine, somewhere informal, relaxed, anonymous. Not dinner, though: the spotlight would be trained on him too closely, for too long. Pop concerts were out, but classical concerts were more than acceptable because they allowed him to play the role of a true aficionado.

He wanted to be in a relationship. He wanted to kiss a girl again, to make love again. (He would have dearly loved a string of one-night stands but lacked the looks, the instant attraction, the nerve, the necessary honesty or the right kind of dishonesty.) He stumbled through a series of fruitless pursuits, often lacking the courage to ask a girl out, being met with refusals when he managed to summon some up.

The break-up with Jessica had brought his self-consciousness to the fore, stripped away any confidence he might have with women. The relationship with Rosalind saw his cowardice take centre stage, as well as his deceit.

And then he met Sally. Sally was an everyday beauty. She was clever, had a good sense of humour, liked clothes and makeup, going out to dinner and listening to music from the charts. She was separated and about to start divorce proceedings. She was a touch taller than Gerard, but she was willing to let that go because he was kind, thoughtful, and generous. He wasn't as kind, thoughtful, and generous as he let her believe, but he could appear to be, which was enough to be going on with.

They went out for meals. They went to the cinema, the theatre and the pub. She told him sex was good. He was certainly willing and giving in bed, but he thought about things too much. He was too concerned about her pleasure, whereas with Jessica and for a while, with Rosalind, he had just done it without thinking, which they all seemed happy with. He didn't mind that Sally seemed less concerned with his pleasure, that sex was something in her gift, that there was a sense he should be grateful, possibly because he wasn't as tall as she would have liked.

And he didn't mind that she talked about her ex a great deal and about the difficulties she was having with the divorce. He minded, although he said nothing, that she said she missed her ex when Gerard brought up the subject of what they should do on New Year's Eve.

And then she called him by her ex's name. She called him Gary.

"What did you say?" Gerard asked. They were in his kitchen, making coffee.

Sally's face was flushed. Her stomach had somersaulted. "Gerry," she said.

It was plausible. She did call him Gerry sometimes. Gerard let it go.

And then she did it again. This came a few months after the first instance. He didn't let it go this time.

It was around eleven o'clock on a Saturday morning. Gerard and Sally had been to the cinema the night before—Clear and Present Danger—had gone back to Sally's, gone to bed, made love, had a lie-in, a leisurely hour or so over breakfast: a normal Friday night, Saturday morning.

While Sally was still in her dressing gown, Gerard showered and dressed. The relationship was at the stage where they kept a few things at each other's place. He was off to meet friends—work colleagues—for a day out at Haydock Park. She was going to stay home and catch up on a bit of cleaning and ironing. He would likely have a couple of drinks at the races but would be back in plenty of time for them to meet at the restaurant he'd booked.

Coming downstairs, Gerard saw Sally curled up on the sofa, reading a magazine, her coffee on the table next to her. The radio was on in the kitchen, the music just about audible in the living room. The TV was on, but the volume was too low to hear. Sally kept the TV on all day, but with the sound down, until there was something she wanted to watch. She liked the company.

"Right. I'm off to lose my shirt," he said. He smiled at her. "Looks like you're all set to get stuck into the cleaning."

Sally looked up. "Ha, ha," she said. "I'm mentally preparing myself for the task ahead." Gerard came over to her. He bent down, and she lifted her head, and they kissed. "You going to be warm enough?" she asked. He was wearing a polo shirt, chinos, and a light jacket. "Weather's due to change, it says."

"I'll be fine. I'm not expecting to spend too much time away from the bar, anyway." Sally smiled. "Right," Gerard said. "I'll be away. See you at the restaurant about eight."

"Yes!" Sally said.

Gerard left the living room door open when he went to the front door. He was just about to open it when Sally shouted, "Back some winners for me, Gaz."

A perfectly ordinary scene changed in that moment. Both Gerard and Sally froze. Without moving, staring at the door, Gerard said, "What did you say?"

Then he turned and stepped into the living room doorway. Sally was still on the sofa with her legs up beneath her. Involuntarily, she was gripping the magazine tightly. Her face was red.

"I..." she began. "I just...said..."

"Never mind." There was no mistaking it, no room for doubt. And it wasn't just the name; it was the familiar form of the name. That twisted the knife. "I heard what you said."

And then he left the house.

The day at the races was completely spoiled, of course. He kept up the pretence with his colleagues, didn't mention it to any of them, he backed a horse in each race, even coming out on top by the end of the day, but he thought about nothing else. He and Sally had been going out together for nearly a year. Gaz, she called him. Fucking Gaz.

It was a long-planned day out with a group of men and women from his department at work. A team-bonding exercise, a reward for all their hard work, a chance to forget all about work for people who worked together every day of the week. Some had brought their partners with them, giving others a glimpse into their personal lives, showing the human being behind the business suit.

Gerard had suggested it to Sally when the jolly was first announced.

"No," she said. "Thanks, but you'll have more fun without me." And then she added, "Besides, I went on enough nights out with Gary and his mates from football. Stuck at a table with all the other wives and girlfriends while he was at the bar, laughing with the lads."

She mentioned Gary often. Why wouldn't she? How couldn't she? That was what he told himself. And what he told her, too. "You talk about whatever you need to," he said to her. The message being, 'I'm understanding, empathic, secure.' The truth being, 'I'm actually tired of it, to be honest, tired of spending so long hearing about you and your ex when I'd rather be talking about us, or me, or anything. But if I say anything, you might begin to see how insecure I am. You might not like me.'

He'd wanted her to come to the races with him. He liked being with her. He loved her, or told himself he did, at least. And she was beautiful, too, of course, in a conventional way, and dressed stylishly. He wanted to show her off, make his colleagues see there was more to him than the actuarial whizz who could be a bit of a laugh but was possibly a touch on the dull side. If he could get a girl like Sally, well…

But now, standing on the balcony of the bar the company had booked, overlooking the finish line, seeing a horse he'd backed come in first at 7-1 beneath the grey sky, a little chilly, wishing he'd at least put a sweater on, well…how would he introduce her?

"Hi, everyone. This is Sally. We made love last night. She wasn't as involved as I'd have liked her to be, but that's probably because she was thinking of her ex-husband, Gary. Or Gaz, she calls him. Calls me, too. Anyone need another drink?"

On the coach back to Manchester, the atmosphere was a bit subdued compared to the journey to the racecourse. Most people had drunk a bit too much. The plans for a raucous continuation of the day with a session in town were being quietly shelved in favour of a takeaway and an early night. Some were still up for it, but not Gerard, not with the prospect of dinner with Sally ahead.

Although it was quiet, and he had a double seat to himself, Gerard found it hard to think about what to do. The rug had been pulled from under him with one word. He kept hearing it and seeing her frozen, flushed face as he turned around.

He stared out of the coach window at the flat fields they were passing, the green of the grass dulled by the grey clouds above and, gradually, he was able to turn down the volume on Sally's voice. He began to consider what to do.

He knew exactly what he should do, of course. There was no way the relationship could continue, no way he could carry on seeing Sally. It wasn't simply that she'd called him by her ex-husband's name (twice: he had always known she'd called him Gary that time). It was the way she did it, the context, the circumstances. It was all so casual, so familiar, so domestic a scene. So ordinary and routine, as if she was so relaxed, she had slipped back to where she wanted to be. This scene still featured Gary. It excluded Gerard, airbrushed him out and replaced him. How often had she caught herself and shut the name in her mouth? How often had she said it and Gerard not heard?

He knew exactly what to do. He had to end the relationship. There was nothing to think about, really. And Sally couldn't blame him, couldn't expect anything else, really. He didn't even need to summon up any courage to do it. He didn't need to worry about hurting her or letting her down. What she did was worse than what he was about to do. It was a given, the only response.

And yet...

He knew he ought to. He knew he wouldn't. He had every intention of doing it, but he knew he wouldn't go through with it. Sitting by himself on the coach as it approached Manchester, he tried to put his finger on the exact reasons. A swirl of reasons and accusations, a mist of self-knowledge, jumbled through his mind. Need, fear, cowardice (even though no courage was required, except the courage to be alone), lack of self-esteem, lack of pride, the need to appear the bigger man, magnanimous, understanding, mature, reasonable. The jibes and rationalisations cavorted inside his head, taunting, specious, truthful, full of false reassurance, comforting, needling, weak.

He asked the driver to let him out early. It was around seven, and he was just a short walk from Sally's house, which, he knew, would be entirely different from the place he left just a few hours earlier. His departure roused his colleagues temporarily. They sent him off with cries of 'Moneybags' and 'Give us a tip for Monday', given his success at Haydock. He smiled and waved and thought they might look at him in a different light after all.

Sally answered the door so quickly that Gerard wondered if she had been there waiting for him all day. Or expecting someone else. He toyed with the idea of saying something along those lines, or told himself he did because, really, he wouldn't have said anything like that in a million years. Too nice, too reasonable, lacking the nerve.

Sally threw her arms around him, pressed her cheek against his chest, pressed her arms against his back, and held him tightly. She didn't need to say anything. He could tell everything he needed to know from the way she hugged him.

She did say something, however. "I didn't think you'd come back. I need you, Gerard."

Gerard held her tightly. He told her it was all right, everything was okay, he understood. Reasonable, controlled, full of understanding. He said, "It's okay. We'll be okay."

He was wrong about the hug. Over the course of the next few months, he sensed Sally drawing away from him, no longer needing him. She became impatient with him, made no secret when she found him tiresome and complained that he was too compliant. For which he apologised, of course, instead of fighting back, which made things worse. He thought she'd have liked him more if he had left her when she called him Gaz. Respected him more, certainly. And he would have respected himself more.

She didn't end things well. He realised one day that she had stopped calling and that she was often out when he called or knew it was him and didn't answer the phone. After a week or so, she finally called him and told him she no longer wanted to see him. Two years ended just like that.

He took it badly. He pestered her, finding reasons to phone her and call around to her house. He still remembered the hug. He was convinced this was a bump in the road, that she still needed him. But he eventually got the message. For a while, he wondered if she had gone back to Gary. He wondered if, whoever she was with now, she ever got his name wrong and called him Gerry. And then he stopped caring.

This was the point at which he started to believe a relationship would never happen, that he wouldn't get married, wouldn't have children, and would spend his days alone. This is where he started to accept it, and also to crave it. Not just because he preferred it that way, which, in truth, he did. If he thought about it objectively, honestly, there were plenty of times with Sally and Rosalind when he wished he was alone, happy in his own company, not having to do what they wanted to, not having to pretend. But also because of his weakness, his need for sympathy and understanding. He found he wanted people to look at him and say, 'Poor man, all alone, and he has so much to offer.' He wanted to say, "Ah, well, it's just not for me. It's just never worked out. Don't worry about me. But, of course, do worry about me."

Once, when he went to see his mother, he tried to tell her of his loneliness, of how much he missed Sally.

She said, "When you were a child, you always cried for longer than you needed to, past the point where you were still in pain, past when the hurt stopped."

And then they talked about something else, and Gerard resented his mother's lack of sympathy and her knack of seeing through him.

There were relationships after Sally, but he entered into all of them expecting them to fail, and his self-denigrating comments wore the women down one by one. They weren't looking for a strong, silent type, but they did wish he would shut up at times or stand up for himself. No one wants a weakling.

He began to develop a romantic image of himself. Sad, brave, stoic, overcoat collar turned up against the elements, walking alone at dusk back to his books and his music, back to the consoling glass.

Chapter Eleven

Then

Gerard gets away with it!

Of course, when he did it, when he got the name wrong, it was okay. Well, perhaps not okay, if he really thought about it deeply, but he didn't. He could excuse himself, or just overlook it and move on.

Whenever he thought back to this particular incident, when it came unbidden to mind, he tried his best to believe the lie he told at the time and usually succeeded.

This was with Rosalind, around a year into their relationship. There had been some months of passionate, frequent, enthusiastic sex with no complaints from either party. Gerard was especially taken by the wild exuberance Rosalind displayed and her willingness to initiate proceedings, in contrast to her demeanour out of bed, which was undeniably cute and appealing but with a dash of uncertainty and diffidence. There had been regular trips to the cinema, meals out, meals in, pubs, clubs, plays, the ballet once, an opera.

But things were settling. Good humour and periods of silence replaced excitement and energy. Rosalind was yet to become aware of how much of an impact Mark was having on her. Gerard had yet to admit to himself how much he wanted to sleep with that stylish girl he saw on her way to the bus stop most mornings or how much he wished he had kissed

Mary-Jane at that party, but he did take care not to mention to Rosalind that he often ate lunch at work with Sarah.

It was a Thursday evening. They were in Rosalind's flat, in the front room. They had finished tea, and the radio was on. Rosalind was flicking through a listings magazine while Gerard was reading the evening paper. In the kitchen, Naomi, who owned the house, was washing the dishes, trying to make her pointed tuts and sighs heard over the music, as she wasn't sure Gerard had got the message when she said, too loudly and with an edge, "I'll wash up, then, shall I?"

Naomi came in when she heard Rosalind squeal.

"Listen!" Rosalind was shouting. "Just listen to this!" She bounded over to where Gerard was sitting, a look of amusement on his face, and showed him the page she had open. She was grinning, thrilled. "Joe Jackson's playing at the Palace!"

Naomi stood in the doorway, watching Gerard's reaction. She was older than Rosalind by about ten years, divorced, and regarded herself as the younger woman's wise counsellor. She had long since decided that Gerard was wrong for Rosalind and had told her so, albeit not in so many words, and also in exactly that many words.

"Oh, yes," said Gerard. He was a fan, too, although not so obsessed as Rosalind was, and had seen Joe Jackson once in his early days when he was more than happy to stand sweating in a packed crowd. He didn't know why, but he never let Rosalind know how much of a fan he was and would talk him down when she talked about how much she loved his music. He was condescending. "Not as good as his early stuff," he said when Rosalind went into raptures about his changes of phase.

Rosalind put her arms around Gerard's neck, like a daughter hugging her father.

"Oh, please, let's go!" she said. "Please, please, please!"

More and more, Gerard liked staying in or just going down the road to the Sergeant-at-Arms.

"Why don't you go?" he said. "I'm not sure I like the latest stuff he does."

Rosalind let go of Gerard and looked hurt, frustrated.

"Is she really going out with him?" Naomi sang in the doorway.

"Okay, then," said Gerard.

Rosalind kissed him hard on the cheek. "I'll get tickets first thing tomorrow," she said, and she skipped back to her seat. Naomi stared at Gerard until he looked back at her, and then she went slowly back into the kitchen. Gerard furrowed his brows to suggest he didn't know what her problem was, but he knew exactly what her look meant and couldn't, if he was being honest, argue with it.

He called Rosalind 'Jessica' in the foyer before the Joe Jackson concert. They bumped into a woman Gerard worked with, there with her husband. Gerard had met him a couple of times before, and so did the introductions.

"And this is Jessica," he said, introducing Rosalind. He fumbled his way out of it because his work colleague had the same name, but he knew what he'd done. The moment the name left his mouth, his stomach lurched, and he felt his face glow with panic. He glanced quickly at Rosalind to see her reaction and told himself he'd got away with it, although he couldn't be sure. He hadn't. Rosalind knew exactly what he'd done. She said nothing, just enjoyed the concert less than she was expecting. Gerard convinced himself it was a genuine mistake, that he hadn't meant *his* Jessica. He believed himself and knew at the same time that he was lying.

The incident affected both Rosalind and Gerard. It further chipped away at Rosalind's opinion of herself, which was becoming increasingly fragile. She felt like second-best but also that second-best was as much as she deserved, maybe even more than she deserved. She wanted to speak up, to confront Gerard, but was unable to do so, held back by a need not to be alone, by a creeping anxiety that she would collapse if she tried to stand without help.

For his part, Gerard continued on a road of self-denial. He was finding it more and more convenient to lie to himself, to justify his own responses, to blame others rather than take responsibility. His regret for causing Rosalind hurt was turning to resentment that she was making him feel this way. He was irritated by what he perceived as her weakness. He wanted to be free of her but felt he couldn't because she would break if he did end things. Or so he told himself. In reality, he was simply too much of a coward to say the words.

Having told himself that getting her name wrong was a genuine mistake, that he did get her mixed up with the Jessica he worked with, he moved on to an occasional admission that he did say his Jessica's name because he still wanted her, and not Rosalind, but he blamed Rosalind for not being Jessica.

And so on they stumbled, both of them unhappy, both apparently facing a life with someone they didn't want to be with, until Rosalind summoned the courage to end the relationship when she found someone else she thought she would love forever and be happy with forever and whom she thought would support her forever. She turned out to be wrong then, too.

Chapter Twelve

Now

Why had she called? What made her want to see him and then say so little when she did? And why couldn't he pack this day away as an aberration?

Gerard couldn't concentrate and couldn't adapt. He could have gone swimming later than his usual time but didn't, unable to accommodate change or interruption. He picked up his schedule as best he could but couldn't settle.

Instead, he wandered through his flat, looking closely at the life he had built for himself. Everything precise, everything exact, all gradually accreted since he first moved in thirty years ago. In the second bedroom that no guest had ever slept in was his desk at the window. Papers, pens, laptop, printer, the house phone that no one called. Straight lines. Neatly arrayed, no carelessness. Accuracy. Clarity.

In the kitchen were the cutlery and crockery, the toaster, the kettle, the pots and pans acquired at great expense for their looks and name. In his hall and living room, he looked at the paintings on the wall—originals, all—and at the furniture, the table and chairs, the sofa and armchairs, the occasional table on which sat the chessboard where he played through practice games and examples from the newspaper. Every item had been methodically researched, with time taken to source, to create not comfort but the look he wanted to give, the impression he wanted to create, of a man of taste and refinement, a man unhindered by needless ornamentation, a man who knew his art, shrewd, insightful, a man who followed his own reason.

The novels were arranged in alphabetical order, the non-fiction according to category. He had read them all, but how many could he remember? How many had left him immersed or moved? How many had been bought and read to fit the image he wanted for himself? To paper the person he wanted people to see? It was the same with the CDs: modern jazz, 20th century avant-garde.

Here was a curated life. Here was the man he wanted to present. But how many people even saw it or gave any thought to him once they had seen him?

He took out a CD he had ordered recently from a small label specialising in contemporary music. He'd seen the label mentioned in a newspaper or magazine, and it struck him as a suitable new detail to add. He put it on. He waited. He watched the timer rise. No sound, and then suddenly a note, played on a piano, deep and long. And then nothing, until a chord, the notes soft and clashing. There was no sense of time in the music. No rhythm or logic that he could perceive.

I feel nothing, he thought. I don't know what I am supposed to feel.

The phone rang. Before he answered it, he looked at his watch and saw that it was somehow 11pm. Inside and outside his flat all was dark.

"Will you come over?" Rosalind said. "Tomorrow? Will you come to the hospital in the morning?"

Gerard said yes because he couldn't say no, and Rosalind ended the call.

Rosalind had dislodged him, knocked him off-kilter, and he couldn't fit himself back in.

He didn't want her. He didn't want her back. He felt nothing when he saw her. No desire, no regret. Sympathy, of course, for what she was going through, but a sympathy that was easily dismissed and forgotten, as he might do when watching the victims of disaster on the news or passing a homeless person in the street. Enough sympathy to donate by text or to dig into his pocket for change. But nothing more than that, nothing that lasted much beyond the end of the report or the turn of the corner.

Maybe regret, actually. Not for what happened with Rosalind. Not for the way the relationship diminished and closed but for the past. Rosalind was the past, and he had blocked that out for the most part. Some flickering flashes came to him now and then, of course, but they were fleeting phrases and images in his mind. This was concrete. This was flesh and blood. Loose flesh and thin blood. A hand he had taken, a body he had held, a mouth he had kissed. A woman he had made laugh and cry and gasp. A woman who had made him laugh and cry and gasp—a woman who now, like him, felt nothing except maybe an itch, a reminder.

He didn't want the past. Gerard only wanted now, and he had constructed a life that gave him now.

The next morning, he set off in his car at just gone eight and drove to Liverpool.

Chapter Thirteen

Now

Rosalind was allowed to stay in her son's room for as long as she wanted; visiting hours didn't apply to her, not with the end liable to happen at any time. She had dozed fitfully through the night in the chair alongside her son's bed. She was woken by her phone vibrating and buzzing. She could have answered it but chose not to. She could have answered the phone and said, "Hello, Mark," and then explained where she was and how their son was doing. Jack wouldn't have minded. He wouldn't have noticed, wouldn't have known, lying as he was in his hospital bed, unconscious, his skin first stabbed and slashed and then pricked, tubes shackling him, drips feeding him, machines monitoring his pulse and heartbeat and blood pressure. She wouldn't even have had to lower her voice.

But she didn't. She'd call back later or text.

She looked at her watch and remembered Gerard had said he'd come over. When she called him yesterday, she said, "It's Ros." For a while, when they were going out together, a serious, stable couple, progressing, meant for each other, a unit, when they went to the cinema every weekend and ate in cheap restaurants and cooked for each other and made love every time they went to bed together, Gerard had called her Rosa. It didn't last; it didn't sound right on his tongue or in her ears, but she went along with it, happily, happy that he wanted his own special name for her. Her father called her Rosie, and Gerard was disappointed that had been taken. He could have used it himself; she wouldn't quite have minded, but he wanted a name for her that only he used. For her part, she never called him Gerry or Ged, which was what all his friends called him. She kept to Gerard, special, rather than formal, his proper name.

She never felt like a Rosalind. She felt she should have been something simple and ordinary. A Jenny, maybe, or a Cathy. Now she was Ros, and she wished to be a Rosalind. Rosalind was a rich girl's name, a name for a special girl, marked out for success and happiness. A Rosalind wouldn't be in this position, wouldn't be at her son's bedside while he fought for his life after a brutal, unprovoked attack. A Gerard could be the father, though, just as easily as a Mark.

She went to her son's side, taking care not to so much as brush against any of the tubes or wires. She reached over and put the back of her fingers against her son's cheek. She felt not the firmness of a young man's cheek, not the friction of the stubble that had grown since the attack, but the barely-there softness of a baby's skin. He was hers, and hers alone. And he wasn't a young man; he was a month-old baby sleeping soundlessly in her arms as she held him in the dead of night, frightened to move in case he woke and also not wanting to move because she had never been more content.

It was just approaching nine when she decided to leave. She told herself there was no point staying any longer, there was nothing she could do, that she'd be back again soon, that anyway the nurses had her number if she needed to get back urgently. The truth was she simply couldn't bear to stay there any longer, in the too-warm room where the silence was broken by the machines beeping and buzzing and clicking, or the sudden opening of the door and a nurse or a doctor bustling in, full of understanding but their minds on a dozen other demanding patients, a quick nod and raise of the eyebrows and maybe a smile to acknowledge her presence, which they'd sooner not have, not because she was being difficult, but because there was nothing to say to her. They were embarrassed by constantly saying nothing over and over again.

Her back ached, her head throbbed, her skin felt like it was contracting, stretching over her bones, about to tear open. She had only arrived yesterday, taking the first train up as soon as the police contacted her, but time had changed, and it felt like weeks already, a long, futile vigil. She told the staff she was leaving and double-checked they had her number.

The hospital felt deserted; the empty lift came quickly. People must stop being sick at the weekend, Rosalind thought. Only the dying remain.

She trudged to the seating area on the first floor, at the front of the hospital, overlooking the entrance, the road down towards town. The day was bright and cold. The smokers at the entrance huddled as close as possible to the door. Hospital staff in Crocs and socks and scrubs risked the traffic to make a dash to the sandwich shop opposite, too cold to wait for the pedestrian lights to change.

Tables and chairs filled a central space, two floors high. Around the seating area were shops selling tea and coffee, sandwiches, snacks, newspapers, toiletries, some books, some toys and pocket-sized versions of board games. A few visitors and patients and staff sat scattered around the mostly empty tables. Rosalind bought a paper and a coffee and then stood bemused, unsure where to sit, spoilt for choice until she finally decided on a table next to the ceiling-high window at the front of the building. Beneath her, ambulances came and went, cars came and went.

She thought vaguely she might look out for Gerard to arrive but didn't. Instead, she ignored her coffee and unthinkingly turned the pages of the newspaper until she arrived at the puzzles page. The night before, the cleaner mopping the floor of Jack's room told her that crosswords were just the thing for this kind of situation. "Or sudokus. Word games, you know," she said. "A book's no good. You can't read. Can't follow a story. But a puzzle does the trick for a while. See a lot of the visitors here doing puzzles."

So Rosalind found a pen in the bottom of her bag and tried to fit numbers into squares and letters into spaces while upstairs her son was dying, or probably dying, or maybe fighting for his life.

She didn't know if her son was fighting for his life. She couldn't be sure. Maybe it was just the tubes and drips that were doing the fighting. It was just a convenient phrase. A nineteen-year-old man is fighting for his life in the intensive care ward of the Royal Liverpool Hospital after being stabbed outside a city centre nightclub in what police are describing as an unprovoked and brutal attack.

How is he?

You know. He's fighting.

Well, he was always a fighter, wasn't he?

That wasn't how Rosalind would have described Jack. That's not the first word she would have thought of. Mischievous, clever, loving, thoughtful, caring, yes. Fighter? No. She hoped he was but knew that it probably wouldn't matter, that it was just something people say in these situations.

She thought, *Gerard couldn't remember my name. It has been thirty years, but then what's thirty years? Thirty years is nothing. Nineteen years is less.*

She saw a voice message on her phone from Mark and listened to it, in case it said he was coming up. Rather than call back, she texted him, a curt Stable. That would suffice, she decided. That would keep Mark at bay, keep Jack hers alone. They were long past the stage where they left kisses at the end of every message, and she couldn't remember the last time they had so much as kissed each other goodnight. For the moment, they still shared the same bed, although they never dressed and undressed in front of each other. They had seen each other naked countless times, of course, grabbed needily for each other, caressed each other tenderly, held each other passionately, but now their bodies were private, concealed, snatched back, an unwanted reminder of the relish with which they had once sought to touch and kiss and pull close.

She went to bed much later than he did anyway—purposely—and would now often fall asleep on the couch with the sound down on the television and only join him when she woke during the night. She knew that she would soon stay on the couch when she woke and planned to keep a blanket in the living room for when that time came. Mark wouldn't care or would just accept it without saying anything. If their son came through, they would formalise their separation. They couldn't move apart. Neither could afford a place of their own, but they'd be able to divide the small house they'd had to move to into demarcated zones and maybe create time slots for the use of the bathroom and kitchen. If he died...well, nothing would matter anyway.

She turned to look out of the window, or face it, at least. Rosalind didn't know why she had contacted Gerard or what she wanted from him and didn't bother trying to explain it to herself. There were no reasons; her son's stabbing had closed the door for her once and for all on rational explanations. Random occurrences and actions and events, that's all there was. Unmotive. Unreason.

She had thought about calling him almost as soon as she knew she was coming up to be with her son. Gerard lived just thirty miles away. They could meet if they wanted to, have lunch, maybe. She even thought she might stay with him and take the train over and back each day; once he found out what had happened, he'd be bound to offer. These thoughts came to her unbidden, as if someone else was telling her of the possibilities she faced. They weren't ideas or suggestions Rosalind was consciously making for herself; they were self-generating fantasies that chased and harried through her mind. Another person had dialled the number and handed her the phone when Gerard answered.

Chapter Fourteen

THEN

They had known each other since nursery and attended the same primary and secondary schools together, always sitting together whenever possible. Rosalind and Sian had been best friends from the day they met, and they remained best friends, although by the time they reached around the age of fourteen, Rosalind didn't actually like Sian much. She was relieved when Sian left school after her O levels to study at the technical college, while Rosalind stayed on in sixth form.

Rosalind was interested in studying and was drawn to other students who felt the same way. Sian lost interest in lessons. She never said much to Rosalind, but she nastily mocked the students who did their homework and stayed in to revise, and Rosalind felt these pupils were proxies for her. When Sian left school, Rosalind felt free to be something approximating herself.

Still, they talked on the phone often and met up at least once a week, in the pubs that didn't enquire too closely about their customers' ages and, at the weekend, at any of the town's nightclubs, for which they could easily make themselves look old enough. They might have met up more often, but Sian started going out with Steve and much of her free time was, understandably, taken with him.

Rosalind was fine with that. She and Sian had less and less to say to each other and were obviously moving in different directions. They had little in common other than that they were best friends. Sian read magazines and historical romances, listened exclusively to music from the charts and wore ra-ra skirts. Rosalind liked plays, poetry and novels translated from the original language into English and listened to the *John Peel Show* and wore T-shirts featuring the names and logos of obscure bands.

Sian thought Rosalind was a snob who thought she was too good for Corby; Rosalind thought Sian was a bore who thought the world ended at the town's limits, but they kept their opinions to themselves because they were best friends.

Rosalind did think she was too good for Corby, and, for that matter, thought she was better than Sian. Except for one thing—Steve. Not specifically Steve. She didn't lie awake at night wishing he was hers, although she liked him well enough despite the fact he didn't like Two-tone music and had a perm. But he was a boyfriend, which was something Rosalind didn't have. Rosalind lacked a boyfriend, which meant that Rosalind lacked something. Something within her.

She didn't resent Sian having a boyfriend; she resented not having one herself, although this did turn into a resentment of Sian for having a boyfriend. Whenever Sian mentioned Steve or said the word 'boyfriend', Rosalind felt she was doing so pointedly, which was galling but handy in a way because it allowed her to justify her growing dislike of her best friend. To be fair, Sian often did say the word pointedly because she knew it irked Rosalind, but she justified doing so to herself because Rosalind so often lorded it over her with her talk of obscure bands and comments about books which she knew Sian hadn't read, and the way she went on about the Treaty of Versailles which she was studying at A level.

When Rosalind said she couldn't go out one Friday night because it was the sixth form dance, Sian said, "Oh? Who are you going with?" She knew fine well Rosalind wasn't going with anyone.

"It's not some high school prom, Sian," said Rosalind.

"No, but..." said Sian. They were talking on the phone, so Sian had no need to hide her satisfaction.

"I'll just go with the gang." Rosalind didn't need to explain who the gang was. Delicate boys, sensitive over-thinkers who liked plays and poetry and who stopped doing PE as soon as the school let them and who were all desperately in love with Rosalind, the only girl in the group, but who couldn't bring themselves to do anything about it. And she didn't need to explain that she'd spend much of the evening wishing someone would ask her to dance and pretending she was glad no one did.

"Have a good time," said Sian. "Steve and I are going to the cinema, I think."

She said it lightly and matter-of-factly and with a note of triumph.

Things got worse when Sian and Steve had sex.

"We did it!" Sian told her, again on the phone. Rosalind didn't need to be there to know that Sian was lying back on the bed, kicking her legs in the air. "Steve and me. We did it!"

Steve and I, thought Rosalind, though she couldn't be certain.

It had been on the cards for a while. Sian had often mentioned they were going to. It was just a matter of finding the right time. Rosalind held back. She didn't want to seem keen to find out all the details.

"His mum and dad went out last night, so we had the house to ourselves," Sian said. Rosalind had so many questions and wanted to hear more but didn't want to hear more. "He was so lovely. I love him, Ros. It was so good."

Rosalind thought Sian probably didn't know what good was, although she acknowledged to herself that she'd have a better idea than her.

It seemed every girl in Corby had a boyfriend, but the lack of one preyed on her mind really only when it came to Sian and Steve. She didn't like Sian having that edge, even sharper now she and Steve had had sex. Rosalind was ahead in all other considerations, was lapping Sian in fact—in her mind, at least—but this single issue seemed to allow Sian to wave carefree while Rosalind huffed and puffed past her. Rosalind wanted to be able to say, "I'm going to the cinema with my boyfriend." And now she then wanted to be able to add, "After which we'll have sex."

She was bothered about still being a virgin, and she wanted to lose her virginity before she went to university, where she was sure people would be able to tell, and it would mark her out. As far as she could gather, all the other girls in sixth form had lost theirs, although she couldn't be sure because she didn't have any female friends other than Sian, who, increasingly, didn't count. Still, picking up snippets of gossip and overhearing snatches of conversation seemed to be the general direction of traffic.

And the girls seemed different, too. More sophisticated, more grown-up.

Even Sian, in her ra-ra skirts and big hair, back-combed to within an inch of its life, seemed to have an air of worldliness which Rosalind's knowledge of TS Eliot and the Treaty of Versailles couldn't counter. Rosalind didn't even have the option of looking down on these girls because she had no religion to give her a sense of untouched contempt, and all the books she read and all the plays she saw and all the subtitled films she watched encouraged her to casually float above outdated social conventions. And she just wanted to. She was curious and felt desire.

There was also pressure from her mother. Not specifically to have sex, but at least to show some interest in boys. More than once, Rosalind's mother asked if she was a lesbian, asking aggressively, nastily, until the question became an accusation.

Try as it appeared she did, her mother couldn't hurt her. It wouldn't be long before she was away to university, and then she'd only be back for brief holidays, so Rosalind shrugged that pressure off. She couldn't shrug off the pressure she put on herself, though, and didn't want to. She felt a craving and was going to do something about it.

With the start of university just under two months away, Rosalind considered her options. She was sitting in Corby Central Park at one of the café's outdoor tables. It was a baking hot day. She was wearing a straw sunhat and a too-big, black Slits T-shirt that had been eagerly lent to her by one of the boys in the gang. She felt the white football shorts and black PE pumps finished the ensemble off nicely but wished she had brought sun cream with her because she didn't want to risk her skin losing its whiteness. In front of her was a selection of books, some reading for the History course she was going to take, a couple of novels, Martin Amis and Edna O'Brien, and a packet of ten Benson and Hedges because she'd started smoking ready for university.

The café was closed. There were no shouts coming from the park lake; all the boats for hire were tied up, banging together and against the concrete jetty. The park was deserted, and the streets had been deserted, too, making Rosalind's journey on her bike more relaxing than usual. Everyone was at home, glued to the royal wedding on TV. When Rosalind told her mother she was going out, her mother said, "Don't be long.

You'll miss it." And when Rosalind had said she didn't want to watch, her mother had looked pointedly at the empty armchair where her dad used to sit, muttering, "What kind of girl doesn't want to see a wedding?" Rosalind smiled, knowing he'd have made some non-committal comment and given her a wink while her mother wasn't looking.

She pushed away all the books but one, her journal, to which she sporadically committed her secrets. She opened it at a clean page, wrote the date and a title — 'Possibles' — on the top line and underlined both with a ruler. Then she scraped her chair back and put her feet up on the table, there being no café staff around to tell her to get her feet down or other customers to give her disapproving looks from which she'd instantly shrink.

She looked again at the title and giggled, thinking that 'Runners and Riders' might be better, but she decided against changing it because that would mean tearing out this page and starting a fresh one. She was unable to cross out mistakes. Regardless of where she made an error on the page, she had to start again.

She jiggled the pen between her teeth. This wasn't going to be a long list, but she wanted to at least feel she'd given it due thought.

Kev.

Pete the Punk.

Finbar (whose real name was Stewart but who had seen a documentary about Travellers on TV one night and came into school claiming to be the seventh son of a seventh son, and Finbar seemed as good a nickname as any from then on.)

Malcolm.

Pete the Gay Prog (*He should really just be Pete the Gay or Gay Pete the ex-Prog*, thought Rosalind now he no longer liked prog rock. But she kept it as it was.)

That boy on the train back from Sheffield.

Kev, Finbar, the two Petes, and Malcolm were the boys in the gang. By this time, things had progressed, although to call it progress was stretching things. Things had moved on. Rosalind had now snogged all of them once, apart from Pete the Prog, who became Pete the Gay Prog after he announced he was gay, cut his hair, stopped wearing flares, started reading Jean Genet and only listened to the Tom Robinson Band and the Ziggy Stardust album, which he carried with him under his arm everywhere he went, a throwback to his prog days.

In each case, Rosalind had initiated the kissing. She knew if left to the boys, nothing would ever happen. In his kitchen getting coffee (Finbar), at the front door of her house one night after being walked home (Malcolm), in the sixth form cloakroom (Pete the Punk), and in a graveyard when she asked Kevin to help her shift the lid of a small tomb to see if there was a skeleton inside (there were only crisp packets and cigarette butts).

The kisses were clumsy and awkward, too aggressive or too passive, not in the least arousing or satisfying, although she was impressed that Malcolm had the gumption to put his hand on her breast, even though he didn't move it once it was there. She kissed them all over the course of three weeks and, after each kiss, said she didn't want to take it further because she didn't want to spoil things with the gang. She felt guilty that she had lifted their hopes and then dashed them, that each took his turn being taciturn with her for a few days, but assuaged her guilt because she had waited until the A levels were over so none of them would be distracted from his revision.

She wrote their names down on the list even though she knew they were non-starters. The same applied to that boy on the train back from Sheffield—Barry. They'd both been for an interview and a tour around the university, and though they hadn't spoken during the day, they decided to sit next to each other on the train when they met and got chatting on the platform.

He was changing at Derby to get a connection to Nottingham while she was going straight through. Barry was tall, athletic-looking and blond. He was chatty and funny and knew all the bands she knew and had read all the books she'd read and more besides, although he wasn't snobbish about his reading like Rosalind was, and said he'd much rather read Tom Sharp than Camus, which he said he didn't really understand, but Rosalind thought he probably did, much more so than her, anyway. He played a lot of sport and liked Sheffield, but he still had a couple of other places to go to, like Liverpool and Manchester.

Rosalind thought he was perfect. When the announcement came over the tannoy that the next stop was Derby, she moved from her seat opposite him to the seat next to him and said that she had an interview coming up at Liverpool and maybe she'd see him there. And then, not caring about the other people on the train seeing them, she leaned over and kissed him. They kissed for a long time, and she put her tongue in his mouth, and he pulled her closer to him.

She was convinced they would meet in Liverpool when she went there for her interview, but there was no sign of him, and she bitterly regretted not giving him her phone number but had decided to leave it to fate, which, she was sure, would be on her side, and then it turned out it wasn't.

She crossed out all the names on the list one by one, neatly, with a single line. Then she reached for the pencil case on the table and took out a red pen to write the one name on the list that would fit the bill, knowing that this was the only name she should have written in the first place.

Steve.

And then, switching back to the black pen, she wrote 'Definite' in brackets.

She smiled. No nerves. No doubts. Just excitement, and absolute certainty. She smiled and clicked the top of her biro with a sense of satisfaction. "A job well started is a job half done," she said aloud, remembering one of her father's favourite sayings. And then she felt a little sheepish for quoting her dad when she was making plans to lose her virginity. And that made her giggle, after which she lit a cigarette, leaned back in her chair, and enjoyed having her feet up on the table.

She felt very sophisticated, almost as if she had actually done it already, and began to understand why the girls at school had all started to seem different. The fact she was planning it all out so deliberately added to her sense of worldliness. She was a woman of poise, an individual who cared not for the bourgeois constraints of a society tied to antiquated mores. She worried momentarily that an outfit of Slits T-shirt, football shorts, floppy sunhat, and black pumps and socks might jar with her new-found polish, might not appear as French as she hoped (and Rosalind felt French was the most appropriate nationality for this incarnation). She dismissed the thought quickly. *The élan comes from within*, she told herself. *Style has nothing to do with clothes, but with personality.*

Nevertheless, she thought that when the time came, she ought to be wearing something more apt, maybe even something beguiling.

She wasn't sure Steve did beguiling. He didn't seem the kind who needed to be beguiled. No boy she could think of did. And that brought another thought into her head. What if he didn't want to? This, too, she dismissed easily. She was a girl. He was a boy. Of course he'd want to. She'd seen more than enough films to know that. Probably even Pete the Gay Prog would want to.

Still, new clothes would be nice, a way of marking the occasion. Maybe even a dress! She couldn't remember the last time she'd worn a dress, although she could easily remember the last time her mother had urged her to.

Rosalind decided it was time to make a new list. Few things made her happier. She stubbed out her cigarette, making a mental note to switch to Gauloises, turned to a clean page of her journal and delved into her pencil case for a suitable colour pen.

A week later and she had everything she thought she needed. She bought a short, but not too short, summer dress from Top Shop. It had a zip up the back. That would be a nice job for Steve. New pants and bra, too, from Marks and Sparks. She already had a pair of white Converse high-tops that she thought would bring a touch of jollity while also allowing her to avoid heels, which she hated. She practised with makeup but was happy with her hair. No way was she going down the back-combed, legwarmers and ra-ra route. She made a special trip to Boots in Peterborough for condoms.

The only thing she didn't have was the opportunity. She only ever really saw Steve when he was with Sian, and she couldn't very well broach the subject then. And she didn't want to call him out of the blue. It didn't seem the kind of thing you could bring up over the phone.

And then the opportunity presented itself. Much to her annoyance, Sian had to go away on holiday with her family to Devon, which meant she would miss the big party Sarah was having.

But Steve would be there. And Rosalind had been invited, too.

When the night of the party arrived, Rosalind took her time getting ready. She washed her hair, leaning over the sink, and then had a bath, adding the scented bath cubes she'd picked up in Boots in Peterborough the same time she bought the Durex. (She felt buying only the condoms would look a little too obvious, and added a toothbrush, as well, although she felt no awkwardness pointing to the packet of three behind the assistant at the counter.)

After the bath, she padded into her bedroom, where she took off her dressing gown and looked at her reflection in the mirror. Save for the towel wrapped around her hair, she was naked. The scent of the strawberry bath cube drifted from her skin. Lying neatly on her single bed were the clothes she had laid out earlier. She stood frank and open in front of the mirror, her arms at her side, striking no poses. She looked at herself for a long, still time and then reached across her body with her right hand to her left shoulder. She drew her hand down her arm, slowly, lightly touching her soft skin, and then across her breast and down to her belly. Without knowing the word, she felt she was anticipating something akin to a sacrament. A milestone, certainly.

She was pleased with what she saw and felt, and she smiled, and then she grinned broadly. She took the towel from her head and began to blow dry her hair, happily staying naked. When she finished, she laid the warm hairdryer on her lap. She looked at the clothes on her bed. She thought about the look on Steve's face when she told him what she wanted.

Those were the words she used in her mind. She said them out loud.

"What I want," she said. "This is what I want. This is what I want."

She repeated the words not to convince herself but because of their truth, as if it was registering properly only for the first time now.

She looked at the clothes on the bed, then reached for her handbag, where she'd put the condoms into a zipped compartment that could have been made for the job. She took them out and looked at the packet, turning it over in her hands. She'd taken the wrapper off as soon as she bought them to save time. Now, once again, she took one out of the pack. She ran her finger along the serrated edge and pressed her thumb against the ridge of the condom, feeling it through the foil.

The night she bought them, Rosalind had toyed with the idea of taking one out of its foil, to get a closer look, maybe even to slip one over a banana. She'd heard that happened in some sex education classes. Not that they had introduced such things in her school yet. There was only Biology and whisperings in the playground. In the end, she hadn't. She decided to leave it to Steve. He'd done it at least three times, according to Sian. Or she'd figure it out for herself when the time came. How hard could it be? She laughed when she thought that.

She wasn't laughing now. She felt serene. As she got dressed, she became more fully aware of her feelings. These clothes weren't for Steve; they were for her. She wasn't doing this to get at Sian, or to be like the other girls in school, or to head to university with experience of more than just books and records. And nor was it some landmark on her journey to becoming a woman, or an element of some frivolous game of let's pretend. This was a statement of who she was and what she was, and she was going to enjoy it, relish it all.

Dressed, Rosalind put the Gauloises and a disposable lighter into the small handbag where she kept the condoms and then put the bag on crossways, from the left shoulder to her right hip, the thin strap running between her breasts. She put on her denim jacket and checked herself in the mirror, liking what she saw, feeling she looked like the person she was.

Her mother tutted at the jacket.

"I hope you're going to take that off when you get there," she said.

"Not all I'll be taking off," Rosalind muttered. And then, louder, "Bye, Mum. Don't wait up."

The bus ride took longer than she expected, but she enjoyed the meandering route as the summer's light slowly faded, and took the opportunity to say goodbye to the town she would soon leave and to which she only intended to return for brief visits—university holidays, the odd weekend, her mother's funeral.

The party was well underway by the time Rosalind arrived. She squeezed her way through to the kitchen, leaving three of the four cans of beer she'd picked up at the off licence, and then made her way upstairs to find somewhere to leave her jacket and check out suitable locations. She knew Sarah quite well but had no idea she lived in such a big house—detached, spread over four floors, and full of nooks and crannies, not to mention a short flight of steps on the top floor that curled up to a small bedroom. There were posters on the wall and toys on the bed. Sarah's little sister's room, Rosalind guessed.

The ground floor and the basement were the party spaces. Rosalind spotted Steve early but was in no rush and happily made her way down to the basement to sip her drink and dance. She felt free, especially as none of the gang was there. They'd been invited—pretty much the entire sixth form had been, as well as Sarah's old friends who'd left, which was how Sian got an invite—but they'd all been adamant they wouldn't go.

They all came out with reasons:
It'll be boring.
The music will be crap.
It'll just be the in-crowd.
Who wants to dance anyway?

I just hate them all.

Rosalind knew they were simply scared and wished they weren't. They were shocked when she said she was going. They went quiet and hoped it didn't mean she was leaving them.

After an hour or so, Steve appeared in the basement, lingering on the edge of the dancefloor, not quite alone but not quite with anyone either. Rosalind, who had been dancing on the fringes of several groups, slowly shimmied her way over towards him. She looked past him several times until she made it look like she'd only just seen him. She waved him over and gave him a warm, encouraging smile when he protested he didn't dance.

He shuffled awkwardly in front of her. She danced freely in front of him, as she would have done had he not been there, feeling the music course through her, singing along with the lyrics. When the song finished, he stood still, not knowing whether to stay or leave.

Rosalind stepped towards him. She touched his arm, pulling him slightly down towards her, and stood on tiptoe to whisper in his ear.

"Look what I've got," she said. She stepped away from him and opened her handbag, lifting the condoms out just enough for him to see the packet. Then she smiled. "Wait a couple of seconds, and then follow me."

Steve did as he was told. She knew he would, never once feeling the need to check he was behind her. In the bedroom she had selected earlier, at the top of the steps, she lit a cigarette and waited. Sure enough, soon the door opened slowly, and Steve edged in, nervous, uncertain.

Rosalind flicked the cigarette out of the window and then turned to look at Steve. She had learned of sex from whispers in the sixth form common room, from Sian's sighs and tender expressions, from bland illustrations in biology textbooks, from novels and films. She had wondered if she would assume a role, become another person. But standing there, saying nothing, looking at Steve, she realised that wasn't happening. If she was becoming anything, it was a newly discovered version of herself. She was acting this way because this was a dimension of who she was.

She stepped towards him but eased past him to push the door closed then she faced him. She took off her handbag and then turned around so Steve could see the zip on the back of her dress.

Over her shoulder, she smiled and said, "Would you mind?"

Steve struggled at first but pulled the zip down, and Rosalind let the dress fall to the floor. She drew Steve towards her and kissed him on the mouth, one hand behind his head, the other pushing up his back.

She looked at the soft toys on the bed and said, "I don't think we'll be needing those, will we?" Steve hurried to throw them on the floor while Rosalind took the condoms from her bag. "These, though..." she said, holding up the packet.

Afterwards, they lay naked, side by side, both panting, both breathless, Rosalind thrilled, exhilarated. Looking at herself from outside, Rosalind liked what she saw. She had loved every moment, every kiss, every caress, every thrust, every wave washing over her as she came. She could feel every inch of her skin. Suddenly, she burst out laughing.

"What is it?" asked Steve.

"When Jenny came in," Rosalind said. She laughed again. While they were making love, another girl had opened the door, Jenny, looking for a spare room for the same reason as Rosalind. Steve had buried his face in the pillow when he heard the door, but Rosalind looked cheerfully over his shoulder, smiling brightly as Jenny said, "Oops!" and then, "Hey, Ros! Good for you!" before backing out of the room.

"You don't think she saw it was me?" said Steve, anxious in case word got back to Sian.

"Not the way you hid," said Rosalind, still giggling. "Unless she recognised your bottom."

"Sian mustn't find out," said Steve. "I love her."

"She won't hear it from me," said Rosalind.

Rosalind was closer to the wall. Now, she climbed over Steve, pressing her hand on his chest for leverage. She took a cigarette from the packet, lit it, and stood naked at the open window, enjoying the feel of the cool air on her skin.

"Do you want to do it again?" said Steve.

"What, now?"

"No, I mean..."

"What about Sian?" She turned to face him, noting the look on his face as she did so. She liked her body tonight and liked that he did, too. "I thought you loved her."

"I do." He took his eyes off Rosalind and looked up at the ceiling. "But...it's just...well, that was nothing like with Sian. She...you were just..."

"We'll see," said Rosalind. She threw the cigarette out of the window and began to get dressed, an extended version of the girl who had put on these same clothes just a few hours earlier.

We'll see, she said, but she didn't need to see. She already knew. They wouldn't. What had begun as a project to lose her virginity, to be ready for university, a reconnaissance mission to scope out the lie of the land and get to know the terrain, to be able to blend in, had ended as something else, taken on unforeseen consequences. The land she had discovered was a part of herself she didn't realise existed. She loved the sense of control, as well as the relish, the appetite she'd had, and the abandonment of control. As pleasurable as the joint expedition had been, she didn't need Steve now. He'd done his bit and, anyway, she didn't want to hurt Sian, to make things complicated, to take her place next to Steve.

Dressed again, she partially opened the door. Steve was still naked on the bed.

"Don't forget to put those toys back," she said. "And get rid of the evidence." She nodded towards the used condom and empty wrapper by the side of the bed. "Although I'll take these, I think." She went back and picked up the packet with the remaining two condoms. "See you downstairs!" She kissed him and left the room.

Chapter Fifteen

Now

Gerard had left Rosalind firmly in the past, left more or less everything firmly in the past, where he wanted things to be. He had made a simple, uncluttered life for himself. He wanted things to stay that way, with no interruptions, no lightning attacks from history, no unplanned excursions or mercy missions where he could serve no possible purpose.

So he was angry as he got in the car and started the engine to make the trip to see her, so deeply accustomed to being undisturbed that he managed to resent her for her plea and even resent Jack for being stabbed. But he also knew how unreasonable he was being and how inhuman his feelings were.

In the car, the motorway traffic light, he considered his reaction, considered why he had felt so annoyed. He remembered that time, when they were a couple, that she'd been in that accident, slipping on the ice and breaking her wrist. He'd rushed to her then, dropping everything and hurrying to the hospital.

Just a broken wrist, an inconvenience, a nuisance, nothing more. But he left work and got to the hospital in time to pick her up and take her home. He insisted she pack a bag and come and stay with him for a few days, at least. He wrote messages of love on her cast, cooked for her, helped her wash. They joked that sex would require a few adjustments, but they'd manage somehow and they did. He drove her to and from work. He couldn't do enough for her, and they spent evenings together reading and watching TV and listening to music, a happy couple.

How he had changed. Now, her son was fighting for his life in hospital, and he begrudged changing his schedule for a few hours to be with her and help her.

How he had changed. He had unsubscribed from this list. Partly by accident, partly intentional, his feelings had calcified over the past few years. He had shut down. Like the owner of a holiday home at the end of the season, he had gone through the rooms of his house, shutting the windows, closing the curtains, throwing sheets over the furniture, unplugging the appliances, turning off the lights, locking the doors. Room by room. He had retreated, the past an enemy, and found sanctuary in his small flat and his unvarying routine.

Then he felt ashamed and then resented the shame he felt. He tried to reject the memories the contact from Rosalind had dredged up. That small, slight young woman with the open face and wide eyes, always ready to laugh — for a while, at least — that curious thing she did with her voice, twisting the vowels when she found something appealing.

There had been a time — they'd been going out for maybe six weeks — when he felt things were moving too fast, that he was seeing her too often. He suggested slowing things down a little, and Rosalind took it to mean he wanted to split up. She left his house in tears. It wasn't what he meant at all, but he was content with the way things had turned out. And then, some days later, she called, crying again, and said she just wanted things back the way they were, and Gerard had said okay, and that night they went out for a drink as if the hiatus had never occurred, and they went back to hers and made love and the next day wandered round the shops and went to the cinema.

He wished he had never said okay. Weakness, fear, a desire not to hurt. Just weakness, really. He wouldn't be in this situation if he had stuck to his guns back then, had said he thought this was for the best. But what situation would he be in? What situation was he in? He knew he would never meet anyone. He longed to meet someone. He was content to be alone, satisfied to be part of the pattern that had been woven around him and that he had helped to weave. He hated the thought of being alone, a forgotten cast-off, an unfancied sample. He was stronger now. He was just as weak as ever.

He parked in the multi-storey opposite the hospital, crossed over the road, past the smokers, and through the doors. And there was Rosalind, sitting in the communal area fringed by outlets—coffees, teas, sandwiches, magazines, newspapers, thoughtless gifts—at a table by the floor-to-ceiling windows. Her drink was untouched, the paper on the table open and folded to the puzzle page, no clue solved.

It was a long time since Gerard had had any conversation beyond the passing pleasantries exchanged in shops and cafés—the weather, the football, the cricket, how busy it was, how quiet it was. He struggled to think of what to say, hoping that Rosalind would turn her gaze from the window and notice him and say something herself. He studied her, beyond the shock of the day before. Smaller, maybe shrunken, still slight, the natural soft brown hair blending with the oncoming grey, and still the shortish cut that somehow expressed both a strong and frail character, as well as now a want of attention and care.

He looked at the paper on the table.

"Not much progress with the crossword," he said.

Rosalind turned slowly, looked down at the paper, up at Gerard. "No," she said. "The clues don't make sense to me." It was as if she had always known he was there or that he'd just popped to the bar to get another round.

Gerard had wrapped up warm against the cold, and now the heat of the hospital pressed in on him. He felt his shirt beginning to stick to his back, and he quickly took off his coat, scarf, hat, and gloves. He gestured vaguely towards one of the cafés around the seating area.

"I'll just go and…" he said. "Want another?" Rosalind's coffee was cold. She nodded. "White, no sugar?" Confirming the past. And she nodded again.

When he returned to the table with the drinks, Rosalind was staring out of the window again. Gerard avoided any serious talk, anything deep. Not that he intended to explore things later; that was simply the way he was now and probably always had been. He picked up the pen and paper and looked at the clues.

"I try and do one a day," he said. "Try the keep the brain active. My age, you know. Normally do the Telegraph. I know, I know, Tory rag, but the crossword's good. Helps to get used to the setters." He heard himself talking too quickly, desperately, hating the void. "Oh, here we go." He put in an answer. "That should get us going."

"Jack is dying," said Rosalind. She was still looking through the window, just speaking out loud rather than speaking to Gerard.

He put down the pen and paper. "Right," he said. "I'm sorry."

"The doctors and nurses haven't said anything," she said. "They come in and look at his charts, adjust the drips and replace the transfusion bags and nod at me. I'm in the way. They'd rather I wasn't there."

"I'm sure that's not the case." He couldn't rise above platitudes.

"And how would you know?" She turned to him now, eyes and voice full of vitriol. "Tell me that. Just how the fuck would you know?"

Gerard's face froze, shocked, confused, uncertain how to respond. He said nothing, thinking Rosalind would apologise, explain away her outburst as being down to tiredness, fear, anxiety, but she didn't. She was tired of saying sorry, tired of explaining, happy to lash out without apology or reason. It was just her now and Jack, and they were the only two that mattered.

"What was the clue?" she said.

"What?"

Rosalind nodded at the paper.

"Oh, right, yes." Gerard picked up the paper and read aloud, "Satisfied now dates changed."

"How many letters?"

"Five."

"Happy?"

"No."

"Happy's five letters, though."

"Yes," said Gerard. "It's sated." Rosalind looked blank. "It's an anagram," Gerard explained. "Of dates. Satisfied now dates changed. You see?"

"Oh," said Rosalind. "Do you want to go somewhere?"

Gerard looked unsure. "Don't you need to...? To stay here? With Jack?"

"He's not going anywhere."

"But what if...?"

"They've got my number." She stood up and put on her coat. "Come on."

Gerard hurriedly picked up his things and followed Rosalind down the stairs and out into the cold air. Different smokers who looked just the same as the previous ones lingered around the entrance.

"Where are we going?" Gerard asked.

"This is the last time I'll ever come to this city," she said. "I always loved it."

"I remember."

"I want to see it once more before Jack dies. Before everything dies."

She walked to the road and then down the hill, towards the city centre.

Rosalind was glad to be outside. Outside, she had to concentrate all her energies on fighting the numbing cold that invaded her through her cheap, thin coat, past her thin jumper and T-shirt and into her bones. Walking quickly helped, too. She could forget the thoughts that burrowed through her brain and just focus on moving, breathing, keeping warm.

They walked past buildings in need of attention and shops selling only cheap goods and neglected people and planners' mistakes and compromises.

Rosalind knew where she was going, or seemed to, but maybe she didn't but walked purposefully, nevertheless. The streets were unfamiliar to Gerard, who had visited the city only sporadically, and then for specific events closer to the city centre. He struggled to keep pace with her, in the way of someone oblivious to the destination, and he resented her silence and the apparent needlessness of his presence.

Rosalind wasn't ignoring him, or, at least, had not made a conscious decision to do so. It was simply that nothing was currently prompting her to speak to him or look at him or wait for him to catch up. If he decided now to stop and return to his car and leave her, she wouldn't call him back and ask him to stay with her, although, in five or ten minutes' time, she might do. She was free, but the freedom gave her no release.

Soon, they entered territory more familiar to Gerard, passing the perimeter line where the money was invested and the tourists welcomed. Rosalind stopped at the bottom of a wide, cobbled road that descended towards a roundabout that gave access to the open mouth of the tunnel under the river.

Gerard knew the cobbled road, the site of the city's central library, museum, and art gallery, with a civic hall grandly sitting at its top. He'd been here before, the last time a long time ago, when he still sought culture and enlightenment for its own sake rather than to pad out the traits he'd chosen for his character, when he was interested in things beyond the narrow bounds he'd set for his life, the throwaway thrillers and regular trips to the cinema, always the same cinema, the matinée show, no matter what was playing. He remembered the road had fascinated him because it seemed so much at odds with its surroundings, disconnected from subsequent intrusions by city planners anxious to update.

Rosalind stood still, uncaring, and Gerard felt himself becoming annoyed with her. She had called him here, snapped and sworn at him, and he had no idea what purpose he was supposed to serve for this woman whose skin he'd caressed and whose body had once moved beneath his. He wanted to shake her.

"We're here," she said.

"Here?" said Gerard.

"The first of my goodbyes." She didn't move. She stared at Gerard; some memories stirred, some sort of coherence arriving.

Gerard felt uncomfortable, waiting for her to move or speak, to indicate what would happen next. When she spoke, Rosalind's tone was neutral. She appraised him.

"You're not what I remember," she said. Gerard shrugged and smiled uncertainly.

"Well," he began, but Rosalind continued her assessment. She reached out and touched Gerard's face, making him flinch at the unexpected gesture.

"Slim, still," she said, "but your skin is looser. And your eyes aren't soft and bright anymore. Thinning hair, too."

"You're making me feel like a second-hand car or something," Gerard said. "A horse you're thinking of buying."

Rosalind didn't notice he'd spoken. She ran her hand down his arm, feeling the material of his coat.

"Good quality. Must have been expensive. No style, though. You're bland now. Everything about you." She smiled at him.

More than thirty years had passed, but Gerard recognised instantly the smile Rosalind gave him. One of mockery—condescending, humouring, humourless—a smile that said she saw through him.

He remembered times he'd seen it before. That time she stayed over at his during one of her holidays, so she saw him off to work, like the good little wife neither of them, in the end, had any intention of her being. He called hello to a woman he saw most mornings around this time, a woman he tried to see most mornings around this time, stylish, her hair in a sort of beehive, following her own fashion, slim, attractive, confident. He heard Rosalind behind him, laughing at him, and he turned, explaining she was a neighbour, they always said hello to each other in the morning, but Rosalind still laughed, saw through him, knew what he wanted. She was right, too, which didn't help. He found this girl attractive; he didn't want her to see him being waved to work by Rosalind. He wished he could see her, talk to her, have a drink with her. This was when he was beginning to find Rosalind exhausting—her suspicions, her moods, the onset of jealousies, the questions, and anxieties. But he was too scared to say anything, to make a clean break, to be honest about his feelings. Scared of hurting her too, but more scared of honesty.

"Charming," was all he said, light-heartedly, hiding his annoyance, reminding himself her son was dying.

"We used to talk a lot together, didn't we?" said Rosalind. "Books, films, gossip. It was easy."

"Things change."

"Before we first kissed, I longed for it to happen." She stepped towards him so they were touching. "I wanted to feel your body pressed against mine. I wasn't embarrassed or nervous when we slept together for the first time. I knew it would be good. I knew your body would feel right against me and inside me." Gerard wanted to move away but couldn't. He felt no desire, just self-consciousness, but still couldn't move. "I made love to you with relish and abandon. But then I did with every man I slept with."

Gerard remembered, but he didn't remember Rosalind. He remembered Jessica. He felt he ought to say something, so he said, trying to be jovial, "Where are those two people now, eh?"

"Those people are dead now." Then she stepped away from him. "Let's go to the art gallery," she said.

Chapter Sixteen

Then

Her relationship with Gerard was a fresh memory. Sex with Gerard, however, was not. Sex with Gerard, once so frequent, passionate, energetic, inventive, pleasurable, started to peter out early in the second year of their relationship.

For this, Rosalind blamed Gerard, and she wasn't wholly wrong to do so. He gradually lost interest in sex with Rosalind, becoming increasingly interested in having sex with other women, although he never did have sex with other women. He made tentative attempts and suggestions, but while his heart was in it, his character wasn't.

While he longed for one-night stands with a succession of women or, preferably, intense, secret affairs conducted in romantic hotel rooms on lazy afternoons with women who wanted nothing more than intense, secret affairs conducted in romantic hotel rooms, with maybe the odd candlelit dinner thrown in for good measure, he was scared of Rosalind finding out. He was scared of becoming entangled in fraught situations, and it never occurred to him to say to a woman, "I don't want a relationship with you, but I find your body attractive and your company fun and would love to sleep with you." Honesty and directness didn't come naturally to him. It was only many, many years later, when it was far too late to do anything about it, that he wondered if such an approach might have proved fruitful.

(There was also the issue of his height and stature and lack of immediate impact. He was no romantic lead, no matinée idol. He wasn't the kind to make an immediate impression, certainly not in situations where commitment-free sex might be on the agenda. He had charm, for sure, and a nicely sly sense of humour, and empathy, both faked and genuine, but he was a slow burner, and without broad appeal, and not tall enough. It wasn't always the case, of course— something in Rosalind clicked when they first met, but then the circumstances were unusual, and, besides, she had quirks and weaknesses which left her vulnerable to any man who was relatively nice to her. In general, though, he was the romantic lead's funny and clever friend, the one to whom the woman who fancies the romantic lead can talk, the one the woman who fancies the romantic lead wishes the romantic lead was like, albeit without the ending of the film, where the woman realises the friend is actually the one she loves and wants to share her life and bed with.)

Mark Jones did have broad appeal. He was a long man. Maybe not conventionally good-looking, but attractive, definitely, with twinkling, naughty eyes, a fresh and ready smile, and was never short of something to say. He joked about being skinny, but he was nevertheless confident of his appearance—confident generally, in fact, which appealed more than anything—and fit, too, a keen sportsman. Almost tall enough to be gawky, nevertheless he moved easily. All this appealed to Rosalind, although she told herself it didn't matter and tried hard not to see the glaring contrast to Gerard. That was too shallow for her to think.

What she preferred to find attractive were the things others couldn't see — the sensitivity, the doubt, the shyness behind the constant jokes and fast talk. She could see those things. She insisted she could see those things.

Rosalind knew for a long time that she and Mark would sleep together, long before they started going out together, perhaps even from that night at the holiday camp, when she first felt she could perceive those hidden qualities and that he had chosen her to reveal them to.

They behaved like a couple before they became one. Rosalind never lied to Gerard—not explicitly—but she was canny enough to give the impression that she was going out either alone or as part of a group of friends when, in fact, she was just with Mark. (And she was deluded enough to think her ruses worked, and completely missed the mark in thinking Gerard cared.)

They never went anywhere in the evening, only during the day, to a gallery or for coffee, Rosalind feeling that daylight gave their meetings respectability and plausible deniability. Night-time would have meant a date, would have proved intent. Likewise, they didn't do anything that could be classed as date activity. There were no trips to the cinema or restaurants, just meetings for coffee, mainly, and a Latin dancing class. (That was a borderline matter for Rosalind, and she trod carefully. She told Gerard, "Some of us are signing up for this dance thing." Which was true, although by "some" she meant "two". She even suggested Gerard might join in, certain that he wouldn't. While she denied to herself that Mark would inevitably be her partner in the class, she hoped he would and made sure he was.)

In effect, then, her relationship with Mark overlapped with her relationship with Gerard, even though Rosalind did enough to more or less convince herself it didn't, to maintain the moral high ground that no one was, in fact, contesting. It was important to her to feel she was being honest, to be able to say she was doing the right thing in the right way.

And it was important for her to be able to say there was no one else. She was actually a touch put-out that Gerard didn't ask. She wanted to tell him she was leaving him because it was the right thing for her (which it was), the right thing for both of them (which it was). And she liked the idea that she was stepping out onto the tightrope without a safety net, her head held high, looking forward and up and towards hope, not down. If she looked down, of course, she would have seen the safety net. She knew she was going to break up with Gerard and knew that Mark would be her next partner, but she wanted to give the whole situation a veneer of surprise.

She felt enormous relief after she told Gerard it was over. She called briefly at Mark's and then went home, happy and exhausted, waking late the next morning even happier, refreshed, full of an energy she'd not felt for a long while. Hungry, too, actually ravenous enough to want to eat.

She was delighted that things were sorted, and even though she had become generally wary of telling Naomi too much too often, she told Naomi the news as soon as she could. Naomi was even more delighted than Rosalind, thrilled Rosalind had, finally, seen sense and taken her advice. Naomi suggested they celebrate with a boozy lunch. Rosalind was uncomfortable with the idea of celebrating the end of the relationship. Gerard wasn't a bad man by any means; it just hadn't worked out. Naomi sensed her hesitation and was having none of it.

"Come on, Ros," she said. "You're free! Let's go out and celebrate. What you need is a few glasses of wine and a big bowl of pasta. You'll need your energy," she added with a wink. She shooed Rosalind upstairs. As Rosalind went into her bedroom, Naomi shouted, "And put on your glad rags! You never know!"

Rosalind didn't quite know what Naomi meant by that and was slightly resentful again of her urgings, but liked the idea of a glass of wine and something to eat. Lunch with a girlfriend, which Naomi was, at a push, felt nicely grown-up, too. She put on some make-up and changed her top.

"Well," said Naomi when Rosalind came downstairs. "Not quite what I was hoping for, but it's a start." She grabbed her house keys. "Come on, then. I've just called and booked Guiseppi's."

Rosalind was caught unawares by this. The situation, to her, didn't call for somewhere you had to book. It was more of a turn-up-and-grab-a-table kind of a meal. And certainly it didn't call for Guiseppi's, which was at the outer reaches of her budget. Rosalind had been thinking more Pizza Express. Guiseppi's was a sophisticated bistro for when you needed a special restaurant. And for evenings only. Lunch there was for proper grown-ups, not for the likes of Rosalind, who was really only just trying on an adult's clothes. Still, it was booked now, and maybe lunch at Guiseppi's was something she should get used to. Maybe the adult's clothes would fit her.

Once inside, however, Rosalind had to fight against feeling intimidated. The other customers—women, mostly—were young, beautiful, and effortless. The weather was warmer than she expected, so she felt flushed and regretted bringing a jacket, even though she stubbornly insisted she was fine when Naomi told her to take it off and ignored Naomi's suggestion to undo a couple of buttons on her top. Confronted by the menu, which, from habit, she read from right to left, she became reluctant to eat, though very hungry, and ordered a salad she no more than picked at.

The drink was welcome, though, the first sip of the ice-cold Frascati reminding her how tense she'd been these past months. Naomi ordered the sharing charcuterie plate as a starter. She pressed Rosalind to eat, saying again she would need her energy, but Rosalind was somehow revolted by the sight of the plate and left Naomi to wolf down the slices of cured meat while she dealt with a few olives.

Throughout the meal, Naomi did most of the talking, eating, and drinking. Especially the talking and drinking, a second bottle arriving before the first was quite finished.

"Well," Naomi said, raising her glass. "Here's to finally getting shot of that awful dullard. You should have done it ages ago. Are you going to eat that tiramisu?" Rosalind shook her head and pushed her dessert, which Naomi had ordered for her, across the table.

"Gerard's a nice man," she said. She meant it. Gerard was, all in all. Naomi grunted. "It just wasn't meant to be. We weren't right for each other."

"He was like an anchor tied round your leg," said Naomi. "Honestly, and they call women the ball and chain."

Rosalind disagreed but didn't say so. Naomi was wrong about Gerard, and Rosalind had never understood what it was she had against him. One thing, though, was that she had wasted precious time in a relationship she knew was over and had known was over even before the moment a move north was suggested. She thought about that while Naomi drank and talked, and couldn't remember whether she or Gerard had suggested it, couldn't actually remember when it was first mentioned. Perhaps it never was. Perhaps neither had suggested it, but each of them thought the other had and felt unable to object for fear of hurting the other. *Or just for fear,* she thought.

Rosalind felt a little woozy. She had only had two glasses of wine at most but had barely touched her food, had barely eaten anything much for a day or so. Naomi, though, as well as asking for two coffees, insisted on ordering another drink.

"A digestif, don't you think?" she said. "We're celebrating, after all."

Rosalind wasn't sure what a digestif was, although she was certain everyone else in the restaurant did. She also noted that Naomi had said *we*.

When the two Limoncellos arrived, Rosalind took a sip of hers, grimaced, and then drank the rest of it. It was the final straw for her, and she slipped from fairly sober to mildly drunk. Naomi had put away far more than Rosalind but seemed unaffected. She became louder, yes, but she usually did during the course of anything but the shortest conversation. Rosalind had no doubt she knew what she was doing and was happy for everyone else to know what she was doing, too.

As the waiter approached with Naomi's second Limoncello, Naomi said, "There's one thing I must say to you, Ros."

Rosalind said, "Yes?" She had no idea what was going to come next, but certainly wasn't expecting what did follow.

"Cocks," said Naomi.

Rosalind snorted, half-appalled, half-amused. She leaned over the table and whispered, "What? Naomi!"

"Cocks," Naomi repeated, ignoring Rosalind's hope that she would match her whisper.

Rosalind tried again. "Naomi, don't."

"Oh, don't worry." Naomi leant back in her chair and gestured around the restaurant. "They'll all be talking about the same thing. And they'll have seen their fair share, too." She took a breadstick from the glass on the table, peeled its wrapper, and then pointed it at Rosalind. "You, however, haven't." Thinking Rosalind might not know what she meant, Naomi clarified, "Seen your fair share, I mean."

Rosalind gave up any effort to redirect the conversation. She knew there was no point, and she was almost drunk enough to enjoy the candour. Almost. Naomi leant forward towards her, looking around, checking the other diners for range. Rosalind came closer to meet her, expecting but not getting a change in volume.

"How many?" asked Naomi.

"Naomi," said Rosalind in protest. "I'm not going to..."

"Oh, go on." She sounded a little exasperated, and Rosalind didn't know if she meant it or not. "Come on, tell me."

Rosalind didn't answer at first, though she could have told her straight away. "Four," she said quietly. She wasn't sure if she counted Steve. For some reason, Steve seemed to belong in a separate category, as he was an exercise in removal, like a visit to the doctor to get rid of a minor ailment. Also, she thought her conduct with Steve might be something she ought to be a little ashamed of, at least when admitting it to others.

"Four!" Naomi practically shouted the number. "And how old are you?"

"Twenty-eight," said Rosalind. She was going red now. "Well, five, actually," she added. She thought four was plenty, but felt she needed to include Steve now, to up the figure to a total Naomi might find acceptable, and resenting that she felt it necessary.

"Five's hardly any better, is it?" said Naomi. She seemed genuinely affronted now. "And you slept with them all, I take it?"

Rosalind noticed how Naomi seemed to have isolated the body part in question as if it wasn't connected to a man.

"Yes," said Rosalind, insistent. "Of course I did. What else?"

Naomi ran both her hands through her hair, scratching fiercely at her scalp.

"Plenty else," she said. "Twenty-two's my tally. Twenty-seven if you count hand jobs." Rosalind didn't know what to say and said nothing. "We need to address this matter now." Naomi had got past her horror and became business-like. "What you need to do is get out there, back in the game. Play the field. Have some fun. You need to get into double figures before you're twenty-nine."

Rosalind found herself thinking through the logistics. "But I'm twenty-nine in November," she said. "That's..." She did the sums. "That's only four months away."

"Plenty of time," said Naomi. She drained the last of her Limoncello. "Come on. Pay the bill. I'll leave the tip." When she saw a flicker of protest on Rosalind's face, she said, "I paid last time."

Yes, thought Rosalind, *but that wasn't at Guiseppi's*. But she did as she was told.

Naomi wanted to wander around the shops. Although Rosalind wasn't keen, she went along with her anyway. She took off her jacket, the better to enjoy the sunshine. The sun in the empty blue sky made the city different. The buildings gleamed, the pace slowed, doors and windows opened. People smiled, people lingered, just enjoying being out, being unhurried.

Naomi, having said she wanted to do some shopping, showed no inclination to go into any particular store. While the lunchtime drink had left Rosalind drowsy, Naomi was agitated, excited, intense, gesticulating. Words tumbled out of her mouth as time and people eased by, and she paused only to draw deep on her cigarette.

"You know what you ought to do?" she said. "You ought to do what I did. You know? When I finally got shut of the waster? When the papers came through?" She stopped and gripped Rosalind's arm. "I was out there. Out. There. Clubs, pubs, restaurants, galleries, anywhere I could meet men. Any time of day."

Rosalind gently freed herself from the grip. Naomi raked her fingers through her hair and pulled her bag back onto her shoulder.

"One-night stands, meaningless flings," she said. "Married, single, younger, older. God, it was such a fucking release. Literally. And think they're all the same? You couldn't be more wrong. Let me tell you, they come in all shapes and sizes. And girths. Like you wouldn't believe."

Lazily, hazily, Rosalind wondered when all this activity had stopped. She had rented a room from Naomi for three years now and had never known her to go out with a man, had never known her to have a man over, even.

Naomi was still talking. "Whatever you do," she said, stopping now, turning Rosalind to face her. This was vital. "Don't jump straight back into another relationship. Just do what I did." She gripped Rosalind by the shoulders and looked into her eyes. "Promise me."

Rosalind was uneasy. She smiled slightly, not sure how to take this, and she promised to do as Naomi said. That made Naomi relax, relieved that she'd extracted the assurance from Rosalind, and they meandered through the city centre, slowing to the pace of everyone else. Naomi began pointing out men she considered likely.

"What about him?"

"Ooh, he's all right."

"He looks like he'd know what he's doing."

Rosalind looked but didn't see. She saw couples everywhere, some hand in hand, some pushing prams, all happy, all relaxed, content. And then she saw only young women, alone, in pairs, in groups. Easy, assured, in bright colours and short dresses, long hair flowing. They were all laughing, Rosalind noted. They were all happy. She looked at them and guessed the ages of these free women: seventeen, eighteen, nineteen, twenty-three, twenty-four, maybe the same age as her, twenty-eight, some of them. She felt older than them. She felt older than twenty-eight, or how she thought twenty-eight should feel. She felt the same age as them. She felt younger than them. She felt apart from them. They had a facility, a languid confidence that she never had, that she could only dream of now.

She saw her reflection in a shop window: the short hair, the black jeans, the navy top. She thought back to how she was ten or eleven years ago and saw much the same thing. Dark colours, baggy jumpers, the Doc Martens, the nervousness and envy disguised as contempt and superiority. The camouflage.

Rosalind wondered, Is it too late now?

She looked past her own reflection at the display in the window. She had stopped listening to Naomi. She only knew she was still talking.

It was a small shop, a single-storey independent fighting its corner against the chains and big department stores. A women's clothes shop. Rosalind saw and stared at a dress in the centre of the display. It was loose, cotton, with a skirt that came a couple of inches above the knee, with an elasticated waist and a top with a round collar. The skirt was yellow and the top was sky blue, dotted with white clouds and featuring a bright sun beaming with rays as a child might draw it. Not the figure-hugging dress that the girls she'd seen were wearing, but bright and light, nothing like what she would normally wear.

And she loved it.

"I'm going in here," she told Naomi, interrupting her. "I'm going to buy that dress."

Usually, Naomi in full flow could not be stopped in her tracks. Usually, she would either not notice someone else had spoken or simply talk more loudly to drown out interference. But this statement of intent caused screeching brakes. Naomi looked at the dress, then looked at Rosalind, then looked at the dress again.

"What?" she said. "That dress? You?"

"Yes," said Rosalind. She wasn't going to explain herself or allow Naomi to make her doubt herself. It wasn't that she was being resolute, simply that she'd somehow found herself shifted to a place Naomi couldn't get through to. Naomi didn't know this and would have persisted even if she had.

"It's too childish," she said. "Too bright. It's not sexy enough. No man will want you in that. You've got a good body still. Show it off a bit." Rosalind went into the shop. When she realised, Naomi followed her, saying, "If you've got it, flaunt it."

Rosalind tried the dress on in the cramped changing room at the back of the shop. She loved it, the feel of the material, the brightness, the sunshine of it.

"Let's have a look then," said Naomi. She pulled the curtain back, threatening to break the spell.

"Oh, no," she said. "It's all wrong." Naomi plucked at the short sleeves of the loose-fitting top. She twanged the elasticated waistband. "You can't get this."

Rosalind changed back into her own clothes and took the dress to the till. She hadn't even looked at the price tag. She paid by card and left the shop happy.

Back at the house, later that day, Rosalind thought about calling Gerard to check he was okay but decided to do it later. She told Naomi she was sleepy and went up to her room. There, she laid the dress out on the single bed into which she and Gerard had squeezed so many times in the early days of their relationship. It had been a while since they had done so, both coming to prefer the space of his double bed, first for one reason, then for another.

Looking down at the bed, Rosalind thought about the time Mark would be in it with her. She knew he would be. They hadn't discussed their relationship, hadn't made any plans, or spelt out their intentions. But she knew they would go out with each other, and she knew he would soon be here with her, in her bedroom, undressing each other, pulling back the sheets, falling into bed together, unable to let go of each other.

Play the field, Naomi had said. One-night stands, flings, casual, meaningless sex. Steve apart, Rosalind had slept with four men, all serious, long-term, monogamous relationships. *Whatever you do*, Naomi had said, *don't jump straight into a new relationship*. But that was just what she meant to do.

As she stared at the bed, she wished Mark was here with her. Or Gerard, or Steve, or David, or Barry. Any one of them would do right now. She needed sex right this moment. She needed to feel a man's naked body against hers, to run her hands over his shoulders and down his arms, to feel his lips against her breasts, to feel him pushing inside her.

But she fought against rushing with Mark even though they both knew what was happening, and despite the fact that, to all intents and purposes, they'd been going out with each other for months now. Rosalind wanted to date Mark properly first. She wanted it to look like this was something new and unexpected. Why, she couldn't explain. Certainly, it had nothing to do with anything Naomi had said. And it wasn't to spare Gerard's feelings. He would be in Manchester anyway. There was no likelihood of him finding out. Besides, from what he said the night they split up, he already knew.

So, Mark and Rosalind dated. They went out together in the evenings, just like two people who had recently met and who were tentatively exploring possibilities. They went out for dinner. They went out to the cinema. They met for a drink. They went out for dinner again. They went to the theatre.

They kissed after the third date. Mark, to Rosalind's delight, tried to persuade her to come to bed with him, but she declined. After the second time they went out for dinner, they kissed, and he felt her breast through her top.

Five dates was enough, Rosalind thought. After they came out of the theatre, Mark suggested going for a drink.

"Let's go back to your place instead," said Rosalind. And so they did.

As soon as they were inside the door, he kissed her, and Rosalind kissed him back, hard. She pushed him against the wall and began unbuttoning his trousers, pulling his shirt out of the waistband, pressing her palms against his back. She fumbled in her bag for a condom and pushed it into his hand.

"Bedroom," Mark said.

"No," Rosalind said. She gripped his jacket and pulled him back to her. "Here."

She made him lift her up and pulled him so he pressed her against the wall. She clawed at him. She gripped his head in her hands and kissed him passionately, needily. She was hungry, voracious, desperate to feel him inside her. She felt starved. She was starved. She wanted release, abandon, departure.

Finished, they went to bed, leaving what clothes they'd taken off in the hall, finishing undressing in his bedroom, leaving the clothes where they fell. After a few minutes, Rosalind reached for him again. She felt his arms and chest, reached down the length of his legs. He felt strong, but she didn't say so.

"You're all elbows and knees," she said, smiling. "All arms and legs."

"Long levers," Mark told her.

"Hmm," said Rosalind. "Talking of long levers." She took him in her hand. "Come on then, Jonesy. Let's be having you."

This was good, different. The girl who had once asked Gerard never to leave her, who had so often felt so fragile, so in need, who had forced herself back to the surface so many times, fell asleep content and certain, sure the frailty would never return.

Chapter Seventeen

Now

But Rosalind didn't move.

"Are we going then?" Gerard said, nodding up the cobbled road. Rosalind shrugged.

"If you like," she said.

"It's not what I'd like," he snapped. "You asked me over, remember? You called me."

"Come on then," said Rosalind. She took two steps and then stopped. The defiance she felt earlier, the readiness to say what she wanted, had left her on the walk from the hospital. "I'm sorry. You can go back if you want."

"No," Gerard said. "Let's go." He felt guilty and irritated. He was right to be irritated by her, he thought. There was her self-pity again, the relinquishing of will, the taking on of blame. But her son was dying, he reminded himself. She could be however she wanted. Gerard had no children and couldn't imagine what she was going through. He said the words to himself: *I can't imagine what she is going through,* to suppress any reactions as they walked up the slope, past the central library.

Similar words had been said to him in the past, back in the days when he was at work and chatted to colleagues about this and that during coffee breaks and in the comments exchanged in the moments before meetings got underway.

You've no idea what it's like.

You're so lucky.

I mean, she's gorgeous, but right now, I envy you.

You can't imagine what it's like.

And yet he was wrong, and they were wrong. He could imagine and did so now as he had done in the past. He imagined standing alongside his wife, gripping her hand, and saying weak words of encouragement as she went through the pain of childbirth. He imagined taking the child, red and squalling, eyes squeezed shut, nodding his thanks to the midwife who bustled through the process; she'd seen it all before, had three of her own, and stared down into the face of this miracle worker, this magician who would cast a spell over everything he or she touched. He imagined telling his wife, "It's a boy" or "It's a girl." And then silently vowing his life now belonged to the child, his or hers, to do anything they wanted with it. He imagined the Christmas shows, the night-time feeds, rows about homework, talks about problems, first football matches, boyfriends calling and girlfriends not calling. He imagined the phone call in the middle of the night from the police, from the hospital, from the friend who saw it all but stood aghast and aside, helpless as the unprovoked and brutal attack occurred.

All scenes from the film of the life he hadn't led that he projected onto a screen in his mind.

Rosalind was walking in front of him. Always slim, always so breakable, he saw her now shrivelled inside the thin coat that had long since needed replacing. He watched her climb the steps of the gallery and use more strength than it should have taken to push the heavy wooden door open and step weak into the foyer.

"Is this okay?" she said.

"Fine," said Gerard. He felt remorse and responsibility. "Have you eaten?" The gallery coffee shop was just beyond the front desk, flanked by the stately staircases that ran up to the exhibition rooms. Rosalind shook her head, barely perceptibly. "Let's sit and have something," he said. "Then we can look at the gift shop and then go. No need to look at any of the paintings." He could manage small talk, clichés, and old jokes.

The coffee shop was more or less empty. Gerard got two coffees, water, and, for Rosalind, a sandwich that she didn't ask for.

"When was the last time you ate?" he said. He kept his voice low. The rich, dark wood panels and the marble staircase both demanded hush. Heavy wood and glass doors sealed in the noise from the children's art room just off the foyer, where boys and girls were making Christmas decorations.

"Old habits," said Rosalind. She didn't like to eat, and the sandwich, too full, with too much relish, repelled her. But she forced herself to take a bite and then finished it all greedily without saying a word, pushing the food into her mouth, her cheeks bulging like a woman starved. Gerard watched her, appalled and full of pity.

"So what happened?" Gerard asked.

"There's no short answer to that," she said. Gerard was puzzled. He didn't know what she meant and shook his head.

"No. I mean, what happened to Jack?"

"Oh, of course. Jack. Do you mind if we don't?" Such polite syntax.

"Of course not."

"Tell me how you've been."

"What?" said Gerard. "Since 1989?"

"Don't." Gerard said nothing more, annoyed again, his irritation without a target. "Do you still have the paper?" she asked. "From the hospital. We could do the crossword."

"I left it on the table."

"Oh."

"I can buy you a new one. If that's what you're worried about."

Rosalind didn't notice the heat in his words.

"Are you sure the answer wasn't happy?" Rosalind asked. "To that clue?"

"It was sated," said Gerard. "An anagram of dates."

"Sated," Rosalind repeated. "Satisfied." She laughed without humour. "I've had enough."

They sat in a silence that was uncomfortable for Gerard but that Rosalind didn't appear to notice. His presence was providing no solace — she didn't even consider if that was what she wanted — and nor was it a burden she wished away. For his part, Gerard continued his slalom of resentment and sympathy. He didn't know what he was doing there, but he knew he couldn't leave, but there was more to that than support for Rosalind. He wanted to stay because he was clinging on for a reason he couldn't name. At the same time, he wanted just to stand up and walk out and breathe in the damp, cold air and let the past he shared with Rosalind slip away again.

"I came here, you know?" she said.

"Here?" said Gerard. "The gallery?"

"No. I mean, yes, I used to come here often. It was calm. But I meant here, this city. Liverpool. This is where I went to university."

"I know."

"I think that's maybe why Jack came here. I used to go on and on about it. About what a wonderful time I had here. The pubs and the buildings and the music."

"Right." Just in time, Gerard stopped himself from asking if it was good to be back. Trite wouldn't play well now.

"I've been back since, of course. Came with Jack for his interview. The docks were derelict when I was here. It was grim, but good, you know? It had heart."

"Had?"

"Had, has. It doesn't matter now. I'm saying goodbye."

"Right," said Gerard. He wanted things light. "I've only been here a few times." He couldn't imagine either of his parents accompanying him on his university interviews. When did parents stop letting go now, he wondered.

"But you live so close," said Rosalind.

Gerard shrugged. "Still," he said.

"I met Andy here."

"Andy? Your old boyfriend?" He wondered how he'd remembered.

"I finished with Andy a little while before I met you." She was playing with a sachet of sugar as she spoke, pressing and twisting it absent-mindedly. "First Barry, then Andy, then you, then Mark. Then no one."

"I don't remember you mentioning a Barry." Gerard thought, like him, she had only slept with one other person before they started going out together. He didn't feel jealous—thirty years, after all—but instead felt loss, wishing he had slept with more women when he was younger.

"Barry was a boy I met on a train, and then I found him again here."

And then she suddenly giggled, and her eyes brightened unexpectedly. Gerard saw a flash of the girl he'd first met at the careers fair.

Rosalind leant in towards him. She lowered her voice. "Actually," she said. "Do you want to know a secret?" Gerard said nothing. "Barry wasn't the first." She giggled again. "The first was a boy called Steve. He was Sian's boyfriend."

"Sian?" said Gerard. Rosalind didn't explain. Gerard wasn't certain she was talking to him.

"We were at a party. Sian wasn't there. Sick or something. She was always getting colds. Anyway, Steve." She put the sugar sachet down. "I was due to go away to university, to come here. I knew they'd done it, and I wanted to do it, too. Who wants to go to university a virgin? I just said to him, Come on. Let's go upstairs. You should have seen his face!" Rosalind's laughter cut through the hush of the gallery. "There! I've never told anyone that before! Is that really naughty?"

Gerard was a virgin when he went to university. He didn't know what to say. He just shrugged. He felt envy. He wished a girl had said that to him, wondered what would have happened if he'd taken a chance like that, to say that to a girl. Come on, let's go upstairs. He knew there were times when he'd wanted to. He wondered if any of the girls he'd spoken to at parties had been hoping for him to suggest it.

Too late now.

Too late now.

"They got married, Sian and Steve," said Rosalind. "When I was in first year. I was a bridesmaid. I gave Steve a wink in the church. At the reception, he wanted me to take him back to my room."

"On his wedding day?" Gerard's outrage was feigned. His envy was real.

"I wish I had done now. Or just slipped into some storeroom close to the main hall. Gone down on him, taken him in my mouth. Or made him come with my hand and sent him back to his seat next to Sian, flushed and confused. It wouldn't matter now, would it?" She picked up the sachet of sugar again, then tossed it onto the table. Her girlish laughter was spent. She was back in the present, with a son dying in hospital. "I hope a girl said something like that to Jack," she said, and then she stood up. "Let's go and look at some paintings."

"If you like," said Gerard. "I'll just finish my coffee."

But Rosalind stood up abruptly and moved away without waiting for Gerard. He hurriedly gathered his things and followed her.

Sudden quickness of movement was followed by fatigue. The climb up the staircase wearied Rosalind; the last few steps, she pulled herself up by the banister like a woman much older than she actually was. Gerard walked at the same pace, reluctantly feeling a duty to be alongside her, even when she lost awareness of his presence.

She stopped on the central landing at the top of the stairs, frozen by the doors which opened off it. The building bore down heavily on her.

"Where do you want to go first?" asked Gerard.

Rosalind shrugged. "There," she said, nodding towards a random door.

"Victorian High Art." Gerard read the sign above the door. "1860 to 1900. A favourite of yours?" Gerard asked. He spoke brightly, trying to keep things light and shallow, his speciality.

"I don't really care," Rosalind said.

They wandered through the rooms, looking but not seeing, unmoved by depictions of myths and gods and whispered confidences, lovers in mourning, stern authorities condemning craven wrongdoers, the innocent in torment, muscular shepherds happening across coy nymphs, Eve tasting of the apple.

Gerard drew Rosalind's attention to the frowning profile of an industrialist's daughter.

"Do you think she ever suggested going upstairs with a dashing young officer she met at a ball?" he asked. His tone was light and false, Rosalind's reminiscence pulling at him, still wishing a girl had said that to him or that he had made the suggestion himself. A memory flashed back. A house party he'd gone to when he'd not been going out with Rosalind that long. She wasn't with him. There was a girl there. What was her name? Mary-Kate? Something like that, two first names with a hyphen, one of them Mary for sure. He'd known her a while, part of the crowd he knocked around with before his relationship with Rosalind took all his attention. Mary-Kate was always making suggestive remarks, not specifically to Gerard, just generally. They'd danced together, crowded close by the press of people, pressed closer. He followed her into the kitchen when she said she wanted a drink. Running the tap for a glass of water, Gerard standing at the door, she said, "I think you should do just whatever you feel. You should grab the chance."

He wondered briefly at the time—and more now, much more now—if that was an invitation to him. She must have felt him pressing against her when they danced, must have felt his desire. He did nothing, told himself she was just talking generally, that her remark wasn't made specifically about him, but it was fear that stopped him, of consequences and explanations and aftermaths, of confrontations.

There, standing in front of this plain young woman, staring at her unsmiling face, captured within the gold-leaf frame, long dead, he fervently wished he had gone to Mary-Kate, Mary-Something, turned her towards him and told her he wanted to kiss her and kissed her and let whatever happened just happen. What would it matter now? Any pain or embarrassment or hurt or apologies or misunderstanding? Any pleasure? What would any of that matter now?

Rosalind considered his question seriously, tried to grasp the girl's character and desires.

"I'm not sure," she said after some thought. "Unlikely, I'd say, though she might have wanted to, or wanted him to."

Gerard felt stupid for asking.

Rosalind moved on, and Gerard followed, going where she went. They meandered like a river on low ground.

Gerard stopped pretending to be interested in any of the paintings on display, focusing all his energies on his growing impatience and frustration. *I've work to do*, he told himself. *I need to be doing my work, and she hasn't shown the slightest consideration for my needs, for any demands on my time.*

Even as he told himself these things, he knew it wasn't the case. He was well ahead of schedule, and there was plenty of time to meet his deadline. Besides, he only really did the work to keep himself busy, to fill his time with the methodical, monotonous, meticulous checking of figures and accuracy and facts and grammar and clarity and phrasing.

Still, his agitation crowded out the truth, which was simply that he didn't want to be here with Rosalind and her tragedy, that he just wanted to be back within the architecture he had built around himself, and so he maintained his level of resentment. He felt summoned by Rosalind, had come as a favour, and she had shown no gratitude, hadn't even given any indication as to what she wanted from him. And there she was, just wandering aimlessly around the gallery, drifting past the paintings with barely a glance.

Gerard had taken a seat on the bench in the centre of the room, preoccupied by his irritation, and so didn't notice straight away that Rosalind had stopped to study one of the pictures. She was staring intently at it, taking in every aspect. He came over to see what had wrapped her attention.

The picture she was studying was light and bright. The backdrop was taken up by a gleaming white wall, inset into which was a statue of the Madonna and Child. Beyond the wall, the sky was blue, with a couple of fluffy white clouds. In the foreground, to the left, a young boy, possibly an altar boy or novice monk, stood holding a staff topped by the crucified Christ. To the right, a monk in white and grey robes was placing a bishop's mitre on the head of the young woman in the centre of the frame. The mitre was red, with a black devil diving downwards, holding a trident or spear. Another mitre, this time black with a stabbing red devil, had been placed on a white stone wall.

The young woman wore her long black hair loose. Her face was maybe a little pale, but her expression was set at rest, neither smiling nor frowning, defiant nor terrified. Her eyes looked upwards, expecting the mitre to be placed on her head as if she were at a fitting. She held her arms straight down in front of her, one hand holding the other, a little child's pose. Over her white tunic, she wore a red tabard with yellow-orange flames licking up from the hem. More winged devils frolicked over the tabard.

Between the young woman and the boy was a large plant pot. A flaming torch had been pushed at an angle into the soil. The monk, realising he needed both hands to put on the mitre, must have jammed it there, the only thing at hand that would serve. The altar boy had his hands full with the cross, and it would hardly have been right to ask the woman to hold it.

"Did we used to do this?" she asked.

"This?" said Gerard.

"Galleries, Victorian High Art. I can't remember. I came here often when I was a student. When I needed calm and coolness. When things were too frantic and jumbled."

"Pubs, we went to," said Gerard. "The cinema. Clubs now and then." He didn't want to remember. He'd shut everything away. The lid came loose now and then of its own accord; he wasn't going to pry it open himself.

"And sex, of course," said Rosalind. "I seem to remember lots of sex."

Gerard said nothing. He didn't want to remember.

"I used to take Jack up to London quite often. On the train for days out. The Tower of London, Hamley's, museums. He loved the Natural History Museum. I always liked the British Library, the recordings of poets reading their own work. Jack wasn't so keen. This was when Mark still had a proper job, of course. Decent money, before he messed it all up."

"Right," said Gerard. He didn't want to know anything about Mark or their relationship, didn't want to hear if things were bad or good, happy or strained. He didn't want to hear anything. He wanted to be back in his flat, working methodically and meticulously through the texts he was paid to check, looking for grammatical errors, factual inaccuracies, lack of clarity, providing precision. This time with Rosalind was making things blurred.

"Auto da Fé. Spain in the Middle Ages." Rosalind read the card next to the pages. "William Shakespeare Burton, 1893. What does auto da fé mean?" She turned around to ask the question, the first time she'd looked at Gerard since they came into the room.

"Heretic burning," Gerard answered. "Spanish Inquisition."

"She doesn't look like a heretic," said Rosalind.

"I guess they come in all shapes and sizes."

Rosalind laughed. She put her hand on his arm. Lightly, briefly. An intimate, casual branding, a claim, a signal sent from light years away, received by puzzled monitors. She didn't seem to even know she'd done it. She took her hand away, but he kept looking down at where she had placed it.

"She's very calm, isn't she?" said Rosalind. "She's facing unimaginable pain and yet she seems quite relaxed about it all."

"Faith, I guess."

"She knows she'll be saved," said Rosalind. Gerard wanted to move on, but the painting held Rosalind. "I suppose you're in favour of it all."

"All what?"

"Burning heretics. Isn't that what they taught you? At that school for clever Catholic boys that you went to?"

"No." He didn't want this conversation, any conversation.

"And what about faith? You must approve of that, surely? Don't tell me you've stopped going to Mass."

"No. I still go."

"Why? Why do you still go?" All the time, they stayed looking at the painting, not at each other.

"Habit, I suppose."

"You always went, didn't you?" She turned to look at him now. "Every Sunday, and other days. What did you call them? Holidays?"

"Holy Days of Obligation."

"Obligation," Rosalind echoed. "I remember you with that smudge on your head. What was that all about again?"

"Ash Wednesday."

"All the time we were together, even though we were fucking. Sometimes straight after we fucked."

She spoke at a normal volume, but the quiet of the gallery made it seem she was shouting. The gallery attendant standing by the door—a young woman dressed in a blue sweater, black skirt, blonde hair tied back in a ponytail—looked over sharply and then looked away. Rosalind caught her look and smiled mischievously and mirthlessly at her.

"Stop it," hissed Gerard furiously.

"Stop what?" asked Rosalind. Wide-eyed, disingenuous. She'd enjoyed saying the word, liked the sound of it, liked that she never spoke like that normally.

"Just stop it."

"Don't you like that word? Or is it the act itself? We all do it. Even her." She nodded over at the attendant, intently staring straight ahead. "Actually, not me, come to think of it. How about you? Fucked lately?" Gerard pushed her towards the door and out of the room. "Easy, tiger." She laughed out loud and ran through the new room and into the next. Gerard stood just inside the door. It would have been easy to leave, walk out of the room, down the stairs and out into the street. He could just walk back to his car and drive home to Manchester and never have anything to do with Rosalind again. Instead, he walked after her and didn't know why.

He found her eventually, after searching through three different rooms.

Rosalind had stopped thinking. She had given up, surrendered to forces which had possessed her, or rather dispossessed her of will and control. There was a dream she'd had often, long before the unprovoked attack on her son, in which she was driving a car up a hill. The incline became steeper and steeper until it was almost vertical, and the car could no longer grip the surface and gravity sent it plummeting downwards, tumbling over and over towards the ground and never crashing. Waking up, sweating, panicked, she'd shake her head to make the dream itself fall out and then, scared to go back to sleep, she would make herself a cup of tea and watch television until the sun rose and it was time to drag herself into the day. Now she wished she could just crash, have it over and done with. That would be better than this tumbling, this never knowing which was up and which was down.

She saw Gerard come into the room, saw the look of anger in his eyes. Rosalind smiled brightly and approached him, putting one foot directly in front of the other, like a model on a catwalk, or a tightrope walker on a high wire.

"Welcome to British Art," she said. She spread her arms wide and turned first one way and then the other to encompass the room. "From 1880 to 1950, this period was dominated by the two world wars. The works on display here mirror the political and social upheavals of the era, with examples from the Camden Town artists Laura Knight and Lucien Freud. You'll see experiments in colour, materials, and techniques, as the artists of the period searched for a way of express..."

"What do you want, Rosa?" said Gerard. "Please. Tell me what you want."

"I don't know." She looked beaten, suddenly much older. "I'm sorry. I'm so weary."

They stood in the centre of the room, neither looking at the other, neither looking at anything.

The exhibits on the walls ignored them, concerned only with themselves: an abstract mother and child; a self-portrait of Lucien Freud, in shabby overcoat and round glasses dwarfed by a potted yucca, the tips of its leaves dry and cracked; Lowry's stick figures crowding around the fever van in a tight terraced street overlooked by a church. A pair of young innocents mutely swore eternal love beneath the boughs of a blossoming tree. Two French cyclists, too full of themselves, flirted with a coquettish girl who had their number before they even opened their mouths.

"Rosa," said Rosalind. "You called me Rosa."

"Did I? I must have..."

"You are the only one who's ever called me that. Mark calls me Lindy. Called. We don't say each other's names anymore, really." She placed her right hand flat against the side of her head, leaned her head slightly to the right, and stared past Gerard to a point on the wall. "Do you ever look at homeless people?" she asked.

Gerard looked puzzled.

"Homeless people?" he said. What was the right answer? There was a young woman he often saw sitting between the paper shop and the deli where he bought his coffee. He gave her money every day, the change from his coffee, but look at her? No. He saw her but didn't look at her. Rosalind wasn't really interested in hearing his answer.

"I do. I look and I wonder. I look and I wonder what brought you here? What happened to you that you ended up sitting in this doorway, wrapped in rags, grimy fingers, dirt under your nails, a chewed paper cup at your side, coppers and the odd pound coin?"

"I suppose..." began Gerard.

"Increments. Tiny increments. Wide, shallow steps down a steep path. Or one seismic event. One crashing moment that sends you lurching and spiralling." She rubbed her head vigorously. Her tone changed. "It was Mark's idea. To call Jack John. That's his Christian name. John. C of E; not that we go, of course. You don't need to, not if you're C of E. That was always your joke, wasn't it?" No jokes for a long time for Gerard unless you counted cheery remarks across shop counters, which he didn't. "I wanted to call him Alasdair with a d. Or Alexander," she said. "Something Scottish. You remember my dad was Scottish?"

"Yes," Gerard said. He did remember. He met him once, a tough, taciturn man. Rosalind adored him, and he adored Rosalind, which she knew, though he never showed it.

"Alasdair Jones," said Rosalind. "I took Mark's name when we got married. Became Mrs Jones. But Mark insisted on John. I said if he was going to be John, then he'd be Jack. Mark called him Johnny, and then JJ. I've only ever called him Jack. His friends call him Jack. Mark still calls him JJ. How's JJ, he says now, when he talks to me. We only ever talk about him, nothing else. If we talk at all. Jack is fine, I say. Only he's not, is he?" Jack was the last rope tying her to the quay. Now that was loosened, slipping off the mooring post. Gerard began to move away, but Rosalind called him back. "I want you to look at this," she said and led him to a display of Second World War art and artefacts, all encased in a glass cabinet.

"I have one of these," said Gerard, pointing to a chair on display. "Designed by Ernest Race. Made from metal formerly used in RAF planes." Trying for chit-chat again. Showing off, too, demonstrating his sophistication, the worldliness that he kept on display.

Rosalind wasn't listening.

"Look at this," she said. She directed him to a painting that dominated the small display.

In the centre of the painting stood a young man in an ill-fitting suit. He wore large glasses. His black hair was cut short and he was unshaven. In one hand, between his thumb and forefinger, he dangled a black rat by its tail; his other hand, by his side, was clenched, in anxiety more than anger. A white rabbit peeped from his jacket pocket. His feet were bare. He was looking off to his left, uncertain, wary, confounded.

The figure filled the length of the frame, standing in or on water, dwarfing the scenes of nightmares or depictions of fears enacted in miniature around and above him. Devils, a naked woman, a parachutist tumbling as his chute failed to open. Christ on the cross stood on a distant hill. Flames rose from a crater and elsewhere danced inside a cave. Figures, their limbs twisted, crawled to shore and rolled dice. The colours were muted, mainly blues and a pale sand, but also dripping blood and orange flames. The failed parachute resembled a shroud. Elongated animals pulled the cart on which the naked woman sat.

"Albert Richards," read Gerard. "British War Artist. There's another of his here, this one, Sappers Erecting Pickets in the Snow. Looks cold." Trying for weak humour again, something non-committal. Rosalind was transfixed. Gerard's words were irritants. She suddenly didn't care about any painting other than the one she was drinking in, memorising every detail. Gerard continued reading the brief biography. He couldn't see what had so gripped Rosalind. "Born Liverpool 1919. Died, killed in action, 1945," he said, keeping it factual.

She heard that. "Killed in action." She muttered the words to herself and thought of her son, lying dying in hospital. "Let's go," she said.

Downstairs, she stopped and bought two postcard copies of the Richards picture. She put one in her pocket and kept the other in her hand.

Outside, at the bottom of the gallery's steps, Rosalind no longer felt how cold it was. She looked up and down the street, uncertain where to head next. Gerard assumed she was thinking she ought to get back to her son's bedside. He himself was simply anxious to get back to Manchester. He'd done some sort of duty by coming over, perhaps even served a purpose. There was nothing for him to say, nothing he could do, no more he wanted to do. He would say goodbye and then, maybe…maybe text Rosalind in a week or so, find out her son had died, write a platitude in a condolence card with a picture of a lily in soft focus on the front, send the card, forget about Rosalind.

Gerard said nothing, though. He was leaving it to Rosalind, waiting for her to say she was getting back to the hospital and that he should be on his way, too; thanks for coming over. He had his response ready, had it all planned. He'd tell her he just had to pick up something from the shops so he wouldn't have to walk back with her. He was even keeping an eye on the traffic so he could dash across the road once he'd mumbled a goodbye, and 'I hope it all goes well,' and maybe 'I'll be in touch.' He wouldn't want to be, of course, but he couldn't not check how things were, could he? And it was preferable to 'Let me know how things go,' which would've put the ball in her court.

But Rosalind wasn't thinking any such thing. She was trying to decide whether to go up William Brown Street, towards the station, or back down, for a last look at the central library. She decided on the former.

"Lime Street next, I think," she said. She had taken Jack to the library the last time she was in the city and seen the new extension. Fresh and sleek, the staircases angling upwards through the air had shaken her with their newness, and moving from the gleaming extension through the door to the old library, with its dark woods and ancient stillness, had made her feel like she had stepped back in time.

She thought she might keep the library for last and maybe go there alone, although stepping back in time was no longer an option for her. She was stepping out of time, taking a scenic route to oblivion.

They crossed the cobbles and went to the top of the street, turning right and walking past St George's Hall, guarded by stone heroes of forgotten campaigns, its thick and sturdy columns pacing the length of the building, a touch severe, restrained, confident of its superiority, but kindly, nevertheless.

"Have you ever been inside?" asked Gerard.

"No," said Rosalind.

"I've been a couple of times," he said. "A while back now. A concert. And a chess tournament."

"Were you playing?" asked Rosalind, surprising Gerard with a show of interest.

"No. Just watching."

"You watch chess?" Gerard's show of polish fizzled out.

Rosalind stopped opposite Lime Street Station, and so Gerard did, too. He tried to see what she saw, tried to imprint on his mind the curve of its roof, the broad steps leading to its entrance, the hustle inside. But that wasn't what she was doing at all. She was reassembling the building as it was when she attended university in the city. She saw it hemmed in and hidden by misguided office blocks. She saw it grimy and dark, abutted by a neglected hotel, long since disused. She saw a waif-like girl struggling with a backpack nearly as big as her, arriving scared and excited, timid and thrilled, stepping out into a rainy city that she would embrace and that would embrace her. And then, once assembled, she deleted the image, just as she had wiped clean all trace of the art gallery she'd just left. She still held the postcard of the painting that had so struck her, but it wasn't a souvenir. She intended it as a prompt, a reminder of her future.

As fearful as she was, when she stepped off the train at Lime Street in September, 1981, the prospects were far too good to allow her worries to take control of her. Yes, she was a young woman in a big, strange city. And yes, she was on her own for the first time in her life and would have to fend for herself. But, on the other hand, she was a young woman in a big, strange city. And yes. Yes! She was on her own for the first time in her life and would have to fend for herself.

The death of Rosalind's father meant there was no longer a check on her mother's comments. She could take her foot off the brake. Rosalind's clothes, her manner, her friends, her insistence on going into sixth form, her desire to go to university, they were all fair game. Why do you want to do History? What's the point? Why can't you be more like your brothers? Why haven't you got a boyfriend? Do you have to dress like that?

She washed against Rosalind, eroding her. Rosalind didn't surrender, although her forces were depleted. And she launched her own guerrilla attacks, goading her mother, dressing in such a way that would provoke her, jeans and baggy T-shirts, jumpers that were far too big for her, charity shop skirts that almost dragged on the ground. She read while her mother watched TV, curled up on the couch with a book as her mother tried to concentrate on the soaps, infuriating her, silently and deliberately.

She left all that on the train. "Please ensure you have all baggage with you when disembark." But of course, it stayed hiding away inside her.

Liverpool was grimy and grey that early autumn morning, beaten down, suffering. Rosalind responded to that. She embraced and absorbed the city, found a rhythm in its streets and in the language of its people that she hadn't found before. Even the tense moments, the signs of trouble, the locals looking for students to beat up, the raised eyebrows at her accent. There was always that spirit, that defiance. She left, though. She left to take a job almost as far away as it was possible for her to go without leaving the country. And why? Because she told herself that she had taken her share. She didn't deserve any more.

She stood now on the pavement next to Gerard, but only vaguely aware of his presence, just as she didn't fully register the people passing around her or the vehicles passing her on the road. She saw herself walking out of the station, and she felt a sudden burst of energy. She knew these streets; the map was still inside her. Even though the shops had changed, and new buildings masked her old layout, she still knew where to go, the shortcuts to take.

Rosalind quickly glanced right and stepped out into a gap in the traffic, dashing across to the middle of the road and then crossing to the other side, sure of herself, nineteen again, part of a laughing crowd of students at the start of the pub crawl that would take them along Lime Street and then Renshaw Street, a half in each and then a kebab and the bus back to Wavertree.

Gerard was taken by surprise. He waited until the lights changed before he crossed, by which time Rosalind was darting past the taxi rank, surefooted, certain, unthinking. It suited her. She could just be. Or not be. She could dissolve into some kind of nothingness, some form of remote control, and just be moved and positioned and repositioned.

Rosalind reluctantly stopped when Gerard caught up with her and pulled at her arm.

"Where are you going?" he asked.

But the spell wasn't broken. She fired out the route like a machine. "Left onto Skelhorne Street and then down Hilbre Street. Over Copperas Hill, along Hawke Street, past the bottom of Royal Mail Street, past the Adelphi car park, and then left up Brownlow Hill." She didn't know she knew the names. She barely recognised her own voice. "That'll bring us out at the back."

"The back?" Gerard said. "The back of what?"

Rosalind didn't answer. She was set off again, with Gerard struggling to keep at her pace. Until finally, she was stopped at the steps leading up to the Catholic cathedral, on the opposite side from the main entrance. The machine that had fired out the route with such certainty had departed.

Gerard was breathless; Rosalind wasn't.

She was now an almost twenty-year-old student with a nineteen-year-old son, a nearly sixty-year-old woman in her first year of university who had tracked down Barry by searching through the lists on the English Department noticeboard, whose relationship with Barry had turned out to be no more than a brief fling. It had left her superficially one of the sophisticated girls she saw confidently striding through the union, sure of their appeal, delighted with their technique, gliding through lectures and tutorials and bars and gigs and beds. She was in disguise, though, and she knew it; aware of an unease and reluctant to acknowledge it.

Which was how she ended up here, at the cathedral, so many years ago, having told the friends she wasn't sure she liked that she couldn't go to lunch with them and would see them in the lecture hall.

"It's changed, of course," she said. She had paused to give the next stage of her goodbyes a proper moment. She was looking at Gerard, but he wasn't convinced she could see him. "None of this was here." She looked around at the expanse of paving surrounding the cathedral, an apron of slabbed stone. "It wasn't so neat and elevated. I don't mean they've raised it. I mean, it's grander." She began walking slowly around the perimeter of the building. "Have you ever been inside?" she asked.

"Once," Gerard said.

"Really?" She could remember him now. "I would have thought this was right up your street."

Gerard shrugged. "I was early for a concert at the Philharmonic and came in to have a look round." He resented her jibe, felt protective of his beliefs, wondered briefly if his beliefs were real or just habit, unwilling to engage with either Rosalind or himself.

They reached the entrance to the crypt, a side door that opened onto a staircase that led down to the beginning of Lutyens' vision that was never realised above ground.

The entrance was panelled in floor-to-ceiling glass, and on the glass were etched the names of the dead, memorialised by the donations of the living. Looking from the outside, they appeared backwards.

Rosalind read out the names as they appeared to her. "navilluS maiL. devoleB rehtaF. 3002-9491. naloD ylloM. 1102-8591." She giggled. "You'd be yhpruM drareG. I'd be dnilasoR something. I make more sense like that. I'm Rosalind backwards."

She pushed through the door and looked at the names from the inside, reading them in the correct order. "They don't make any more sense from this side," she said.

Chapter Eighteen

THEN

January 1982. It was the invisible girls who saw her first, who spotted the tears. Rosalind had fought them back from the moment her tutor returned the essay and she read his comments. She had fought them back on the bus back to hall, gulping down air and holding her breath to keep the tears at bay. She walked as fast as she could from the bus stop to hall but, once through the doors, could hold them in no longer. She dashed along the corridors to her room, head down, her bags slipping from her grasp, overheated despite the cold of the day.

But the invisible girls spotted her yards from her door and saw her upset. It was just one at first, returning from the bathroom, but then others sensed it, noted the bleeps on their radar, and soon doors opened, and three girls guided Rosalind back to her room, where they sat her on the bed and encouraged her to let it all out.

A boy, they assumed, not worth crying about. Don't waste your tears. Men are bastards.

What do you know about boys? Rosalind thought fleetingly, spitefully, in spite of herself. *How many do you know? How many have you had inside you? I've had two.* But that nastiness left her as soon as it arrived almost. She accepted their concern easily. There'd be time to resent it later, in a week or so, and then she could dismiss them. She would no longer see them. Rosalind would return to the fringes of the cool and admired while they would ease back into the walls, with their prim haircuts and old lady blouses, accustomed to their place in the reserves.

But when Rosalind told them the problem, they laughed. Is that all? You had us worried for a minute. You should see my essays.

The girls left Rosalind's room, disappointed it wasn't something juicier—a break-up, unfaithfulness, an unwanted pregnancy. Rosalind started crying again as soon as the door shut behind them, the dregs of her previous tears.

The end-of-term essay she'd left with her Medieval History tutor before Christmas had come back littered with scathing comments: Immature evaluation. Lacks credibility. A very shallow reading of the matter.

Rosalind didn't need to read them again, but she did anyway. She needed to suffer. She was incredulous, too, though. She never got bad marks. She never got bad marks! And she'd tried so hard with the essay, like she did with all her work. She'd had to sit through the whole tutorial, the minutes ticking by like days, while the tutor and the other students blithely chatted about Matilda or Maude and the White Ship and the Anarchy and how it was being back after Christmas.

For a while, she thought about contacting her old History teacher at school. Mr Fitzmaurice. She loved Mr Fitzmaurice. A grandfatherly figure, he would work in his classroom over lunchtime or sit and read the paper and eat the sandwiches his wife made for him, always cheese and tomato, and he'd let pupils come in and sit, too. They could read or chat quietly or play chess. He knew there were pupils who needed sanctuary, an escape from the corridors and the playground. Rosalind would read there and always hoped he would note her book and make a favourable comment. She would photocopy the essay and send it to him, see what he thought. He'd be on her side.

In the end, she didn't send him the essay. He'd just be disappointed in her. Instead, she rewrote it.

Rosalind didn't sleep for three nights. As soon as her lectures were over, she went to the library. As soon as the library closed, she went back to hall and worked at her desk. She didn't eat. She re-wrote the essay from scratch. If she made a spelling mistake or needed to cross something out, she would tear the sheet from her pad and start the whole page again.

She wasn't sure what day it was when she finished or what time. The weather had been grim and dark, the days merely a slightly brighter version of the nights, the sky in a bad mood, ready to lose its temper.

Satisfied it was perfect—not just the best she could do, but perfect—Rosalind slipped the essay inside a plastic wallet. She dashed out of hall and ran to the bus stop, where she stood without a coat, unaware of the cold, muttering demands for the arrival of the bus into town.

It turned out it was a Friday, late afternoon. When she arrived at her tutor's office, he was just packing his briefcase to head home for the weekend.

"Miss Duncan," he said. "You're rather early for Monday's tutorial." He didn't seem surprised to see her. He always called her Miss Duncan; he called the other students by their first names.

He took the essay from her and put it in his briefcase with his other papers.

"I'll read it over the weekend," he said.

"Read it now," said Rosalind. Tiredness had stripped her of reason and manners, but there was something else, too, a voice that didn't seem to come from her.

"I said I'll read it over the weekend," he told her. Cold, hard.

"Now," she said. Almost begging, her own voice returned. "Please," she remembered to add.

"Very well. Wait outside."

Rosalind did as she was told. She leaned against the wall and slid to the floor.

He came out of the room half an hour later and handed the essay back. Looking down at her, he said, "Better." He walked off down the corridor, and Rosalind stayed slumped against the wall, unsure if she could get up.

She felt the cold as soon as she stepped outside the department building. She had no coat, and when she looked down, she saw she was wearing just a T-shirt, jeans, and trainers, and she was almost certain she hadn't changed in days. At the bus stop, she realised she didn't have enough money for the bus fare back to hall. She walked the four miles, felt she deserved the cold slog back.

She got back to hall just as her fellow students were making their way to the canteen for their evening meal, and she wondered how long it had been since she'd eaten. Instead of joining them, though, she headed in the opposite direction, back to her room. She undressed, showered, and then went to bed, too tired to feel anything but exhaustion, expecting the relief to arrive when she woke.

Rosalind slept until the early hours of the morning. Relishing the silence, the secrecy, the darkness outside her window, she went to the small kitchen at the end of the corridor and made herself a coffee, which she took back to bed. She looked at the essay again. The tutor hadn't written any comments on it, but he had said "Better," and that was all she needed. Still, though, unease stayed with her, small, nagging, persistent, worming its way through the relief and sense of satisfaction.

The shock of the critical comments that accompanied her first effort came back to her, and she cast aside the second essay and retrieved the original. She read through the tutor's remarks again, punishing herself, exposing herself to their vehemence and scorn.

And now, any sense of accomplishment, any idea that she had got herself back on track, left her. She remained troubled throughout the weekend, staying in her room for the most part, leaving only to go to the hall vending machines for chocolate and cigarettes.

She tried to read but couldn't. She told friends who knocked on her door that she'd join them in the hall bar but didn't. The thrill of the first term had gone, the passion with Barry spent. She told herself there was still fun to be had but wasn't convinced. Something had changed. Something had dented the one certainty she had: her intelligence, her academic ability. She swore she would cut back on her social life, work harder, work for longer. And so she did. She surprised her friends with her diligence, shocked them with her doubts. She slept less, ate less, drank less, socialised less, worried more, needed more.

The term dragged on remorselessly. Spring struggled to arrive. Rosalind was unable to shrug off her anxiety, although she kept it at bay most of the time. One day, the first bright day in weeks, with Easter approaching and the dread of returning to Corby and her mother starting to press against her, she left her friends at the end of the last lecture of the morning, telling them she had something to do and would see them later. They were used to the more sombre, more isolated Rosalind now, a little tired of her too, so didn't try to persuade her to stay.

Rosalind walked. She headed towards the top of Mount Pleasant with no purpose, no reason why. Still without reason, she stopped at the foot of the steps leading up to the cathedral. She craned her neck and looked up at the spiked crown spearing the sky, and then walked up the steps and entered the cathedral.

She ignored the central area, ignored the colours drifting inside the crown, the sun shining weakly through the stained glass. She found a side chapel, without knowing what a side chapel was, and sat down. She stared past the small altar, past the bank of votive candles shimmering their desperate and dutiful prayers and saw only the blank wall ahead of her. The choir was rehearsing. She was aware of the music but unable to follow it. She let her mind empty.

She continued to return to the cathedral, irregularly, never with any sense of purpose. She didn't want God, didn't want religion, but she liked the stillness, the hush, the cool, the space.

Some sort of consistent happiness came back to her once that term was over, but she was never sure of it any longer.

Chapter Nineteen

Now

Entering the cathedral, Gerard dipped two fingers into the stoup and made the sign of the cross, enjoying the familiar sensation of the holy water against his forehead. Then he stepped forward, rested his left hand on the end of the last bench and genuflected.

"Finished?" said Rosalind. She could feel herself lurching again, could hear herself speaking loudly, inappropriately so, and could do nothing to stop it. "All done? Feel better now?"

Gerard ignored her. He was taking in the cathedral. His previous visit had been perfunctory, something to kill time. Now he wanted to see it properly, to feel it, to feel something, without Rosalind's sniping remarks, her grief, her storm-tossed intrusions. And so he paid her no heed.

He looked up first, drawn to the crown at the highest point of the round church, and then down past another crown, close, almost threatening, to the altar beneath. Like a stone dropped into the centre of this calm pool, the benches for the congregation rippled out from the altar. Beyond them was a wide walkway running just inside the perimeter of chapels, and he looked at these too.

He saw the choir stalls, empty now, although there was some soft bustle around them. In the chapel closest to the stalls, two choristers were practising, maybe some preparation for an Advent service. They stopped and started, listening to the advice of the woman taking the practice.

Typically, he wanted to recognise the hymn they were singing. He wanted to know the designation and purpose of each chapel. He wanted to know who had designed the stained-glass windows in the crown, who the architect of the cathedral was, the date it was built, the significance and history of the round shape.

He knew nothing. He was unable to tell Rosalind anything, unable to impress her, unable to fight against the need to impress with his knowledge. And he knew he would find out later. Byrd, Piper, Gibberd, and also Lutyens and Pugin ("Not many know that..."), the Blessed Sacrament, the Lady Chapel, St Joseph. He would find an opportunity to tell—maybe Rosalind, or the woman in the newsagent or the man who served him in the deli, or some other close stranger—and he would reel off the names as if he had long known them.

He suddenly hated the shell he had constructed for himself, wished he could feel as deeply as one of the devout and prayerful people kneeling alone around the cathedral, wished he could just let the notes of the hymn being rehearsed simply soar inside him. But he knew he couldn't, so he stopped hating the shell and told himself it was more than a coating, that it went deep inside him, that it was him.

Sunlight drifted downwards. Gerard began to walk around the cathedral, and Rosalind walked beside him.

"I never prayed here," she said. Her voice was soft now, respectfully hushed.

"No?" said Gerard.

"I never believed," she said. "I never wanted to believe."

"What did you do here, then?" Gerard asked. He felt the superiority of the devout, in possession of the gift non-believers would never receive.

"I sat. I just sat. I liked being alone. It suited me." They walked in silence for a while. "You're alone," Rosalind said. "Does it suit you?"

Gerard had his arms behind his back. He was looking everywhere except at Rosalind.

"Yes." It was both the truth and a lie. Then he said, "No," and that was also both the truth and a lie. And then he said, "I don't know," and that was closer to being a lie than being the truth. Reluctantly, he remembered the first time he and Rosalind made love. He remembered she was wearing black underwear. He remembered how wonderful it was to feel her naked body against his naked body.

"Why do you believe?" said Rosalind. "How? How come?" Gerard didn't answer. He was wondering if there might be a chance he would feel Rosalind's body against his again. Or any woman's body. How many chances had he missed? Not for sex. Not now. Just intimacy. Simply to reach out and gently touch the face of a woman who wanted to be touched by him. Just intimacy. Just knowledge. But he'd made his choice. "Did your parents push it on you? Is that it? Is that all?"

Yes, thought Gerard, *that might well be it. That might well be all.* But he said nothing. He was long accustomed to avoiding the truth.

Rosalind shrugged. "I don't get it," she said. "Any of it." They walked to the door. Gerard wet his fingers with holy water, genuflected, blessed himself. "There's something I always wanted to ask you," said Rosalind. Gerard was on his guard, watchful, but he welcomed the apparent interest. Maybe this was a chance to talk about himself. "The night we split up. Remember?"

"What about it?" He was disappointed, wary, cautious, wanting to know where this was going but reluctant to follow.

"You didn't try to talk me out of it," Rosalind said. "You accepted it. Why was that?"

Why was that? Could he tell her? Could he say he was glad, relieved? That it was like a weight had been lifted off him? That for the first time in months, maybe over a year, he felt light and happy? No. He couldn't. He told himself he was saving her feelings, that her son was dying in hospital, and she had enough misery in her life as it was without him making her feel worse. That wasn't it. He could not look at someone and say the plain truth. He could barely admit it to himself half the time.

"I guess," he began. "You were with Mark." Leave it at that.

"I really wasn't, you know," she said. Now she was lying. "I mean," trying to claw back some honesty, "I hadn't slept with him or anything."

"It was obvious," Gerard said. "Whether you'd slept with him or not." He didn't care now and wouldn't have cared then. "You were close to him. Closer to him than to me."

What was he doing? He was too much of a coward to finish with her at the time, had wanted things to end for months, felt himself dragged by dishonesty deeper and deeper into a relationship that was no longer working. But instead of saying that, now, when it didn't matter, he was trying to position himself as the injured party, the one who wanted things to work, who was trying to make it work.

"I wasn't surprised," he said. Although he was, in a way. He knew she was close to Mark, but even so, he didn't expect her to finish with him. She had said so often how much she needed him. Finishing with him had been too much to hope for. And then she didn't need him at all. "The way you talked about him."

"Did I say that much?"

"No. It was the way you didn't say much." Close enough to the truth.

"Did I hurt you? I mean, I must have, I know. But did I hurt you so badly? Don't tell me I'm the one who's made you the way you are now. All the fun drained away." Gerard said nothing. Another failing of his that he hated yet clung to, the need for pity. But he was transparent. "Christ," she said. "Have you ever had an honest day in your life?" *No*, he nearly said. She looked around, felt she'd seen enough, and said, "Let's go."

"You don't want to..."

"What? Pray? Say something to God? No, I fucking don't."

"I was going to say," began Gerard, and then gave up. There was no point. Rosalind was walking away. Even had she stayed standing in front of him, there wouldn't have been any point.

When Gerard came out, Rosalind was standing at the top of the broad steps that led down to a wide pavement and then the road. She was teetering on the brink of the steps. Gerard wondered if he should take her arm, make sure she didn't fall, but he didn't.

"Where to now?" he asked.

"Look down there," Rosalind said. She nodded to the view across the road and down Hope Street, past the Everyman, the Philharmonic, all the way to the Anglican Cathedral. It was a proud view. It suggested activity and achievement. "It seems wrong that it's so much nicer now. Cleaner than when I was here." She began walking down the steps. "It's cold. Buy me a coat."

Hope Street, Hardman Street, Leece Street, Bold Street, Hanover Street... Rosalind knew the route and paid no attention to the incidents in her life that the route held. The Casa, where she danced on sticky carpets. Kirkland's, where she kissed that boy whose name she never knew and would have done more if the chance had arisen and not felt a shred of guilt that she was going out with Andy at the time. The bombed-out church where she fell asleep against the wall after she'd drunk so much her friends had to shake her into semi-consciousness and lift her into the taxi.

These were places that didn't matter now, that she wanted to forget because Jack would never have those experiences. They weren't landmarks. They were just places where things happened to her, things that she once thought might have marked some sort of development, some shift in her process, things to be proud of, to be embarrassed about. Those emotions now meant nothing to her. They were things she'd told Jack about—maybe not the kiss at Kirkland's, at least not the whole story. She wanted to help him learn, possibly just wanted to show him there was more to his mother than being his mother. Less now.

But she paid no mind to them now because they were things outside herself. The gallery, the cathedral, the ferry ride she would go on soon—they were within her. They were places that went beyond the physical, past solid experience and into her spirit. They shifted unshakeably into her soul—if she had one; she wasn't sure—speaking and listening to her very self. And so she was divesting herself of them because she no longer had need of a spirit.

They met daytime Christmas crowds as they arrived at the shopping centre at the bottom of Hanover Street. Rosalind tried to remember what it used to be, this space, Liverpool One, before it was built. The bus station? Paradise Street? The buildings looked unfamiliar to her, sleek and modern, fusing with the older structures around them, although she'd been here before. Not to buy anything, of course. The mess Mark made of their finances saw to that, except that one time, when she came up with Jack at the start of term.

Chapter Twenty

THEN

She took an instant dislike to him. The moment Rosalind looked up and happened to see him walk into the pub, that was enough. There was a swagger about him, an expectation of attention, a sense of I'm here now: the party can start. She couldn't believe it when he came over to where they were sitting, said, "Hiya, Links," to Mike Lincoln, clapped his hands together and said, actually, demanded to know, "Right! What's everyone having then?"

While he was at the bar, Mike Lincoln explained.

"That's Jonesy," he said. Links and Jonesy: Rosalind wasn't the only one to roll her eyes. "Mark Jones. He lives in the house next door to me." And then he added, as if sensing the hostility from the table of teachers, "He's all right, really. He's a banker."

Rosalind beat everyone else to it.

"You're telling me," she said, and everyone laughed.

They were still laughing when Mark came back to the table with his pint and a fresh one for Mike Lincoln. No one else wanted anything. "What's all the laughter about?" He'd squeezed in next to Mike and turned to him. "You've told them I'm a banker, haven't you?" Mike nodded. "Well, they'd have worked it out for themselves sooner or later, I suppose."

This made everyone like him, apart from Rosalind, who stuck to her original judgement.

From then on, Mark joined them often. For quiz nights, trips to the cinema, drinks after work on a Friday when he finished early, ten-pin bowling. He was even there on the trip to Butlin's they went on that weekend, a cheap, out-of-season deal, a chalet for two nights for £10.

The camp they went to was about thirty or forty miles down the coast, still surviving, to everyone's surprise, long past the holiday camp heyday. For once, it wasn't organised by Mike Lincoln, who was the staffroom's social secretary, always coming up with ideas for things for the younger members of staff, the unmarried, the single, the childless, the dissatisfied. Still, despite Mike not organising things, it was made clear that Mark should be included, such was his place and popularity in the group.

It wasn't until they got there that anyone knew the camp was hosting a 50s and 60s music weekend, and they arrived to find a world of drainpipe trousers, ankle socks, DAs, ponytails, swirling skirts, thicker waists, and one-hit wonders.

There were sniggers in the bar that night, mocking comments from the teachers in their twenties directed—out of earshot—at those trying to recapture theirs. A couple of the teachers got up and attempted a jive at the edge of the dancefloor, exaggerating their movements.

Rosalind happened to find herself sitting next to Mark. She noticed he wasn't joining in the laughter.

"Dickheads," she heard him say. He was thinking aloud, not talking to her.

"Who?" she asked. "Them?" She pointed at the dancefloor crowded with forty and fifty-year-olds, moving smoothly and easily and expertly in the clothes they used to wear every day but now only got out of the wardrobe for weekends like this.

"Them," Mark said. He didn't look at Rosalind. He seemed to be growing angrier by the second. "Thinking they're God's gift. Just having a bit of fun, not harming anyone."

Rosalind was confused both by Mark's words and his anger. She still wasn't sure who he was speaking about, not even sure he was talking to her or realised she was there. She was still trying to think what to say when Mark abruptly stood up and left the table. Rosalind watched him, not knowing where he was going, and was glad he left the bar rather than head to the dancefloor.

She waited a minute or two and then, not knowing quite why, followed Mark out. She took both their drinks with her. She felt the cold as soon as she stepped outside but decided not to go back inside for her cardigan. She wandered around until she found Mark sitting on the steps that led up to what she assumed was the chalet he was sharing with Mike Lincoln.

"You forgot this," she said and handed Mark's drink to him. He smiled sheepishly as he took it.

"Over-reaction?" he said.

"No," said Rosalind. "I mean, I don't know. Maybe." She sat down next to him on the step. Her shoulder brushed against his arm, and she didn't move away. "What was the matter? I mean, you're normally..."

"Jack-the-lad?" Mark finished the sentence for her.

"No. Well, yes, maybe. You're never that serious. Not that I've seen, anyway."

"I didn't like what they were doing. Those mates of yours. Sneering. Laughing at those people. What's so wrong with them grabbing a bit of fun? Trying to get back to a time they were happy, no responsibilities. That's all. Not like they have much fun Monday to Friday, is it?"

"I guess not," said Rosalind.

"You think I'm stupid for letting it get to me that much?"

"No, not at all. It's just...it's just I never realised jiving meant so much to you."

They both burst out laughing.

When they finished, Mark said, "Still think I'm a complete banker, then?"

"Oh, no. Who told you? I guess Mike must've."

"He did mention it, yeah."

"Well, no," said Rosalind. "Not a complete banker, no. Jonesy." Very deliberately, slowly, she poked Mark's arm with her index finger.

Mark looked at her. "Jonesy," he said. "You've never called me that before. Never called me anything before."

Rosalind shrugged.

Mark picked up the packet of cigarettes from beside him on the step, took one for himself, and offered the pack to Rosalind. She took one, squinted when he lit it for her, coughed slightly and then played with it, watching the smoke rise straight in the still air.

"You don't smoke, do you?" said Mark.

"Not often," said Rosalind.

They were quiet for a while after that, an easy silence, both taking sips of their drinks, staring straight ahead. They could hear laughter from inside a nearby chalet and the muffled introduction of another one-hit wonder being welcomed to the stage, and a slow song starting.

"Appropriate," said Mark.

"Hmm?"

"This song. *Silence is Golden*. The Tremeloes." He spoke in a stage whisper.

Rosalind giggled. She shivered and, in doing so, moved closer to Mark so their shoulders were touching. She didn't do it deliberately and didn't move away.

"So," she said. "Big fan of the Tremeloes, are you? I've barely heard of them."

"What?" Mark pretended to be outraged. "Never heard of the Tremeloes! Brian Poole! Here Comes My Baby! I'm shocked. Shocked!"

"I take it you're a big fan, then."

Mark settled, and his voice returned to its usual volume. "No, not at all, really," he said, chuckling. "My mum was, though. Well, my mum just loved music. The radio was on all day from the moment she stepped into the kitchen. Records, too, although it was the radio she listened to mostly. My dad bought her a transistor so she could listen to it round the house while she was doing the housework." And now his voice became softer as the memories returned, and Rosalind warmed to it. "She'd sing, too. Lovely voice, my mum. I used to think she knew the words to every song they ever played. Turned out she'd make them up if she didn't know them."

"How about your dad? Did he like music, too?"

Mark shrugged slowly. "Dad?" he said. "No. Not pop, anyways. He was a good bit older than my mum, so he couldn't understand what she saw in all of that. This is the 60s, of course. It was all new." Mark mimed a man taking his pipe out of his mouth. He was his dad now. "Philippa!" Mark barked. "He always called her Philippa when he was cross, or pretending to be. What's all this racket? I'll have none of that under my roof! It's all long hair and revolution! And then he'd give her a smile and a kiss and go off into his study with the paper."

Rosalind smiled and pictured the scene for herself, longing to be in it.

"A study, eh?" she said. "Sounds posh."

"Oh, yes. Can't you tell?" said Mark. "No study for you, then?"

"No. And not much in the way of music, either. Not that it was a bad childhood, at all."

"Did you…do you…get on with your mum and dad?"

"Past tense for my dad," said Rosalind. "Present for my mum." She shifted her position, though not so much as to move away from Mark, but as if the movement was needed to collect her thoughts. "I do, I suppose. Get on with them, I mean. Got on, for my dad. Usual arguments with my mum as a teenager. Well, unusual, if I'm being honest. But the usual frustrations with her now. Always wanting to know when I'll settle down and get married."

"You're only…what? Mid-twenties?" asked Mark.

"Yes, but that's leaving it late, so far as Mum is concerned," she said. "Married at seventeen. Mother before she was nineteen."

"With you?"

"No, my eldest brother. I came along much later. Bit of a surprise, as far as I can gather."

"And your dad? He…?"

"Died when I was fourteen." Rosalind finished the sentence for him. "I loved him very much, and he loved me very much. Didn't say it. Never needed to."

"You miss him?"

"Every day." Then she laughed. "I think he thought I was a boy, you know?"

"Surely there must have been a clue," said Mark. Rosalind laughed.

"Football, fishing, fixing things," said Rosalind. She smiled at the memory. And now she mimicked her own father. "Come on, you. We need to work on your heading! And out we'd go to the park. Stay there for hours."

"Your accent changed then. Doing your father's voice."

"Scottish," said Rosalind. "Mum, too. Moved down to Corby before I was born. He was a steelworker; she was a housewife."

"You never picked up the accent?"

"No. Much to my dad's dismay." Again, she mimicked her father. "Och, how is it we have this English cuckoo in our nest?"

Mark took a sip of his drink.

"What did you mean then?" he said. "When you said about your mum. Unusual arguments."

"Another time." They were both struck by the fact there'd be another time.

It was a clear night. The moon was full, and its light gleamed off the chalet roofs. In other circumstances, Rosalind might have found the effect to be eerie, but she found it pleasantly mysterious and captivating tonight. Again, their talk of family over, they shared an easy silence until Mark spoke.

"Interesting man, Billy Butlin."

The new subject took Rosalind by surprise.

"Who? Billy Butler? The disc jockey?"

"What? No, Billy Butlin. Who's Billy Butler?"

"He was on Radio Merseyside when I was at uni there," she said. And then, in her best Liverpool accent, she shouted, "Hold yer plums!" She giggled again, and Mark laughed with her.

"I really don't know what you're talking about, my dear," he said in his finest upper-class twit.

"Sorry," said Rosalind. "Take ages to explain. No, go on. Billy Butlin. In what way interesting?"

Mark smiled broadly. "I'll need a moment to collect myself. Lost my train of thought when you offered to hold my plums."

Only a week ago, Rosalind would have viewed this remark with contempt, further evidence of Mark's crass and cocksure manner. Now, she shrieked with laughter and mock indignation. She pushed Mark with both hands.

"I did nothing of the sort, and you know it!" she said. "*Hold Your Plums* was the name of a game show on the radio."

"A likely story!"

They laughed and settled, and Mark started to tell her what he knew of Billy Butlin, the entrepreneur who accidentally found himself serving on the Western Front in one of the Bantam battalions in World War One when all he actually wanted was an 'I Volunteered' badge, and who went on to build holiday camps around the country.

"Billy Butlin," Mark said when he finished. His left arm swept across the scene in front of them. "Master of all you survey." He cocked his head towards her. "If he's still alive."

"Fascinating," Rosalind said. She meant it. "How do you know so much about Billy Butlin?"

"Just things you pick up. I like history, but the interesting footnotes. Not the dates and things like you teach."

"There's more to it than that," Rosalind said, and then she realised. "You know what I teach."

Mark ignored the comment. "You must be cold. Let's go back inside before I start boring you about the stars and how you can find Sirius by looking for Orion's Belt."

He stood up, and Rosalind, with a reluctance that surprised her, stood up, too.

"Another time," she said. And then added, again to her surprise, "I'll hold you to it. Jonesy."

It was a short walk back to the bar. Rosalind walked slowly, stopping now and then to look needlessly down the paths between the lines of chalets, some with lights on, most in darkness, their occupants here for the music revival and not prepared to miss a minute. Mark was happy to keep up with Rosalind's pace.

A few steps short of the door, hearing the one remaining member of the original Freddie and the Dreamers line-up performing a rousing I'm Telling You Now, Mark said, "So who will you be coming to Butlin's to hear in twenty years' time? Part of an 80s hits weekend."

Rosalind stopped and looked at him. "Me?" she said. "Oh, there's no question. Joe Jackson. Love him, absolutely love him!"

Mark held the door open for Rosalind and sang, "Don't you know that it's different for girls?" as she went through past him.

Back inside, nobody had noticed they'd been gone.

Rosalind gave no conscious thought to the time she'd spent with Mark that night, didn't mull it over at all, didn't talk about it to anyone, but, from that night on, whenever they went out in the group, she always found herself sitting next to him, and on the same quiz team, and at the same alley when ten-pin bowling. And when any of her female friends in the group rolled their eyes at something he said or did, she said nothing but thought they didn't know him like she did. And she let no one else hear her calling him Jonesy.

Chapter Twenty-one

Now

"Is this where you wanted to come?" asked Rosalind. They were standing outside John Lewis, its windows glowing with festive lights sparkling around expensive gift suggestions. A family of feature-free mannequins were wrapped in scarves and cheery sweaters, winter dresses, thick cords.

"I was just following you," Gerard said. He looked at her. She was shivering. "Come on. Might as well go in here. Let's get you that coat you told me to buy." Resentful, but accurate, so deniable. "And then we can get you something to eat." Thoughtful, generous, making his generosity and concern clear, and his lack of concern for himself.

Inside the shop, it was too warm for everyone except Rosalind. Shoppers loaded with bags and coats bumped and squeezed their way around more mannequin families in matching Fair Isle sweaters lounging on plinths. There were elegant fountain pens in spotless cabinets, red and gold table centrepieces, stationery ideal for the teenage girl, and tie pins for the golf fanatic. None of these was for Rosalind and Gerard.

He touched her arm and nodded towards the escalator in the centre of the store. They rode up to women's fashion beneath glittering stars hanging from on high.

It was less crowded in this department than on the ground floor. Gerard watched a man wandering helplessly around the displays, looking bemused and clueless at the dresses and tops. He wondered if there was a fork in the road that might have led to that being him, eventually picking out a skirt that would have delighted his wife until she surreptitiously changed it for one in her size and colour.

He shook the thought from his mind, contented himself in his isolation, as long as someone noticed it and felt pity and thought, what a shame, a nice man like him. Not that anyone would look at him and think that now, as he played his imposter's role of solicitous husband taking his wife to buy her the new coat she deserved because she thought only of the children and put everyone else first.

"See anything you like?" he asked her.

"You don't have to do this, you know?" Rosalind said. "I don't even know why you are."

"Because you need one." He thought, *Yes, I do. You told me to, remember?*

"You're not doing it out of guilt?"

"I've nothing to be guilty about," he said. His voice was sharp. He believed it. Rosalind didn't but said nothing.

She went immediately to the practical, the sensible, the sturdy, well-made, shapeless, and functional. She checked prices first and then sizes before pulling out something grey and padded. She put it on and said, "This will be fine. And it's not too expensive."

Gerard recognised his own traits in her, the self-pity, the self-abnegation, the don't-worry-about-me-I'll-be-fine disingenuousness. He could tolerate it in himself, deny it even existed, but it annoyed him in her.

He remembered a call from Rosalind a couple of days after they'd split up. He was at home, packing, getting ready to make the move north, the move they'd sort of intended to make together, even though they'd never properly discussed things, simply left things unsaid, assumptions made, hopes that it would never happen hidden.

Rosalind had wanted a favour, some minor, intimate thing; he couldn't remember what. Maybe help fix something in her flat or give her a lift somewhere. Gerard had wanted to refuse. Simple as that. He'd wanted to refuse, to tell her that was the kind of thing a girlfriend asked of a boyfriend. That that was no longer their status. That the past two or three years meant nothing now.

But he didn't say those things. He hesitated but soon enough said he would. He carried the heavy object or gave her a lift or fixed the washing machine, whatever it was. Whatever it was, he'd done her the favour.

Then, as now, he couldn't simply state his case, couldn't articulate his feelings. Fear. Fear of honesty, fear of directness. The clarity he had achieved in his life now was just a façade. He had merely stripped away all occasions when clarity was required, when confrontation may be unavoidable, when it was necessary for him to say clearly what he felt and what he wanted.

"Put it back," he said. "It looks like you're wearing a tyre." She liked that he said that, and let him steer her towards more stylish, more expensive coats, thick and rich in wool, lined and fitted, in a range of colours. "Get one of these," he said. Impatient, in charge, tired of the weakness.

"You choose for me," said Rosalind. Meek, submissive.

Gerard looked at the coats carefully, picking out one or two and holding them by their hangers against Rosalind before moving to a different display full of duffle coats.

"What size are you?" he asked.

"I told you. I've not gone up a size since I was eighteen." Playful now.

"What size are you?" he repeated.

"Eight," she said, back to meek.

Gerard flicked through the coats and found one in her size, bright red. He handed it to her, and she looked immediately at the price.

"Gerard," she said. "This is…"

"Just try it on."

She did as she was told and luxuriated in every aspect of the coat: the warmth, the thickness, the rich softness of the material, even the wooden toggles she fastened gleefully.

"I don't look like Paddington, do I?" she said. Playful once more. "This is beautiful. And exactly the thing I'd choose myself."

"It suits you."

"What about the colour? Not too bright?"

"It suits you," he said again. "Look at yourself in the mirror."

Rosalind went over to the full-length mirror on the wall. First, she stood straight in front of it, and then she began to pose, turning one way and then the other, hands in pockets, hands out of pockets. And then she stood looking straight at herself again. Softly, slowly, she began to cry, her tears gently rolling down her cheeks and onto the soft fabric of the coat. She did nothing to stop herself crying or to wipe the tears away.

To a soundtrack of easy listening Christmas instrumentals, Rosalind watched herself cry. She might have crumpled to her knees, but she needed the pleasure and pain of seeing the coat, its newness, its spotlessness, its quality, wrapped around her shrunken, spare body, its vivid colour serving only to frame her drained and lined face. Her arms fell limp at her sides. She was a helpless child. She watched the blurring reflections of oblivious shoppers, lifting hangers, touching material, examining price tags, and wanted them to both remain oblivious and rush to hold and support her.

Gerard didn't notice she was crying at first. When he did, he involuntarily took a step back, embarrassed, fearful, constricted by so many years of disengagement, of empathy felt only at a remove.

"What's up, love?" One of the sales assistants, a young woman with an older manner. "The auld feller says it's too expensive? Mean auld skinflint."

Rosalind smiled and sniffed. "No," she said. "It's my son. My boy, Jack. He's in hospital, dying."

The sales assistant put her arm around Rosalind and looked over her shoulder at Gerard, who managed to free himself of his restraints and step towards them. He patted Rosalind awkwardly on the back, and the sales assistant passed her over.

"Buy her the coat," she said. She smiled. "No arguments."

Gerard attempted something like a smile and thought about giving some sort of innocuous explanation but didn't. Before she moved away, the sales assistant touched Rosalind's arm, nodded over towards the tills, and said, "Ladies over there, love. If you want to fix yourself up."

"I wouldn't know where to start," said Rosalind.

Gerard helped her off with the coat.

"I'll go get this," he said. He knew it would be stupid to ask if she was all right. She wasn't.

"Thanks. I better try and make myself presentable."

Gerard didn't lie, didn't say she looked fine. "I'll see you in the restaurant. Top floor."

Rosalind nodded and they went in their different directions.

Lunchtime was more or less over, but the restaurant was busy nevertheless. Still, Gerard had no problem finding somewhere to sit. He chose a spot in the far corner, by the window, with a view between buildings of the river and the Wirral. He sat with his back to the window, the bag with Rosalind's coat on the floor next to him, an actor again, playing the husband who has bought the present his wife will be anxious to see, while she buys the cards and the scarf she hopes his one surviving uncle will like when Gerard brings him to the house from the retirement home on Christmas morning.

He didn't consider how many other people in the store or out in the streets, shuffling from shop to shop, might also be playing roles. Gerard had spent too long wrapped up in his own constructions to consider others might also be struggling. He assumed everyone else was fine.

He saw Rosalind enter the restaurant and stop to look around for him. He didn't try to attract her attention and didn't wave or gesture in any way when she spotted him and came over. She moved quickly, her head down, embarrassed, and not wanting people to see her face, to know that she'd been crying. When she sat down, Gerard didn't ask how she was, but anyway, she said, "Better now." Then she said, "Thank you for the beautiful coat." A dutiful child expressing gratitude to a maiden aunt who expected it. "I don't deserve it."

"Stop it, Ros," Gerard said, intolerant.

"Sorry."

Gerard stood up and said he was going to get something to eat and asked if she wanted anything. Rosalind said a coffee would be fine, but Gerard said that was ridiculous and that she must eat something, that she needed to keep her strength up. He forced himself to swallow his anger and tell her to stop wallowing in misery, but this was a reaction from thirty years ago, and he didn't say anything because he remembered it didn't matter now. He didn't remember that the grief and misery were justified and the wallowing was justified.

The restaurant was self-service, with an archipelago of islands presenting salads, sandwiches, hot meals, cakes, pastries, drinks. Gerard was hungry but reluctant to eat much with Rosalind opposite him. Enjoying a meal together was taking the impersonation too far. He got himself a coffee and some fruit and joined the longest queue in the restaurant, for the Christmas specials. When he came back to the table and put the tray down, Rosalind reached immediately for the fruit.

"No," said Gerard. He handed her the plate, laden with ham, turkey, stuffing, roast potatoes, parsnips and Brussels sprouts.

Rosalind looked at the plate and felt sick. "I could never manage all this," she said. She picked up her knife and fork and tentatively cut some meat, putting it in her mouth fearfully.

For God's sake, just eat it! Gerard kept his screams inside his head. "Just eat what you can," he said. "And throw that old coat away as soon as you can."

Rosalind ate silently, small forkfuls, long, difficult chews.

"You know," she said. "There were times when I was with Mark, in the early days, I mean, that I wished he was more like you. When I was dithering or anxious. Confused. You were either tender and helpful or told me to pull myself together. Mark just stood there. He didn't know what to do. Didn't tell me anything."

Gerard pushed away the plate from in front of him. He felt he needed space for what he was going to say, though he hadn't planned it. It just didn't need clutter.

"I was glad we split up," he said. Not spiteful, no venom, no desire to hurt.

"What?"

"I didn't try and stop you, or call you, or try to get you back," he said. "It was because I was glad we split up. I was relieved. It had all become too much, all too difficult."

Rosalind had been hungrier than she'd realised and had begun to eat with real need. Now, she pushed her plate away, too.

"Well," she said. She touched her hair, looked down and around, smoothed her hands along her jeans. She felt awkward. She didn't know where to look or what to do or say. "I mean…" she began but couldn't think where to go from there. Still the Christmas music continued, still the indistinct buzz of talk and activity from all around them. Only they were motionless.

Gerard felt nothing, certainly not relief or the sense of a burden being lifted.

"I'm sorry," he said. "I don't know what made me…I just…"

"No. No, it's fine. Honestly." She tried to make light of it. "It's good to know. And there was me thinking I'd ruined you for other women. That you are alone now because of me."

"No," said Gerard, without knowing quite what he was saying no to.

"I mean, I didn't really…" But she stopped. "I did sometimes, you know. That's the truth. This past day. Now and then. And other times, too. Before. When things weren't going well with Mark. Things are never going well with Mark." Her voice was drifting. "I hoped you were alone because of me. Not nastily, you know? And not wanting you back. Funny, I don't think I ever wanted that. I just wanted that impact. To have made that impression. Sometimes I feel I leave no trace."

Gerard sat back in his chair.

"Well," he said. "I've said it now."

"Yes," said Rosalind. "Yes. And I'm glad you did. Honesty. At last. It's good to know."

Gerard clearly felt that was that. He began peeling and cutting up his fruit. He knew how prim and fastidious it made him look, but control was important, and he couldn't risk biting, crunching, dribbling juice.

Rosalind was overfaced by her plate. Her instinct was to move it aside, leave it to congeal, stare down the emptiness gnawing away at her stomach, but she was too hungry to push the plate away. She delayed matters with a comment.

"Three hundred pounds," she said. Gerard looked up, wondering what she was referring to. "You didn't even blink. Did you even look at the price tag? I can't remember."

"Eh?" said Gerard. "Oh, the coat. It's a good coat."

"But I'm nothing to you." She picked up her fork. "You said so."

"Not nothing." He wiped his hands on his napkin. "And I didn't say that."

"You thought it. You think it."

Gerard wanted her to be nothing to him, but she wasn't. He didn't know what she was to him, but she wasn't nothing.

"That's nonsense," he said.

A couple came and sat on the table next to theirs. Rosalind heard her voice grow slightly in volume.

"Are you very rich?" she asked Gerard. "Do you have lots of money?"

She noticed the woman at the next table look across at the man with her. Only a quick glance, but enough to let him know this could be interesting, that they should keep quiet and listen. Gerard noticed the same look. He leaned forward, kept his voice low.

"Rosalind," he began.

"Well, do you?"

"No." He sighed and leaned back, giving up. "I'm comfortable," he said eventually.

"Mortgage?" Rosalind asked. Gerard shook his head. "Savings?" He nodded. "Tell me about your work."

Gerard looked at Rosalind, unsure what mood she had shifted into, unsure if he was about to invite more mockery. He shrugged and began.

"It's nothing, really," he said. "Proofreading, checking figures, some editing. Commercial publications, internal documents. For the company I used to work for, and a couple of others now, too."

"Used to? Who do you work for now?"

"Myself, I suppose. I took voluntary redundancy a couple of years ago. I just drifted into consultancy work. The company asked me to have a look at something, and it just grew from there."

"Voluntary redundancy. I never knew that."

"No reason you should."

"No. Did you want to go? Did they push you out?" She seemed to be reaching at something, anxious for particular information. "Did they offer you a good package to leave?"

"It was okay."

"Which means it was very good," said Rosalind. She gripped her knees more tightly. Resentment flashed across her face.

"It was okay. I had been there a good while."

"So you manage okay, then?" She was trying not to sound too interested. Gerard remembered the effortlessly casual dropping of Mark's name into conversations.

"Oh, yes. I've got savings, too, of course, and the company pension." He felt guilty for the obvious discomfort he was making Rosalind feel and didn't stop. "Private pension, too. And the flat's long since paid for."

Rosalind said nothing for a while, then changed the subject, trying to stop it nagging away at her.

"What does it involve then?" she asked. "This work."

Gerard shrugged. "Checking for accuracy, clarity of expression..."

"I mean, do you enjoy it?"

"It's not the kind of thing you enjoy, really. Very dry."

Once again, Gerard was being dishonest. The work was dry, certainly, and it wasn't the kind of thing to be enjoyed, but it fulfilled a need in him. It absorbed him, killed time that might be spent thinking and reflecting. There was no creativity, no blurred lines, no grey areas. No gaps, no cracks, no chinks of light. It allowed him to keep things sealed.

"Pays well, though?" Rosalind said, back to the only theme that interested her now.

"I guess so. Depends what you mean by *well*. More than pin money." Vague enough, not boasting, and no consolation to Rosalind.

"And you do it every day?"

"As and when. When the work comes in, you know?"

"Is it hard to come by? I mean, do you advertise or have a website or something? Could I Google you if I wanted to hire you?"

"Word of mouth. I don't go looking." And he added, "Don't need to." A twist of the knife he wasn't sure why he was holding.

"I need my life editing. I need someone to proofread it for errors." And the advantage went to Rosalind. She had wrested back control of proceedings, turned things from him back to her, from his situation to her plight. Her plight, her circumstances, her situation, her state of affairs. Her specialist subject, to which she returned again and again, alone, or with the one friend she had managed to retain. More often alone, though, monologues and dialogues and re-draftings whirring through her head, honing, refining, cutting and pasting, then ripping up and throwing in the air, only to pick up the pieces and re-assemble them, approaching the subject from a different direction. "A generous pension, I'm sure," she said. "With a lump sum, too, no doubt." He shrugged and nodded. "I bet you charge plenty."

"I charge a fair price," Gerard insisted.

"Naturally," she said. "Fairness." She stabbed a potato with her fork and held it up in front of her. "I have nothing. I work full-time, and I have nothing. I'm left with pennies. Buttons."

"Ros, you can't blame me for..."

"Why not? Why can't I blame you? You and Mark." She examined the potato on the end of her fork. "He bankrupted us, you know? Everything in joint names."

"I'm sorry," said Gerard.

"Why are you sorry?" she asked. "I thought you said you weren't to blame."

"I'm not," he said. "I just meant..." He gave up. Just leave her to it, he thought. Let it wash over you.

She pulled her plate back towards her, picked up the knife and fork, cut herself some potato and turkey. It must have been cold, but she gave no indication of noticing. What fresh mood was approaching now? Calmness, and a mild need to hurt. Before putting the forkful into her mouth, she said, "Does it ever bother you?"

"What?" Gerard asked. Now he'd decided to switch off from what she was saying. He was suddenly hungry, wishing he had ordered more, and reached for his fruit distractedly, not paying attention to Rosalind, no more than manners demanded, not expecting anything except maybe another question about the break-up, or the happiness they'd shared.

"That you're not real," she said. Coolly. Sweetly. She gathered more food onto her fork: ham, some sprout, a little potato, a dab of gravy. Daintily, she put it into her mouth, chewed a little, looked at him, raised her eyebrows, eyes bright, smiling. Gerard stopped what he was doing. He thought he'd misheard, or that she meant something else.

"What?" he said. "How do you mean?" He was thrown, still convinced they were at cross purposes, certainly not expecting the insight that Rosalind would deliver.

"I mean. You used to be," she said. "For a while. So I thought, anyway." All the time so normal, so matter of fact, cutting the food, taking mouthfuls, equable, pleasant. "Not now, though." She pointed her knife at him playfully. "And not for a while, I'd wager."

Gerard tutted, exasperated, rolled his eyes. "Ros, for God's sake…"

She continued in the same manner as before. "Let me tell you about your life," she said.

Gerard put down his knife, sat back in his chair, and spread his arms. "Go on, then," he said. "I'm all ears."

"I might not get the details right," she said. "It may be more of a broad brush."

"Oh, no. I'm sure you've got me sized up. After all, we've had a couple of hours together now after not seeing anything of each other for thirty years." He was worried, though, worried that she would be right.

"Well. let's see now." She put down her knife and fork. "Neat, tidy, and orderly, for starters."

Gerard opted for sarcasm. "Oh, straight to the quick."

"Meticulously arranged," Rosalind continued. "Regimented, even, maybe?" She wasn't addressing Gerard. "Yes," she decided. "Regimented. That's not too strong." Gerard sat watching her, pretending not to squirm. "I think your life is perfectly constructed," she said. "Perfectly arranged. Everything precisely selected."

"And what if it is? There's just me, isn't there? Why shouldn't I do everything to suit myself? There's no one else to suit. It'd be stupid not to."

"Because there's nothing else there," said Rosalind. "There's nothing behind the surface. You're a Potemkin village. It's all for show."

"Nonsense."

"And what do you want people to think?" she asked. "What impression do you want to give? Poor Gerard Murphy, bravely going through his days all alone. He deserves more." She stared at him. Gerard met her stare despite himself. "But you don't, do you?" she said. "Deserve more. You know why it's just you? Because that's the way you really want it. You say it like you wish there was someone else, but you don't really. You don't want more. You don't want love and laughter and life. You tell yourself you long for life to kick the doors down, but you don't, do you? You don't want to let go of your misery. You cling to it. Just as long as people see it and say how brave you are. But you can't admit that, so you stay smooth and lifeless, all the while demanding pity and attention that you don't really want. I'm all right. Don't worry about me. A fake martyr. You're a liar."

Gerard tensed, his hands gripping the edge of the table. He wanted to hit back, to spit out his reaction, to fight back, refute Rosalind's observations, especially since she was right. He couldn't say the words he wanted to say, couldn't dredge up the memories, the times he'd bitten his tongue when they were a couple.

"And what about poor Rosalind? How you used to whine about your life! All that anxiety, all that fear and shaking! All that expectation, the demands! And never your fault! You do a good line in self-pity yourself, you know?" Words he wanted to say years ago, that he should have said years ago but didn't,

too frightened to stand up for himself, to lose control. And he certainly couldn't say them now, of course. A dying son wipes out the past. A dying child beats all other hands.

And so he chose another route.

"What's so special about real life?" he asked her. "You always hear people saying it. Live in the real world, they say. Why? They never say why, do they? Those people who go to comic conventions and rock and roll festivals, dressed up in their outfits, their houses and flats adorned like milk bars and spaceships. They're dismissed, laughed at. They don't live in the real world! Well, why should they? All they're doing is getting through as best they can. We all still die, don't we?"

There, he'd mentioned death. He winced inside and was on the point of apologising but there was no need. Rosalind wasn't taken to her dying son's bedside by his words but back much further in time.

Chapter Twenty-two

THEN

"You don't have to do this, you know, Mum?" Jack said.

"But I want to," said Rosalind. She squeezed his hand. "You're my little boy, aren't you?" Jack looked quizzically down at his mum. "Well, maybe not so little anymore."

They were standing in the centre of Liverpool One. Stairs and escalators criss-crossed around them. Shoppers moved up and down, in and out. Department stores, sports shops, toy shops, clothes stores, phone shops, computer games, toiletries, beauty products — they drew money like magnets.

"I'd rather you got yourself something," Jack said. "Especially as...well, you know."

"Don't you worry about that. I've been saving up. Just me," she added. "Not Mark." She had stopped calling Mark *your dad* when speaking to Jack some time ago—a conscious decision. Jack couldn't remember when she started. He just noticed it one time and then every time after that.

"Don't worry," Jack said. "Dad..." And he stopped. His dad had specifically told him not to say anything to Rosalind, though Mark still said, *your mum*, as he knew how she'd react. Jack hoped she hadn't noticed his slip-up. He was always careful to side with his mother, despite his feelings for his dad. Mark understood. It just made life easier.

"So, then," Rosalind said. "What's it to be?" She was being brave. This time tomorrow, she would be at Lime Street, waiting for the train to take her back to Exeter. All those hours, all those miles. She couldn't bear the thought of leaving her little boy, of returning to the cramped little house Mark's stupidity and misjudgement had forced them to move to. It wouldn't be too bad if Mark weren't there, if there were only her. She could cope then, but his presence would make it harder. His clothes, his things, his body, his smells, his breathing. She realised she had drifted off from the present and forced herself back.

"How about a nice briefcase?" she asked.

"Mum," said Jack. "Who carries a briefcase?" He was laughing and she joined in.

"So, not a briefcase, then."

"Or a pair of mittens on a string to go down my sleeves."

"Well, I'm getting you something. What'll it be?"

Jack shrugged. "I don't know. I've pretty much got everything I need."

It was true. He was a loving boy, but an independent one, too. For a while now he had been aware of the distance between his parents and of the money troubles they had. How could he not be aware? So he had taken on a series of part-time jobs. Paperboy to begin with, then behind the counter in the shop, a couple of hours after school and on Saturdays. Then his dad got him a part-time spot in the same warehouse where he worked. Much better pay and pretty much the same hours. He had to give up the running club, but he didn't mind that as much as he thought he would. He could still go out running by himself, which was what he liked most. He didn't need the club vest. He didn't need the competition, the victories and near misses. And he could still see his mates from the club now and then, when they did an early Sunday run or when there was a half marathon the odd Saturday. His boss liked him, so he was happy enough to switch his hours to a Sunday morning if Jack gave him enough notice.

And working at the warehouse gave him the chance to be with his dad a bit more, to see him in a different setting, laughing and joking and relaxed with his workmates, away from his mum. He had to keep things quiet from her, of course. He had to tell her where he was working, but he let her think he was in a different section to his dad.

So, he had his own money. Not loads of money, but more than his friends had. He didn't need much, wasn't fussed about clothes or computer games or going out drinking every night, and there was no girlfriend to help him spend it. Not yet, anyway.

"There must be something you'd like, though," Rosalind said. "It doesn't have to be something you need. It's a treat, remember."

Jack heard the edge in her voice. His reluctance was starting to annoy her. She was still smiling, but her eyes weren't. She could switch so quickly. He looked at the shops around them and spotted the sports shop with a sign announcing a sale in the window.

"Let's look there," he said and pointed to the shop. *A hoodie, maybe*, he thought, *or a pair of tracksuit bottoms. Trainers would be too expensive. She said she'd been saving but didn't say how much she'd got.*

"Really?" Rosalind said. "More T-shirts?" She didn't hide her exasperation. She should have just gone shopping by herself, bought something and given it to him. But then she wouldn't have been with him. She went along with him, though, and they went into the shop together.

Inside, the shop was something of a mess, the sale sign attracting plenty of people on the lookout for bargains and not too fussy about how they searched for them. Jack kept away from the display of quality running shoes that weren't in the sale, and made sure he checked the prices of everything discreetly before he picked anything up.

A pair of tracksuit bottoms, a T-shirt, and a sweatshirt. All in the sale. Three for the price of two. Rosalind paid in cash, taking it from the purse she had cleared especially for the Jack Fund.

Outside, she said, "You do know no girl is going to look at you in scruffy clothes like this, don't you?" Jack laughed. Rosalind looked at his handsome face, saw her tall, fit boy, and knew the girls would be queueing up for him if he walked around town in a pair of pyjamas. That made her feel good, and a little unhappy, too. "I can buy you more, you know?" she said. "I've plenty left."

"I don't want anything more, Mum," Jack said. He held up the bag. "This is brilliant."

He put his arm around her and pulled her close. Rosalind was delighted he felt no embarrassment showing her affection in public. He didn't think twice about hugging her or saying he loved her. Her tall, good-looking, fit, confident boy.

"I've plenty left," she repeated. "How about I buy you lunch? You're always ready to eat."

"Yes, to lunch. But this is my treat." Rosalind started to protest, but he said, "To say thank you."

He put his arm around her shoulders again, and Rosalind felt like crying and wanted to stay this close to him forever.

They went to one of the chain restaurants on the top floor of the shopping centre, where Jack wolfed down a burger and fries and Rosalind felt sick at the sight of the chicken salad she ordered.

The next day, she let Jack insist on seeing her off at Lime Street, only saying there was no need once, just in case. She cried saying goodbye and cried intermittently on the train, not caring who saw the gentle tears drifting down her cheeks.

Chapter Twenty-three

Now

Gerard waited for a reaction to his thoughtless mention of death, but Rosalind was present in body only. And then she was back in the room, material gathered, images viewed. She gave up trying to work out whose life she'd just seen an excerpt of. The man was a stranger; the woman she vaguely recognised but couldn't put a name to.

She shook her head clear, looked at Gerard, smiled brightly. Her eyes twinkled.

"Well, I'm finished," she said. She pressed her hands down on the tabletop and pushed herself up. "Shall we get going? I'm going to throw this old coat away and wear my lovely, new, bright red duffle, I think. Shall we do the ferry now? While there's still some good light left?" She shrugged her arms into the sleeves of her new coat. "Might be nice, though, if it starts to get dark. See the lights from the river."

Gerard stared from his seat at this new version of Rosalind.

"What?" he said. "After...You still want to?"

"Eh?" Rosalind said. She didn't know what he was referring to, didn't know why he was still in his seat. "Why wouldn't I?"

"Because..."

"First, though," she said, not waiting for him to finish. "I'm going to get rid of this tatty old thing." She looked at Gerard and giggled. "I don't mean you." She waited a beat. "You're not tatty." She picked up her coat as if she was sorry she didn't have tongs with her.

"Okay, then," said Gerard. "Let's go." She was several different people, and Gerard didn't know who would appear next, but he was suddenly happy to stay with Rosalind for a few more hours rather than go home and resume his routine, perhaps because going home meant resuming his routine.

Outside, Rosalind went straight to the nearest bin. Rather than throwing the coat in straight away, she went through the pockets. Tissues, a few loose coins, the rail ticket from the journey up. She bunched the items in one hand and stuffed the old coat in the bin with the other. Then she put them in the pocket of the new one.

"Girls love pockets!" she said.

"Why are you keeping those?" Gerard asked.

"Souvenirs of my trip."

Gerard thought she'd want no reminders but didn't press the point.

Chapter Twenty-four

Then

"West Didsbury, yeah?"

Gerard nodded. "Just off Barlow Moor Road," he said. "Top floor flat."

She raised her eyebrows and puffed out her cheeks. "Bit rough round there, you know? Renting?"

"No," Gerard said. "I've bought it."

"Ah, right."

Gerard was in the staff kitchen, making himself a coffee. The woman he was talking to—smiling, friendly, attractive—was on the same floor but in a different department. Gerard had only been there a couple of weeks and was still learning names.

"What's wrong with West Didsbury?"

"Nothing," she said, now she knew he'd bought a place. "Just…My boyfriend's a probation officer. Does a lot of calls on Clyde Road."

But he only heard the words, "My boyfriend". Warning him off. Shields and deflectors deployed, phasers on stun. Gerard got the message—nothing personal, just a necessity for women in this and countless similar situations. (It was one of many such instances for Gerard, incidents that accreted and led to him deciding he would be left behind, and sad acceptance of the fact would be his look). He wanted to tell her there was no need for her to say it, that he knew what she was doing, that he found it conceited, that he wasn't interested anyway, but that would be both confrontational and untrue. Without even noticing he was doing it, the first thing he did on meeting, or even just seeing, any woman he found attractive was to check her ring finger.

"Still," she said. "You've got Didsbury up the road. Different kettle of fish altogether. And there's Marie-Louise Gardens, of course."

"Yes?" he said.

"On Palatine Road, I think. Near the lights. Bit hidden. Built by a woman in memory of her dead daughter. My boyfriend runs past it every day. Sometimes goes in there for a couple of circuits."

No need to mention him again, Gerard thought. He noted the reference to him running daily, too. Fit. Tall, probably. I'll use the gym membership that work gives me. Won't make me taller, though.

Gerard finished stirring his coffee and went back to his desk.

Gerard found Marie-Louise Gardens in his exploration of his new area that Saturday. He walked up Burton Road first, looked in the window of the tired delicatessen, made a note to avoid the couple of dodgy-looking pubs on Lapwing Lane, thought he'd stick to the Barleycorn for an early pint. Closer to his flat, nothing to write home about but nice enough. He walked down Clyde Road, trying to spot parolees, and then up Old Lansdowne Road. The houses were towering and uncared for, the pavements narrowed by cars and bins. He passed a synagogue that felt hidden and a long-established Jewish deli where he thought he'd stop for bagels on his way back from mass every Sunday.

He kept walking down Palatine Road and nearly gave up finding the park his colleague had mentioned—and then he found it. An open gate, a short flight of worn stone steps, a peeling sign curled by climbing weeds. He went up the steps and found magic.

He stayed at the top of the steps for a time, delighted by what was revealed to him: a park, not expansive but big enough, laid out in a rectangle. Within the perimeter path were lawns, with flower beds at regular intervals, neat, without being formal or fussy. Ringing the path, hiding the gardens from the road, tall trees stretched into the sky, their branches swaying gently against the blue sky, leaves of varying greens dancing on the branches. The summer sun caressed everything within the park. Unruly rose bushes filled the flowerbeds, their flowers in bloom and marked by deadheads. At one end of the park was a hut or small pavilion, its first storey of brick, its second topped by mock-Tudor black and white. Gerard was the only one there. He felt he'd found a secret, something once loved but now forgotten. Or maybe just remembered now and then, with good intentions to tidy things up, well-meant but never carried through.

He walked the perimeter path, stopping to sit on one of the benches, its paint blistered and chipped. He listened to the birdsong and promised to come again and often, to bring the newspaper and maybe a flask of coffee, just to sit and be hidden.

He did come back often. He stayed in love with the park, perhaps the only place where he was happy to risk the chance of genuine reflection and real regret. He always thought he had discovered it, this secret location, and wondered for a while if he was the only person who knew of it, so bare and unloved was its beauty for so long.

He wasn't, of course. At some point, a group of local volunteers was established to care for and maintain the gardens. A sense of its wildness and secrecy remained, but it was not so highly classified now. Still, he loved it, and didn't mind that others knew of it, or that it was now tended and manicured. But the nature of his love for it changed, became more a matter of habit, a deliberate act, his visits with coffee and a book or newspaper scheduled in the diary. Now and then, he listened to the birdsong and missed the unpruned rose bushes with their buds shed of petals.

Chapter Twenty-five

Now

Feeling how the cold wind was whipping up through the buildings from the Mersey, Gerard said, "It'll be freezing on the river. Cold enough here. We should have got you a hat and gloves, too." He put his own gloves on, his words reminding him he had some.

"No need!" said Rosalind. She threw the hood over her head and stuffed her hands into her pockets. "Look! Toasty!" She felt the first creepings of frenzied unhappiness. The coat had fitted her perfectly but now seemed to swamp her frame, and she increased the effect by lifting her shoulders and ducking her head.

"You look like a little girl," said Gerard.

"I am a little girl." The frenzy ebbed away.

They joined the back and forth of people between the shops on one side of the wide Strand and the docks on the other. There were more people heading against them than with them, and the crowd thinned further as they approached the Albert Dock, with most people heading left towards the Tate Gallery and the cafes and shops around it. Gerard and Rosalind went right, past the Museum of Liverpool. The newer buildings jutted and curved and reflected, in contrast to the older buildings of the dock, brick red or pale grey, gleaming in the sun, tall and stately and overwhelming.

By the time they reached the Pier Head, they were more or less alone. Only a few hardy souls—one couple and a family with the look of tourists wearily making sure they experienced everything in the guidebook—were queueing for tickets, the wind biting across the river discouraging any others who might have been tempted.

"I took Jack on the ferry the first time I brought him here," said Rosalind. "He was already set on applying. I went on so much about what a great time I had here. But I brought him for a weekend anyway. It was for me more than him, I think. Have you ever done this?"

"Been on the ferry? No. Been to the Tate. While back now."

"It's so different. First time I went on the ferry— what, forty years ago now?—it was all grimy and dilapidated. This, I mean." She gestured around her at the newly built terminal, bright and clean and decorated with posters of old Liverpool, stands full of brochures for cruises and silent discos. "And the ferry was for getting across the river and back. Workers. Not for tourists."

They stood in the queue as the family in front discussed half-price fares and weekend passes. Gerard picked up one of the leaflets and looked at it without reading.

"I'm sure there was a Chinese restaurant upstairs," said Rosalind. "Or a Berni Inn. Do you remember Berni Inns?" Gerard nodded. "My dad loved a Berni Inn," she went on. "And there was a chippy and a paper shop, and the buses used to terminate here. I caught the last bus from here a few times."

Finally, the group in front collected their tickets, and Gerard stepped forward to buy theirs. They moved on and went straight down the ramp to the jetty, where the tyres on the side of the ferry were bumping against the concrete platform. They waited until they were allowed to board.

"It's very brightly painted, isn't it?" said Rosalind. The ferry was decorated in an array of colours: blue, yellow, red, orange, green, black and white, a psychedelia of pattern blocks of circles, wavy lines, stripes, chevrons, checks. "Nothing's grey anymore, is it? Have you noticed?" Gerard shrugged. A lot seemed grey to him. "And everything's better, isn't it?" She increased the emphasis with each question as she asked it. "Brighter, cleaner. All geared for a new way of life, yes? Where we stroll past and barely absorb? We don't do anything. Do you engage? With anything? I don't."

One of the ferrymen beckoned the few people forward, up the gangplank and onto the ferry.

"It's all to do with the past," Rosalind said. "All this newness. It's just the past."

Once on board, they made their way to the top deck. They stood on the bow, alone, while the handful of other passengers stayed in one of the lounges, out of the elements. The ferry pulled away from the jetty. A voice came over the tannoy welcoming them aboard for this fifty-minute sightseeing cruise on one of the world-famous Mersey ferries, exploring the city's maritime and musical history. The voice continued for a sentence or two more before stopping to allow the opening bars of Ferry Cross the Mersey to take over. For the rest of the cruise, the voice and the music took turns. Rosalind and Gerard shut both out.

"Do you think it's important to be there when someone dies?" she asked. "Were you there for your parents? Or for anyone?"

"Not my father," said Gerard. "He had a heart attack, which killed him pretty suddenly. My mum, though, yes."

"How was it?" The ferry bumped gently through the glass water.

"How was it?" Gerard repeated. "It was like your mother dying. A sudden illness, nothing to worry about, then the examination revealing something far more serious. Fatal. Days to live. She was very matter-of-fact about it. Didn't want me to hang around. Brusque, really. Couldn't see what the fuss was about."

"Was she a Catholic too?"

"Lapsed. Used to laugh at me for taking it seriously. She said goodbye like she used to say goodnight to me when I was a boy. A kiss on the forehead, and then off you go to bed."

"Did you cry?"

"No. Not at the time. Not later even, come to think of it. I didn't know what to do. I felt like a spare part. I felt like the ending had come too soon, like I wasn't expecting it. I was just, sort of, Oh, that's it then."

"What's with all the bright colours anyway? All these zigzags?" asked Rosalind. "Why have they done the ferry up like that?"

Gerard took the leaflet he'd picked up in the terminal out of his pocket. He scanned it. "It's like a dazzle ship."

"A what?"

"A dazzle ship," he repeated. "It was a form of camouflage. For a while, at least. In just the First World War, I think."

"Why?" asked Rosalind. "Wouldn't the colours make a ship easier to see?"

"To disorientate, it says here." He read from the brochure. "The contrasting stripes and curves create an optical illusion that breaks up a ship's shape and obscures its movement in the water, making it difficult for enemy submarines to identify and destroy. Painted in bright colours and a sharp patchwork design of interlocking shapes, the spectacular dazzle style was heavily indebted to Cubist art. The inventor of dazzle painting, Norman Wilkinson, was influenced by avant-garde British painters such as Wyndham Lewis and David Bomberg." He stopped reading and looked back to the Liverpool side. "There's one over there. You see? In the dock. That's done by Peter Blake."

"The Sergeant Pepper man?"

"That's the one."

"It's always the Beatles, isn't it?"

"Except Ferry Cross the Mersey. That's Gerry and the Pacemakers. Anyway, I thought you loved the Beatles. You'd never hear a word against them. Or the city, for that matter."

"That was then." She leant over the railings, looking down into the water, blue-black and white where the ship cut through it. Gerard went to sit on a bench a couple of yards away.

"My coat," said Rosalind. Gerard struggled to hear her with her back to him.

"What did you say?"

She turned to him. "My new coat. It's like a dazzle ship." She moved around the railing, her back to the low sun. Gerard twisted in his seat and had to shield his eyes from the setting sun to look at her.

"What do you mean?" he asked.

"It creates an optical illusion. People see how bright and colourful it is. They don't identify what is really there." Gerard could hear her, just about, over the wind and water, but even squinting, he couldn't make out her features, just her silhouette. "We're both wearing camouflage. You, though..." she said. She was warming to her theme, expounding on the ideas she'd put forward over lunch. "...your camouflage is grey. Your clothes are dark. You merge into your background. And yet the funny thing is you want to be seen. You want people to pick you out, to sense the attractive sadness that lies beneath the greyness. You want that to be your allure. Your brave smile, your doggedness, your steadfast willingness to endure. Your don't-mind-me when all you want people to do is mind you."

"This again," Gerard said. "You've thought about this, haven't you? Given it a lot of thought?" He hated that she was right; he always did.

"It's not really camouflage, though, is it? It's a lie."

"Yes," he said. He brought his hand down from his eyes and turned away from her, tired of trying to make her out. She came and sat beside him.

"When people saw Jack, they saw me. I liked that. That's what happens when you have children. They become the way others see you. And you lose your name. For years, I've been Jack's mum. Not Rosalind or Rosie or Ros. Or Rosa. And I didn't know the names of the other mums. Or I'd know them and forget them. We used to laugh about it, me and the other mums at the school gate." She took the old tissue from her pocket and wiped her nose, which was running slightly with the cold. "I loved it," she said. "I loved that he was my prism. I wanted to be seen through him, and I saw through him."

"Like you see through me?" Gerard said, his face away from her.

Rosalind laughed. "Sulking suits you. You know what I mean. I looked at the world with his eyes. I saw the wonder and the beauty. I kept the conkers he picked from the ground. He'd pick them up and hand them to me, and I'd put them in my pocket. He never asked for them again, but they were there. I'd come across them now and then and feel them, admire their shiny coating, and think, yes, I know why he picked this up. I know why it's important." She stood up quickly, spread her arms wide and spun around. "He took big handfuls of life. Big bites. He gulped it down." Now she mimed a child crying, their face crumbling into screwed-up eyes and downturned mouth, shoulders heaving, breath gasped. "And

I'd cry with him, because he wasn't picked, or a friend didn't invite him." Her face and voice went blank. "And now I see the knifing through his eyes. The knife that stabbed him. The thrust of the hand, again and again, shoving through his shirt. I reach with both hands to the wounds and feel our blood seeping and oozing through our fingers and spreading its stain and taking our life." She knelt down on the deck. "And I fall to the ground, and I hear the footsteps running away, and I cannot stand, and soon I cannot see or hear." She stayed kneeling. "Is this how you pray?" she asked. She pressed her hands together in front of her, fingers to the sky, as a statue or a child might pray. "What words do you say? Do they help? Would they help me, do you think?"

Gerard had nothing to say.

Still on her knees, Rosalind said, "If he's not there, no one will be able to see me. I won't be there." She pushed herself to her feet with an effort. "Of course, the coat will be. They'll see that. But there'll be nothing inside it."

Without either of them realising, the cruise had come to an end. The ferry bumped against the jetty, and the tannoy voice said he hoped they had enjoyed themselves and that they'd come back soon, and souvenirs of their trip were available in the shop by the ticket office, and to have a merry Christmas. Then Gerry and the Pacemakers took over for a final time.

"This land's the place I love," said Rosalind. She moved to the steps, and Gerard followed her down and off the ferry.

The sky had stayed unchanged through the day, a cloudless, icy blue, bright and cold, until now it was suddenly night, with no sense of gradual shift. Across the river, the lights of the Wirral were beginning to glow while the ventilation shaft of the Mersey Tunnel withdrew into darkness. On the Liverpool side, the buildings around them shone and shivered, and red and white lights sped up and down the Strand.

Outside the Pier Head again, Rosalind said, "I need to get those decorations. To go round Jack's bed."

"Really?" said Gerard. Rosalind looked at him. "I mean. Isn't it...?"

"Why not? They'll have to have batteries, of course. No spare sockets. So many machines, all plugged into the wall and plugged into him."

They made their way back towards the department store where they'd eaten. Things were changing. The shoppers were slowing down, thinking about heading home, swapping shifts with Christmas drinkers, groups of men making an early start, hen parties coming out of their aparthotels. Football fans head to toe in red and white shuffled mournfully around, looking to drown their sorrows after defeat in the early kick-off, not caring about the hangovers they'd have to nurse on their Sunday flight home.

The earlier joy had receded, replaced by a grim pursuit of that last gift and a more serious intent to have fun. The lights strung across the streets sparkled. The Christmas centrepiece in the middle of the shopping precinct, a giant cone studded with circles of different coloured lights, glowed with a determination to spread festive cheer.

Rosalind perused the lights on offer, the selection reduced by weeks of being on sale. She sensed she was breaking down and observed with interest how she presented a calm, nonchalant image to the world. She picked up a box and held it towards Gerard.

"They wouldn't let me put tealights up, would they, do you think?" she asked. She heard herself talk as if trying to prepare a room for last-minute houseguests.

"I wouldn't have thought so," said Gerard.

"Fire risk, I suppose. Shame. Nothing like the glow of a candle." She picked up another box. "These will have to do.

There's too many of them—a hundred, I think—and they're all different colours. I really wanted all white. But they run on batteries, and it's not as if there's much else left." She kept the box in her hand and continued to look at the decorations and accessories. "Oh, now, would you look at this? What do you reckon? He'll love this!" Rosalind had picked up a child's Christmas stocking, warm crimson, trimmed in fake white fur. She rubbed it against her cheek. "It's so soft! Here, just feel it."

Rosalind reached over to Gerard and touched the stocking to his cheek. He forced himself not to flinch or back away, disturbed by the gesture and the motive behind it. *What were they now?* he wondered. *What were the other shoppers seeing? Too old to be parents of a child who might need such an item. Grandparents? New grandparents eager to indulge a newborn? What does Rosalind think is happening?*

"It's velvet, isn't it?" Rosalind said. She looked at the price. "Oh, blimey." She smiled. "Oh, who cares? It's only once a year, isn't it?" She put the stocking in the same hand as the box of lights. "And this, too, I think." She had picked up a toy elf, bent at the waist, ragdoll arms and legs sagging. "An elf on the shelf. And now we're done. Let's get these and then go see where he was stabbed."

Gerard took hold of Rosalind's arm and steered her gently to the side of the shop, as far away from anyone else as he could manage.

"Ros. Are you okay?"

She smiled and frowned at him, puzzled and amused by the question. He kept his hand on her arm, and she did nothing to make him move it.

"Yes, I'm fine. Why do you ask?"

"Well, because..." Gerard gestured towards the shopping she was holding. "All this. The fairy lights and the doll and the stocking."

"Yes?" she said, still bemused. "What about it?"

"It's just...you know...you know where Jack is, don't you? You know what's happened?"

"Of course I do, silly." She tapped him on the arm, a gentle smack. "I know he's been attacked and stabbed and is dying." Her tone was light, as if she were explaining patiently to a child. "Oh. You mean the nurses won't let me put the lights up! Well, don't worry about that. I'm sure they'll let me, in the circumstances."

Several parallel strands ran through her, each a different consciousness, each able to view and hear the others. To the strand that was uppermost, she made perfect sense. To the others, it was coherent babble, logical madness. She couldn't control any strand. She couldn't stop herself. And so she continued in the same way, coquettishly asking Gerard to pay for the items she'd picked up, which he did, asking if he'd mind terribly carrying the bag, which he also did. And then lightly stepping out of the shop and into the deeper darkness and brighter lights.

"It's this way," she told Gerard, heading to the crossing on Hanover Street. "I forget the name of the street, but I'll know it when I see it. The place we're looking for is called Chill Bar."

The attack took place in the area between Bold Street and Duke Street, a warren of narrow streets, cobbles, and old commercial buildings having had a change of use, their red-brown-black bricks now decorated in brash neon and peeling posters advertising two-for-one drinks events that had already happened. It was grimy and earnest, having been cleaned since the night before, ready to collect all the glasses and bottles and takeaway cartons that would be dropped or placed or thrown later. Aparthotels announced themselves in silver panels lined with buzzers and intercom panels. Out of their doorways emerged stag parties and hen parties to join the groups in town early, eager to start, struggling to decide which of the identical bars to begin their drinking in. It was untouched by Christmas, unaware of the area outside its confines.

Rosalind and Gerard wandered along, too old, incongruous with her bright red duffle coat and his shopping bag knocking irritatingly against his leg as they walked up and down and across, stepping off the narrow pavements to let more forceful pedestrians pass, stepping back on to avoid the taxis crawling through, looking up to read the neon, moving on to read the next neon.

"This is it," said Rosalind suddenly. She pointed across the street to a sign dominating its brick wall. Up a flight of steps was an open door, dim yellow light peeping out. She crossed the road and stood at the bottom of the steps. Gerard followed. She looked up at the two bouncers flanking the door. They ignored her.

Gerard felt anxious. He didn't want to be here. This area was no business of his. Rosalind's quest—whatever it was she was looking for—was no business of his either.

"Come on," he said. "You've seen it now. Let's go."

"I want to look inside," she said. Her lightness had left her, replaced by caution, fear, uncertainty, need. "You can stay here if you want to."

Feeling he had no choice, though he told himself there was always a choice, reluctantly Gerard followed her up the steps, past the bouncers who barely looked at them, having already sized them up and dismissed them. Their problems would come later. Gerard and Rosalind were nothing to worry about.

As early as it was, Chill Bar was ready. The music was loud and demanding, and the darkness won over the bright, flashing lights from around the room. The server on duty behind the bar, a young woman wearing all black, stacking shelves and loading shot glasses onto trays, couldn't hide her surprise or bemusement as Rosalind and Gerard approached.

"What do you want?" Gerard shouted. Rosalind shouted back that she'd have a dry white wine, and Gerard shouted for that and a sparkling water. When the drinks arrived, Gerard suggested sitting in one of the few seats around the wall, but Rosalind wanted to stay at the bar to ask some questions, even though she didn't know what she'd do with the answers. She wasn't looking for reasons; this was a matter of going through the motions. The only fact that mattered was lying in the hospital dying. She called the server over. Even after the woman turned the music down, Rosalind still had to talk loudly, and raising her voice about the attack on her son struck her as desperately wrong.

The girl knew nothing, and when Rosalind shouted, "I'm his mother," she just shrugged apologetically. Rosalind drank down her wine and told Gerard they were leaving.

The doormen outside were sympathetic but couldn't or wouldn't help. They weren't on that night or were on their break, or it happened around the corner, and the first thing they knew about it was when the ambulance and the police arrived and even then, they didn't take too much notice because, well, it's not like they're not here most nights, is it?

Rosalind went slowly back down the steps and Gerard followed.

"Unprovoked, the police told me," she said. She was just talking, not necessarily talking to Gerard. "Jack was with a couple of pals standing at the bottom of the steps here."

A group of women in high heels and pink sashes teetered their way towards them. They whooped when one of them lost her skirmish with the cobbles and toppled to the ground.

"Not even had a drink yet," said a woman to Gerard as she helped her friend upright.

Gerard smiled weakly. Rosalind didn't even see them. She was looking intently in the direction from which they came but seeing something else entirely.

"Jack's attackers came from up there," she said. "That's why the police don't reckon it had to do with anything that happened in the bar."

"And they just went for him?" said Gerard. "Maybe they heard his accent."

"Is that a reason?" Rosalind said. Her voice was sharp. "Is that a good enough reason to kill?"

Gerard felt like he was being accused. "Reason enough for some," he said. "That's what I meant." He hooked the handles of the bag onto his wrist and pushed his hands into his pockets.

"My Jack was with two others. Two other boys," said Rosalind. "They ran as soon as they realised what was happening." She wasn't reconstructing the scene; she was watching it happen. She walked down the street. Her steps were deliberate paces, alongside the running, terrified boys, alongside her terrified son. After twenty or so yards, she turned left, down another street, shorter and narrower than the one she left. "They ran down here next. They wouldn't have known where they were going, or why they were being chased. Jack slipped. The other two kept running." She stopped walking. "I don't blame them. They might not even have known he fell." She held her arms loose by her sides. "Anyway, he slipped. Or tripped." She pressed her foot down on a loose paving stone. "That's all. Thing is, he could have outrun them all. Good runner, my Jack. I told you, didn't I?" Gerard nodded. "Doesn't seem fair, does it?" said Rosalind, mild and soft now. "That you should die simply because you tripped over. Seems harsh."

For the second time that day, Rosalind knelt. She leaned forward and pressed the palms of her hands into the pavement.

"One of the gang went for him when he fell. Stabbed him," she said. "Again, and again, and again. The police told me how many times, but I'd stopped listening by then. Only certain details matter." She bent down and kissed the cold slab and caressed it with the back of her hand, gently stroking the surface, worn smooth by decades.

Mary-Jane, thought Gerard. *That was her name. Not Mary-Kate.* The name, unbidden, unsought. The memory grew once it arrived in his mind. And so, unable to help himself, while Rosalind tenderly and lovingly pressed her lips against the paving stone on which her son died—because he would die, she was certain of that—while she kissed the stone and felt her baby son's soft cheek, while it was the small hours of a night-time nineteen years ago and Mark was snoring in their bed and she had soothed Jack back to sleep in her arms, Gerard also travelled back in time, to just over thirty years before. He stood in the kitchen of a flat he went to just the once, with music pounding and people dancing in the next room, and watched Mary-Jane get herself a glass of water. He heard her say those words, that people should just act, just do what they felt like at the time, seize the chance, act on impulse. He was there, held back, not acting, yet wanting to act, and making excuses for not acting.

He made himself step forward and reach for Rosalind. Taking her by the shoulders, he gently guided her to her feet. She smiled at him.

"Thanks," she said. She breathed deeply, lifting her shoulders, shifting the weight she carried there, crushing her thin frame. "I'm okay, you know? Even though he'll die, and I'll carry on living." She paused. "He will die, won't he?" Double-checking, not looking for hope.

"Yes," said Gerard. "I think he will."

"And I'll carry on living?"

"Yes."

"It's not fair," she said, a mild observation.

"No. It's not fair."

He saw himself putting his hands on Mary-Jane's shoulders, gently turning her around and kissing her, more than thirty years too late.

An empty space, and then, brisk, business-like, Rosalind raised her eyebrows to bring things to a halt.

"Well, then," she said. "I'll be off."

Gerard was caught by surprise. "Where?" He was anxious, uncertain of where he was or what he wanted.

"Back to the hotel. I'll be at the hospital all night. I want a shower. Get my toothbrush." Reasoned and logical now.

"I'll come with you."

"No need."

"Well, my car's parked by the hospital. I need to go back there anyway. Might as well keep you company." But it was he who needed company. It didn't have to be Rosalind. Just so long as it was someone. His hands pressed against Mary-Jane's back, urgently, needily, pushing her into him. And she responded with as much need, her fingers in his hair, nails digging into his scalp. She pulled away and then took his hand, led him to her bedroom, more than thirty years too late. And in the bedroom, nothing else mattered, just the moment, just the desire, not the outside world, not relationships, not the future, not any possible consequences and repercussions.

"Okay, then," said Rosalind. "If you like. Let's go this way so we can walk down Bold Street. I always liked Bold Street."

Chapter Twenty-six

Then

"He wasn't even the first man to sign it," said Mark.

"Hmm?" Rosalind wasn't paying attention.

"John Hancock," said Mark. "He was the second man."

"Second man what?"

"To sign the Declaration of Independence," he said. "1776. You know. You're the history teacher."

"Who was?"

"Well, that's the point. No one knows. Well, someone must know. But everyone says, 'Put your John Hancock there.' No one says put the name of the other man there. All because John Hancock wrote his name in massive letters."

Rosalind let Mark's words wash around her. She was doing that more and more lately. Mind you, he was talking so much. Wittering on, Rosalind called it.

"What are you wittering on about now?" she'd say, and Mark would smile and apologise and tell her to ignore him, that he was just so excited about it all.

It was late afternoon, and they were at the kitchen table. Jack wasn't back yet. He was staying late at school, helping paint the set for the Christmas play. Rosalind was only paying scant attention to Mark. She was thinking more about starting to get Jack's dinner ready. He'd be hungry. He was always hungry. Boys! She stood up and started getting things out of cupboards, off shelves, from the fridge. Potatoes, fish, lots of vegetables. She smiled to herself, leaving Mark and his prattle far away.

"Don't forget he's got running club tonight," Mark said, sifting through the papers, finding the ones he was looking for.

Rosalind had forgotten. She felt a stab of resentment and anger that Mark had remembered. She had a choice to make: admit her mistake or bluff her way out of it.

"I know," she said. "It's there written down, isn't it?" She nodded at the calendar on the wall. "You don't need to remind me. This is for when he's finished that. He'll need a snack, though. Something inside him."

Mark was still sorting the documents.

"Sorry, love," he said. He was used to her snapping now, so didn't really notice her tone, and, besides, he was too excited by events to take issue. "It's just if you're thinking of heating something up." He looked up at the food on the counter. "You know, fish and so on."

Rosalind tutted and sighed. In for a penny...

"This is for us," she said. "I thought, seeing as you're home early." She started getting more things out of cupboards, from the fridge, off shelves. Bread, cheese, pasta, milk, broccoli, crackers, fruit. "I'm doing him a snack and getting a pasta bake ready for after running."

"Didn't think you ate fish," Mark said. He wasn't poking her. This was just absent-minded chat from him. He was normally good at avoiding saying the wrong thing.

Rosalind said nothing and resigned herself to eating a meal which she would struggle to stomach, just to save face. But then she had a brainwave. She turned up the annoyance slightly.

"I'm not hungry now anyway," she said. "I'll just do yours."

"Right-ho," said Mark. He had all the papers he needed ready. "Can I just get you back here, though?"

Rosalind went back to the table. She stayed standing. Mark gave her a pen and pointed to a dotted line on the top paper.

"Sign here." He turned the page over. "And here." Rosalind scribbled her signature. *Where's Jack?* she wondered. "I like these funny little post-its solicitors use," said Mark. "And here." Rosalind signed her name again. "Oh, you've put Duncan." Rosalind tutted. "Not to worry. Just cross it out and do it again." Rosalind did as he said. "There," said Mark. "That's the last one done." He shuffled the papers back into order. "I'll get these round to the solicitors first thing tomorrow. I'll call Jeff and meet him there. Harris and Harris. We're still arguing over whose name should come first." It was Mark's regular joke, and he'd been making it ever since he first started talking about going into business with his brother. Rosalind screamed inside and went back to preparing the food. "But before that, let's celebrate!" He went to the fridge and took out a bottle of champagne.

Rosalind wasn't sure about celebrating. She trusted Mark—that wasn't an issue. He'd always been a good provider, and she didn't doubt that would continue with this new venture of his. And it wasn't because she was in a bad mood because she'd forgotten about Jack's running club. She had already decided it was Mark's fault for distracting her with those papers she had to sign. It was just that she wasn't that interested. She hadn't paid much attention to all this talk about this new business for all the weeks and months he'd been going on about it. Setting up on his own. Well, with his brother, so not quite going it alone. She was happy enough that he was happy, and happy, too, to sign the papers (Mark had explained why, but she had switched off).

But Rosalind had other things to think about. Jack, of course, first and foremost, but her own work, too. It didn't keep her awake at night, of course, but it was a responsible job, and she enjoyed it, working with the little ones, a teaching assistant now rather than a teacher.

It was nice just following instructions, although she had to bite her tongue at times when the teacher got it wrong. The teacher was a bit suspicious of her, wary, because Rosalind had been one herself. It made her uncomfortable; Rosalind was sure of it. Still, that was no big deal, and it was such a relief to be able to leave the work at the door rather than bring it home. Okay, so the money wasn't brilliant, but it was fine, and Mark brought home plenty. They were never short, far from it.

Best of all, the hours suited her down to the ground. She could drop Jack off at school and be there to pick him up when he finished. She could take him to the library or for a snack and a chat at a café before heading home to make dinner while he did his homework at the kitchen table.

He didn't want lifts now, mind. Getting all grown up, wanting to walk or catch the bus with his mates, to go into town after school now and then. What he should be doing at his age, of course, but still.

Rosalind missed the school run. He didn't know she followed him sometimes or parked up around the corner so he wouldn't see. So he wouldn't feel she was spying. Well, it wasn't spying, really, was it? It was loving, keeping an eye out for him. Funny, seeing those girls come up and talk to him. They looked a year or two older, too. He was embarrassed, you could tell, and his mates teased him when the girls had gone. She should tell him. That means they like you. And who could blame them? A fine, good-looking boy you are.

Rosalind couldn't really share Mark's excitement, though she didn't object to it, didn't think about it much at all. She took just the one glass of champagne and left much of it, forgetting it was there, on the counter next to the cooker. Mark drank more, nearly finishing the bottle, but left some in the fridge, with a spoon in the neck to keep the bubbles.

"That won't be the last time we celebrate with champagne," he said and took his glass and the papers to the spare room, which he had fitted up as a home office.

He was right. It wasn't the last time they celebrated with champagne, but there weren't that many more.

For a while, things were good, to the extent that Rosalind had to look hard for clouds to darken her vision. Mark bought a new car. Mark bought Rosalind a new car. They went to Florida on holiday. It was too hot for Rosalind, but Mark and Jack loved it, which put Rosalind's nose out of joint. She didn't like it when Jack had too good a time with Mark, although she was always able to find some cover for feeling that way.

You'll spoil his appetite.

He'll burn.

He's only twelve, remember.

But what if he falls?

And then things stopped being good, more or less suddenly, as far as Rosalind was concerned. Mark, in fact, had been as much in the dark as her up until a few weeks earlier. He tried to keep it from her, did his best to rescue things. He sold his car, telling Rosalind he was getting lazy and was thinking of getting a bike, and not telling her the money he got for it — selling privately, in haste — didn't fully cover the loan he'd taken out to buy it. He tried cancelling the second holiday to Florida that he'd booked.

"Listen, Ros, I've been thinking," he said. "Why don't I cancel this?"

"Why would you do that?"

"Well, you hated it last time, didn't you? All that heat."

"I wouldn't say I hated it." She actually did say she hated it — more than once.

"Still, I'll give them a ring. We could go camping instead, maybe. Or a youth hostel tour. Somewhere here in England. Keep it simple. Let Jack see his own country first." He didn't want to discuss it in case he ended up on the losing side and saw mention of Jack as his winning card. It was a cynical ploy, but, to be fair to Mark, he was doing his best to keep the bad news from Rosalind, still desperately hoping he could save the company.

It backfired. When he rang the travel agent, he was told it was past the point where he could cancel and get any kind of refund, so he ended up doubly upsetting Rosalind. She made it clear she hated Florida and was really looking forward to a simple camping or youth hostel holiday.

On top of which, of course, he couldn't save the company.

At first, when he finally told Rosalind, it was as bad as he feared. She was furious with him for not paying as much attention to the finances as he should have done, for not working hard enough, for leaving his old job in the first place, for thinking Jeff was a good partner to work with.

"Jeff!" she yelled. "How could you possibly think you could trust him?"

"He's my brother," Mark said.

Mark was at the kitchen table. Rosalind was storming up and down the kitchen. Every now and then, Mark would go to stand up to go to Rosalind but then sit down, correctly thinking better of it.

"He's a waster!" Rosalind said. "I've always said so. I warned you this would happen!" She hadn't always said so. She never warned Mark this would happen. She always said how much she liked Jeff, how much fun he was, how charming he was. She encouraged his drinking.

Things got worse when she found out how much money they owed, and it was they who owed it. Mark had to remind Rosalind she was a director of the company and so shared the liability. Although Rosalind didn't see it as a reminder. She saw it as the first time she'd heard anything about it.

"You never told me!"

"I swear, love, I did."

"Don't you 'love' me." Which could be taken in as many ways as Mark wanted to. Rosalind meant them all.

"I can get my old job back." Meek now, scared, knowing the worst was not nearly over.

The final blow landed when Rosalind said, "At least we've still got the house."

In other circumstances, in other very different circumstances, it could have been a moment of mild comedy.

"Yeah, the house. Funny you should mention that."

But there weren't other circumstances, and the remortgage was very real.

"What?"

"But you signed the papers! Here! At this table!"

She cried: rage. He cried: shame, failure, disappointment, humiliation, loss, responsibility.

And still they had to go to Florida, and what an excruciating holiday it turned out to be. The hotel was all-inclusive, which Rosalind kept on reminding Mark was just as well. She made no attempt to hide her contempt for, disappointment in, and anger at Mark, and she was especially clear about that with Jack. She felt everything she said and did was valid, and Mark couldn't and didn't blame her. He spent the holiday damaged.

Part of Rosalind was enjoying it, though she didn't admit it. At last, she could feel fully justified in believing that the world was against her. And she could rightfully declare Jack as hers alone (Mark having let him down utterly), which was something she'd always felt but not been able to rationalise without lying to herself. She would have gladly swapped the pleasure of being right for a continued pretence, however. The property market was in a slump, and they had to sell at a loss. The house they moved to, which they were renting and could never have afforded otherwise, was cramped, featured worrying damp patches, and was in a part of town that left her feeling uncomfortable. She had to go back into teaching. Any passion she once had for the job mutated into discontent, seething irritation, and resentment. She didn't acknowledge it, but she became her own version of Trevor Jervis, whom she had once despised. In all, then, she hated everything and relished the hating.

Jack took it in his stride, though. Despite Rosalind's attempts to trip him up, she couldn't turn Jack against Mark. Jack's values were admirable. Yes, his father had messed up, but he was only human. And Jack could see he was happier than he'd ever known him. He kept this from Rosalind, of course.

Mark was happier. He never lost his guilt, but his shame shrank to a manageable level. He never really sought that old job. He had a meeting with his old boss – a drink, a casual, careful, coded enquiry – and took it no further. To tide him over, he took a post at a warehouse, handling goods destined for a supermarket chain, and found he loved it. Regular hours, workmates who liked him and didn't care about his bankruptcy and teased him because he was so good at crosswords and always wanted him on their side at pub quizzes. He turned down any promotions that were offered. He didn't want to manage. He didn't want to supervise. He found hobbies. He helped on a workmate's — a friend's — allotment. He took up crown green bowls. He never saw Jeff again. When Rosalind wasn't looking, he spent more time with Jack. He accepted that the marriage was now loveless and grew accustomed to the awkwardness and atmosphere.

Chapter Twenty-seven

Now

They began to walk, past shops, cafés, pubs, clubs, restaurants, people. Gerard didn't notice any of these, preoccupied as he was by the cracks appearing in his walls. Rosalind had taken on yet another different form, feeling happy and contented and part of the flow. She felt snug in her new coat, shielded somehow, too, and liked that she was carrying bags of Christmas shopping, like she was part of the season.

Onto Hanover Street now, and she smiled as she watched homegoers pushing onto already-crowded buses, their windows steamed up or wiped clear by passengers glad to find a seat and eager to see the Christmas lights and decorations they passed. She smiled as she watched loving couples in hats and scarves bundling through restaurant doors. She smiled as she watched laughing groups of young men and women heading to pubs. She smiled to think of the drunken kisses they might share later in the evening. It didn't occur to her to reflect on how that was the way her own son's fatal night out started just a few days before. She didn't reflect at all, didn't question her high spirits, her breeziness, her buoyancy, didn't upbraid or admonish herself. She knew she was no longer in control and would never regain control and accepted the fact. She surrendered to the chaos.

Rosalind's hotel was on the main road that ran alongside the Mersey, but rather than take the most direct route, she steered them left early.

"I think they call this the Baltic Quarter," she said. "Jack told me about it. He likes it."

"Everything's a quarter," said Gerard, unwilling to emerge from his isolation but feeling he had to, for form's sake.

It was an area of tall, red-brown brick warehouses and low workshops, lacking the grandeur and scope of the nearby Victorian docks, built for function rather than appearance, even though their function had first fallen and then renewed into something else, something edgy and youthful, with an air of penniless energy, as young colonisers with no desire to work for anyone else moved in, defiantly rejecting the routes now closed off to them. They passed an artisan bakery, a micro-brewery, a Scandinavian church, a board games café, tiny bars, bicycle workshops, website design companies. But serious money was slowly shifting here, too, as the cranes and boards bearing familiar names and costly intentions bore witness.

"Oh," said Rosalind, pointing to the entrance to a bar. "Jack says he goes there. Long trestle tables, he said, and wild bingo nights. He loves it there."

Eventually, meandering, they reached Rosalind's hotel, on the fringes of the city centre, close enough to be within easy reach of the effects of so much investment without quite sharing the products of the new incoming wealth itself. It was a dull building, thrown up quickly and cheaply according to the formula that worked everywhere the chain alighted, with a jarring dirty yellow sign holding the company logo. But it was cheap to stay there, even though Rosalind was still shocked at the price, not realising how they soared when Liverpool were playing at home, the hotels cashing in on the football tourists who flooded in to proclaim their undying love and strip the club shop of full kits and souvenirs.

There were fans milling around in the lobby when Gerard and Rosalind walked in, making it even more cramped and close than it was to begin with. They were all red and white, all clutching shopping bags, a look of doubt on some faces, confused by the defeat they had just watched, surprised that it had been allowed to happen, that the travel brochure should have mentioned the possibility.

Like Gerard and Rosalind, the fans were only back at the hotel briefly, dropping off bags before going out again to eat and drink, not heading to keep vigil at a hospital bedside or drift back to an empty and accusing apartment.

Rosalind's room was on the first floor. Like everywhere else in the hotel, it was clean, bland, but tired. It didn't seem to Gerard like it was the kind of hotel where the rooms were made up every day, but Rosalind's bed looked freshly made to him until he looked a little more closely and made out light depressions on the top sheet and pillow. Rosalind saw what he was looking at.

"I lay on the bed last night," she said. "I don't think I moved at all. I didn't get undressed. Just lay there and came out in the clothes I slept in." She put her bag down by the door so she wouldn't forget to take the decorations to the hospital and took off her coat. "I'm going to have that shower now."

Gerard sat on a chair by the window. Rosalind began to take her clothes off. Gerard stood up hurriedly.

"Sorry," he said. "I didn't realise." He moved towards the door. "I'll wait in reception for you."

Rosalind took off her top, revealing a thin, plain, white vest, the straps of her bra visible underneath.

"Why?" she said. She looked confused. "You're fine where you are."

Gerard expected Rosalind to move into the bathroom, but she didn't. She continued to undress, tossing each item onto the bed as she took it off. Her vest, her shoes and socks, her jeans, her bra, her pants.

Gerard stared at her. He wanted to pretend this wasn't happening, or that it was nothing out of the ordinary, to just move on as if she was fully clothed. He couldn't. He felt discomfort, doubt, need.

"Why are you doing this?" he asked.

"Doing what?" she said. "Oh, this?" Her voice was blithe and airy. She gestured down her body. "Don't worry. I don't want anything. I don't want to sleep with you. I don't want your body next to mine again or inside me again." She sat down on the corner of the bed. The room was small enough that their knees were almost touching. Gerard shrank back but also wanted to reach out and touch her. He felt himself tumbling. "Now, what was it I was going to...? Ah, yes, I remember." She reached back across the bed to her bag, from which she took the postcard of the Richards' painting that she bought in the gallery. She leaned forward and held it so she and Gerard could both look at it. Gerard shifted his position, moving away but craning to see the card. "Why do you think he's in bare feet?" she asked. She was studying the postcard she'd bought, the self-portrait of Albert Richards. "I mean, it's strange, isn't it? He's in a suit, but his feet are bare."

Gerard shrugged. "Something religious, maybe?"

"How do you mean?"

"I don't know. Don't some cultures insist on something like that? Bare feet for worship?"

"You never could do that, could you? Just say you don't know and leave it like that. It's okay not to know, you know." Gerard was irritated by both the truth of what she said and the familiarity the comment suggested, an intimacy they once had but no longer, a layer of closeness added to the nakedness. "Unprepared," said Rosalind. "I think that's it. All these terrible scenes around him, and he's there in his bare feet. He's not ready."

"He died, didn't he? Later in the war, when he was twenty-five, was it? His jeep ran over a mine. Maybe he wasn't ready for death."

Rosalind said nothing at first.

"Or life," she said. "Not ready for life."

Rosalind subsided back into her study of the picture.

"Why have you taken your clothes off?" Gerard asked, breaking the silence, his body clenched and tense.

"Hmm?" It was like he'd made a casual remark, like they were sitting up in bed together, reading a book, maybe the paper, on a lazy weekend, like he'd made a comment that she'd not immediately caught because she was concentrating so intently. "Oh, I'm going to have a shower." Still concentrating, her mind on the card in front of her. "Silly to keep my clothes on."

"You know what I mean!" He snatched the card from her. "Why..." He gestured towards her body. "Why this? Why this?"

"I'm naked," she replied. Moods, tones, attitudes, responses shifted within her, surging, retreating, swelling, subsiding, weather systems contending. Jaunty became mocking became spiteful became coquettish became louring became resentful became sullen. "It's nothing you've not seen before," she said. "My body was different then, of course, so maybe it is. Looser, duller."

"Rosalind," said Gerard. "What are you doing?" Calm again now, controlled, concerned, or sounding it at least. His tenderness concealed a panic, a desperation.

Rosalind stood up before him. As he had leaned forward, he was only inches away from her and now moved back.

"I'm naked, Gerard," Rosalind said. "This is what I am. Do you see? I have nothing. No defences, nothing to hide behind. I'm stripped."

He felt sorry for her, but he also felt a familiar irritation, familiar from 30 years previously. Sorry for herself. Demanding, needing. He tried to give then but gave up, angered by her lack of action and her reluctance to take control. He couldn't give then, stopped wanting to give then. He could feel himself being drawn back in and also recognised himself in her.

"It's all right for you," she said. "You have your moat and your castle walls, your parapets, your keep."

"I don't know what you mean," he said. But he did, and he knew she was right, so he sat and listened while she explained some more.

"Come off it, Gerard. You know exactly what I mean." Resentment pushed alongside the pity. Her tone became angry. Her fingers tightened and twisted on the card as she pushed it towards him. "Do you know what my picture would look like? My Seven Legends?" she said. "Do you? I'll tell you. I'd be there, naked, in the centre. Grey skin, sagging, creased. And all around me, there'd be Jack. Jack being born. Jack running. Jack falling. Jack being stabbed. Jack dying. And I'd be shrivelled in the centre of it all."

She let the card fall on the floor.

"Rosalind," Gerard said.

"And what would yours look like?" she demanded. "Hey? What would yours look like? Walls. You in the middle and walls all around you, all neat and straight."

"And you? You've knocked the walls down? Thrown the doors open wide?"

"No. I've thrown myself from the highest ledge. The air currents carry me or let me fall."

"Look, I'm..." But she wasn't listening.

"I bet I could tell you what you do all day," she said. "Not the exact details, maybe, but the gist of it. Waking at the same time, the same breakfast, a walk maybe, to get the paper which you read before you settle down to your dry, imagination-free work."

She was right, but Gerard sought to defend himself, show her she was wrong.

"Everyone lives like that, though," he said. "Up to a point. Everyone goes to work at the same time."

She was ignoring him. "And then, just before bed, you do your stupid crossword. Sated. Not happy." Rosalind's fury was spent, tears close now. And then they weren't, and she was in another place, in another situation, in the middle of a conversation no one had started. "No, Jack was never fussed about any team sport," she said. She and Gerard were lovers again, Mark a memory only. They were here to spend time with Jack and had arranged to meet him for dinner — their treat — but there was no rush because he'd be late anyway. Gerard and Jack got on well, Jack having long accepted he was good for his mum. She knew none of this was true but believed it anyway, in the way hotels can make you believe things that aren't true.

She carried on talking. "He played them, though. Fit, you see, and good coordination. Rugby, football. I even took him to watch a few games, now I think of it. Cricket, he played, you'll be pleased to hear. And he was a good runner. Very good. Ran for the county. Musician, too." She paused her brushing and looked straight at Gerard. "Did I ever tell you he played the cello?"

"No," said Gerard.

"Oh, yes. Piano, too — that's what he started with — but the cello was his true instrument. City Youth Orchestra, you know. And he brought it with him when he came up here." Truth met fantasy without changing her tone or knocking her off her stride. "Don't know what I'll do with it now, of course. Shame to sell it, but we don't really have the room."

"No," said Gerard.

"I got on your nerves, didn't I? When we were together. I felt I couldn't do anything right at times, and whatever I did made things worse. Do you remember that?"

"Yes, I remember that. I'm sorry."

"That's when I started to realise I didn't like being with you so much. I tried for a while, but then I realised it didn't work, and I stopped wanting to try and I wanted to spend time with Mark instead." Gerard said nothing. "Did you know?" she asked.

"Know what?"

"That that's why I wanted to spend more and more time with Mark?"

"I don't remember," said Gerard. "It's thirty years ago."

"I think you did know, but you told yourself it wasn't the reason. You told yourself your faults weren't the reason." She picked up the postcard. "It was easier to blame me, wasn't it? Or Mark. Or something. Just not yourself. You always had to be the injured party, didn't you?"

"It doesn't matter now," said Gerard instead of *Yes, I did*.

"I'm going for a shower," she said. She tossed the screwed-up card at Gerard. He let it hit his chest and drop to the floor. Gerard picked it up, tried to smooth it out, and put it in his pocket. Then he took it out again and laid it on the bed.

Gerard thought about following her into the bathroom to say something — anything — but he quickly realised he had nothing to say. He stood awkwardly in the room for a minute or two, listening to the shower, and then decided to go. The best thing would be simply to walk out, saying nothing, with no need to say anything, but he wasn't the type to do that, to leave things abruptly and unclosed. He went to leave but came back. He had to say something, tie things up, make one last plea or statement to show he was the one wronged or misunderstood or hurt, and so he pushed the door open and said her name.

She didn't reply, so he went on.

"Look," he said. "I think it's best if I go." Rosalind heard him and ignored him. *What did he want her to say?* "I'm making things worse staying here." *How could I imagine things could be any worse for her?* he thought, hearing the arrogance of his words but doing nothing to change them. He wanted her to say, "No, you're helping. Please stay." But she didn't. She said nothing.

So Gerard slowly went back into the bedroom, lingered, hoping she might call him back, not knowing why he wanted her to call him back. When she didn't, he left.

Rosalind finished her shower, came out and sat, naked and soaking, on the bed, sobbed, stopped sobbing, dressed, gathered all her belongings, and checked out of the hotel. She walked to the hospital, past Christmas lights and Christmas faces, through Christmas laughter, drunken shouts, and Christmas music.

Chapter Twenty-eight

Then

They came crashing through the back door, all laughter and giggles, merry and manic.

"Don't drop the chips!" Mark shouted.

"I've got them, Dad," Jack replied.

"Shame you don't play in goal for Rovers!"

Rosalind came into the kitchen from the living room. She was torn between anger and delight.

"Shoes!" she shouted.

"Shoes!" Mark said.

"Shoes!" Jack echoed.

Rosalind tipped nearer to anger, unsure if they were mocking her.

"And close the back door!" she said. She heard the edge in her voice and hoped that Mark heard it and Jack didn't.

"Door!" shouted Mark.

"Close the back door!" shouted Jack.

Now Rosalind was certain they were mocking her or that Mark was, anyway. Not Jack. Jack wouldn't, not unless Mark was leading him on. She pretended to sort something in the cutlery drawer.

Mark leant against the back door to take his shoes off. Jack put the bag of fish and chips on the kitchen table and sat down. His cheeks were red and his eyes were glowing with fun. Rosalind saw how cold his fingers were as he bent down to untie his shoelaces.

"Here," she said, moving quickly over to him. "Let me help."

"I can manage, thanks," said Mark, pretending to think Rosalind had meant him. He caught Jack's eye, and they giggled together. Rosalind continued to untie Jack's laces despite his protests.

She nodded at the bag of fish and chips of chips on the kitchen table. "I thought you said you were going to cook," she said. She looked down at Jack's shoes.

His shoes off, Mark took off his coat and hung it on the rack by the door.

"I was," he said. "But JJ said he fancied fish and chips." Mark rubbed his hands together to try and get a bit of warmth into them. "Freezing out there."

"Did he?" said Rosalind. *Don't call him JJ.* She looked up at her son. "That right, Jack?"

Jack nodded. He was sensing something — the usual — and was reluctant to commit to speaking just then.

"Tradition, you know?" said Mark. "After being to the match."

Rosalind stood up.

"Tradition?" she said. "That's the first game you've been to."

She went to the cupboard where they kept the plates.

"Plates?" said Mark. He poked Jack playfully in the side. "We don't need plates, do we, JJ? We can eat out of the bag. With our fingers!"

Rosalind took two plates out of the cupboard. *Don't call him JJ.*

"Please, Mum," said Jack.

Rosalind sighed. "Okay, then," she said. She put the plates back and shut the cupboard door forcefully. "But knives and forks." She rattled the cutlery out of the drawer.

As she was doing that, Mark took three bags of fish and chips out of the carrier and laid them out, one for Rosalind, one for Jack, and one for himself. Rosalind came to the table with two knives and two forks. She saw her portion.

"You didn't get any for me, did you?" she said.

"Of course," said Mark. He and Jack had unwrapped the paper and had started tucking in. "We couldn't get any scallops, though. Don't do them down here."

"What are scallops?" Jack asked.

"Depends where you come from, JJ," Mark said. "Down south, they're a fancy seafood delicacy. Up north — well, Liverpool, really — they're slices of deep-fried battered potato. Your mum loves them."

Don't call him JJ!

"I don't," Rosalind insisted. And then, more sharply than she intended, "Jack! Fork!"

"Well," said Mark. "You used to, anyway. Couldn't stop talking about them."

"Hardly," said Rosalind. Despite her hunger, despite how tempting the fish and chips looked and smelled, she didn't eat, just pointedly squeezed down on the fish with her fork and looked distastefully at the grease oozing from it. Mark didn't notice. Jack did.

"Mum…" he said quietly, leaving it there, enough to urge her to join in.

She smiled at him and prised some fish from the batter and ate it. Wanting more, she stood up and went to the fridge.

"Who fancies a drink?" she asked, meaning only Jack.

"Coke, please, Mum."

"There should be half a bottle of that wine from last night," Mark said. "Glass of that would hit the spot, love."

Happily, she got the Coke; she got Mark's wine with reluctance.

"Honestly, Mum," said Jack. "It was brilliant. I mean, like, we lost, but still. You know?" He pushed his dad's arm. "That man behind us!" He and Mark laughed.

"What are you giving it to him for?" began Mark.

"He's just given it to you!" Jack finished.

"What's he supposed to do, ref?" shouted Mark. "Flipping disappear?"

"Except he didn't say flipping," said Jack. He giggled.

"Don't talk with your mouth full," said Rosalind. She bundled up her food and took it to the bin. "Sounds fun. Will you want to go again?"

"Oh, yes!" said Jack.

"I'll take you," said Rosalind. A statement, not an offer.

Rosalind had her back to the table, so she didn't see Jack look up at Mark, and she didn't see Mark nod his head.

"Okay," said Jack.

Jack and Mark continued eating, but neither finished.

Chapter Twenty-nine

Now

Gerard's car was in the multi-storey opposite the Royal. Although he left the hotel at least half an hour before Rosalind, he didn't reach the hospital long before her. He walked slowly, unsure of the route, unsure of himself, unsure as he left the nightlife of bars and restaurants and Christmas parties and made his way through empty streets.

He never felt confident walking through a city centre at night and was relieved to be back in his car, out of the car park, and on the way out of town and onto the M62.

Relief, though, gave way to the thought of what awaited him back in Manchester, the trudge up to the empty flat, not just empty of people but drained of life and emotion, which he had deliberately created, piece by piece.

When he arrived home, he poured himself a drink. A whisky, a single malt from a small distillery in Scotland, bought through a website catering for whisky connoisseurs. Expensive, of course, and esoteric, naturally, only available in specialist shops or through certain websites. It came with tasting notes, which Gerard read before taking a sip. Rich, complex, and peaty, although not dominantly so, with multiple layers and a complex character, enhanced with the merest drop of water.

Gerard needed more than the merest drop of water; he put a single ice cube in the glass. He knew this was not by any means the recommended way and that real connoisseurs would be appalled, but it was the only way he could drink it, and he told himself he could take it any way he wanted. Besides, swirling the ice in the glass added to the effect — contemplative, brooding, introspective.

He carried the glass across the living room and went out onto his balcony. He looked at the lights in the distance and the darkness of the golf course below and the blackness of the river that ribboned slowly and narrowly alongside the course. *The River Mersey*, he thought, *that works its way through Stockport and around south Manchester before gathering power and breadth as it reaches Liverpool and the Irish Sea. The same river I crossed on the ferry earlier, with Rosalind and the dazzle ship.*

He finished his whisky, rinsed the glass, left it to drain, and went to bed. He slept better than he expected and was woken at just before six the next morning by a phone call from Rosalind, who said the doctor had given Jack just a couple more hours and would Gerard come over to the hospital.

There was no question of getting back to sleep after the call, and Gerard didn't bother trying.

It wasn't the news of Jack's impending death so much, or at all, to be honest. To be honest. It was Rosalind's request that he come over. The bother, the nuisance, the grating assumption that he had nothing better to do, that he would simply forget all other plans and come to her side. Where he would feel useless, ill at ease. More than that — an actor that didn't belong in the scene, or that was needed but not wanted, or wanted but not needed. One or the other, or both.

He got up and made a pot of tea, which he drank in the living room, the curtains open, watching the day first merge with and then replace the dark, gradually, and then suddenly. Another bright day, he thought, cloudless, cold.

He didn't want another day like yesterday when he was ignored and abused, confronted, humiliated, and accused, when the curtain was ripped away. Why did she want him there? What did she want from him? Why did he say yes? And why did he mean it when he agreed to come?

Because he didn't have to go. And even though he said he would, he could simply not go. That was an option, theoretically, at least. He could simply wait until his gym opened and then go for a swim, then mass, get the paper afterwards, a coffee, a pastry. Clean the flat in the afternoon.

He could text an excuse. Better than calling. Better than leaving himself open to persuasion.

The car won't start. It's been funny all week.
I've suddenly started to feel sick. I've felt a bit funny all week.
Or something that aligned with the truth.
I really don't feel it's my place to be there. I'd only be intruding.

Or he could just not bother. Just not go. He could leave Jack dying and Rosalind waiting until Jack was dead, and Rosalind twigged that he wasn't coming. Plenty of people did that, things like that.

Yes, I'll call you during the week.
I'll be in touch in the next couple of days.
I'll write as soon as I get there.

He could come up with a lie that made him sound noble but failing.

I was held up but got there as soon as I could. They wouldn't let me in. Not immediate family. I called, but there was no reply.

No, she'd see from her phone that he hadn't called, and he couldn't call from Manchester pretending to be at the hospital in case she answered and said she'd come down.

I would have called but I didn't think it was right to disturb you. That was better. Safer, and just as noble.

He didn't consider telling the truth.

I'm not coming because I don't want to.

Although he did want to. He needed to. Not to comfort or console or help Rosalind, but for himself. His need for completion. Or a need to hang on, to cling on, just in case. Rosalind had nothing to do with it. This was what he was like. He needed to have the final word, just in case it wasn't the final word, just in case the other person wanted to cling on also.

So he'd go. He'd take his time — shower, breakfast, stop for a coffee and the paper. But he'd go. Of course he would.

Gerard took more time than he realised, and so it was well after ten by the time he left, and the motorway traffic was heavier than he expected. He decided against the M60, not wanting to get snarled up in Trafford Centre queues, and so took the M56 first and then the M6. A north-south artery, the December Sunday traffic was no different from any other day, heavy but flowing, nevertheless. Gerard took his time, staying in the nearside lane, watching cars passing him with football scarves and flags in the back, the colours of so many teams, blue, red, white, claret, gold, green, black. All travelling in hope and expectation, whereas his journey had neither. Death and doubt waited for him. Death he would leave behind on his return — for a while, at least — but doubt would stay with him.

On the M62, Liverpool getting closer, a giant statue overlooking the motorway, a white sculpture of a woman's head, staring out over the six lanes. Spectral, almost, though too substantial to be called that really, unsmiling, neither threatening nor benevolent, staring unseeing and uninterested across the motorway, incongruous, not belonging. The sculpture was on the far side from him, alongside the lanes heading east.

It caught the corner of his eye, failed to register, and then he realised what it was as he passed it. He looked back to see more but couldn't.

There was a queue of cars at the end of the motorway. He waited his turn to go through the Rocket and crawled through Old Swan and along Edge Lane. Traffic thinned when he veered off towards the hospital. He used the same car park as the day before and parked on the same level and in the same spot, a creature of habit and repetition, even though more convenient spaces were available.

There were fewer smokers outside today. Gerard went to the mezzanine seating area, once again going to the same place as yesterday. He texted Rosalind, told her where he was. Waiting for a reply, Gerard looked around. There was a Christmas tree in the centre of the space, tall and artificial. He wondered if it had been there the day before. He couldn't remember it. Few of the other tables were occupied. Those that were had been taken by hospital staff, some of whom wore festive accessories, Santas popping out of the pockets of their scrubs, a couple of porters in Santa hats, next to empty wheelchairs with twists of tinsel round the handles. Despite the decorations, Christmas had barely scratched the surface of the hospital.

Gerard's phone beeped. It was Rosalind replying to his text with a message to go to Room Nine on the fifth floor. He wanted to stay where he was. He wanted to walk out of the hospital and go home. He was scared of further change and just wanted to be gone. Reluctantly, he made his way to the lift.

Room Nine was at the end of a corridor, away from any wards or staffrooms. When he asked for it at the reception desk, the nurse on duty immediately changed her countenance, from harassed and impatient to sympathetic and concerned. She pointed him in the right direction and called him

Mr Jones. Gerard didn't correct her. The door was solid wood, with no windows. Gerard knocked softly and went in without waiting for a response.

He couldn't have known the details, but Gerard had got the essentials right. A bed, two chairs, two bodies, both still, one dead, one drained.

Rosalind was sitting on a chair with her back to the door. Without turning around, she said, "This is where they bring the dead."

Gerard stepped closer and put his hand on Rosalind's shoulder. In her lap was the bag of decorations she had bought the previous day, her hands pressed down upon it, crumpling the thick paper.

"I'm so sorry, Ros," he said. He looked at Jack. A single sheet was wrapped tight over his body, his arms pressed tight against his side. Rosalind had turned down the sheet so his pale, handsome, dead face was visible.

"I'm not a Ros, you know," she said. Her voice was flat, empty, lost. "Not a Rosalind. Never have been, really. Certainly not a Rosie, or a Lindy, a Rosa. They are names that belong to other girls." She scoffed and said the single word again. "Girls." And then she went on. "I don't know what my parents were thinking. Rosalind is a girl from a different place. She is pretty, and she laughs a lot and has friends and has money. She has long, rich hair. She doesn't have a dead son." With an effort, she raised an arm and took a handful of her brittle hair. Gerard thought she might try and yank it out and thought it would come with ease. But she did nothing, just kept her fist against her head, her knuckles against her skull. "I think I'm a Debra, or a Jane, or a Mandy. Penny. Jenny," she said. "Something plain and forgettable. I don't know. Mark will be here soon. He called."

Gerard nodded. He didn't have a clue what to do or say. Even though Mark coming gave him a reason to leave now, a way out, he couldn't move. Instead, he just looked down at Rosalind. He was at a remove, unable to share her pain, only to observe it. Sympathetic, certainly, deeply sorry for her loss – the clichés came naturally – but separated, useless, completely apart. How could it be otherwise? He could not conceive of the pain she must be feeling because he had never had a child of his own, never lost a child of his own, never felt such agony. He told himself these things, told himself he had never felt what she had felt, what any parent had felt, and told himself he could have left the sentence there, just left it at never felt.

It could have been otherwise, though, couldn't it? He didn't mean there was a chance they might have stayed together, that this was a moment among years of moments they might have shared. He just meant that something was missing from him that would have moved him closer, that he had worn away that part of his self that would have allowed him to feel.

Gerard continued to look down at Rosalind. She looked small and fragile, but more than that. She was crumpling, like wrapping paper torn from a present, crushed into a ball, ready to be thrown away. It seemed that before his very eyes, like the trick of a malign magician, she was receding into nothingness.

Gerard thought, *This was a woman I have laughed and cried with. This was a woman I desired. A woman I have undressed, a woman I have kissed every inch of. A woman whose naked skin I have stroked and caressed and pressed. A woman whose body I have held tight against mine. I have held her hand. I have sat in silence next to her. How can this be the same person? How can I? We can't be, that's how.*

Behind him, the door opened.

"Mark," said Rosalind without looking up. Gerard turned around. He had never met Mark but recognised him immediately. Behind Mark stood a nurse, leaning into the room, confused, saying uncertainly, "Mr Jones?" into the room, to Rosalind, Gerard, to Mark himself, or to no one.

Mark went straight to the bedside and fell to his knees. He reached beneath the sheet and took hold of Jack's hand. He pressed his face to Jack's hand and wept.

"Do you remember when he was born?" Rosalind said. Her voice was far away. She was speaking from within a void. "Afterwards, I was wheeled into a room. It was like this. Just the one bed. I held Jack and whispered to him. You're mine, I said. You came in and leaned over us. You took him from me, smiled, and then gave him back to me. I have never known tiredness or happiness like it. We sat there. You in a chair and me in the bed with Jack. At one point, you looked at your watch. Just casual, nothing to it. Habit. I remember thinking, why are you looking at your watch? Time has stopped. There is nothing but this moment forever. Throw away all the clocks and watches." She sighed, drained. "I don't want time. I don't want now. I don't want 'do you remembers?'"

Rosalind still and dying. Jack's dead hand against Mark's cheek, face and hand soaked with silent tears that would never stop.

"Jack changed it, you know," she said. "Changed everything. Mark was at the birth, of course." She spoke now as if he wasn't there, as if no one else was there, maybe not even Jack. "I wanted him there, needed him to help me through it, or thought I did, at any rate. I still loved him at this point. But as I went into labour, I found I needed him less than I imagined. This was when I still loved him, long before I properly stopped loving him, although it might have been the first step away. Mark stayed for a while and then had to leave. He didn't want to, but he had to. It's funny, one of the other mothers, the next day, she said to me she felt lonely, left there just her and the baby. Felt it wasn't fair. I didn't know what she was talking about. I wanted Mark to go. And I didn't feel tired. Everyone else said they felt exhausted, like they could sleep for a week. I sat next to Jack's cot and watched him. Wrapped so tightly, just his tiny face. Nothing mattered after that. I didn't really understand. But I know now. Nothing mattered after that."

Gerard said, "I..." but didn't say anything more. He left the room, and no one noticed.

Gerard took a different route home, all along the M56 until it took him into Manchester. He wanted to avoid the statue of the woman's head at the side of the road. But he also wanted to cross a bridge. The road took him over the Runcorn Bridge, and that was what he wanted. It felt right to do so. He would never go back; neither did he ever leave.

It was mid-afternoon by the time he got home. He was restless, reluctant to go into the flat. There were too many hours left in the day stretching ahead of him, waiting to be filled. But he didn't know what to do otherwise. So he left in his car in his usual parking space and walked to the entrance of his block.

Self-consciousness suddenly took hold of him. It wasn't paranoia, wasn't some manifestation of mental illness. It was the natural consequence of so many years of deliberate and painstaking self-manufacture. He couldn't simply walk to the door, not without some awareness of how he looked, how he moved. It was like he was an actor following direction, the eyes of everyone in the audience on him. Except they weren't. Of course they weren't, and Gerard knew they weren't. And yet he still thought they were.

Inside his flat, he hung up his coat. He tossed the paper on the hall table and sat down on the hall chair.

"This is the chair we saw at the museum," Gerard said aloud. "The one designed by Ernest Race. From aluminium taken from wartime aircraft. The upholstery is RAF material, too."

He sighed. He rested his elbows on his knees, bent over, put his face in his hands. Every move was contrived. He cursed every gesture and expression as fake, learned from scenes he'd seen in films. This is how a man in your situation behaves. These are his movements, his sounds, his thoughts, his actions.

He went to the living room. It was too light yet to close the curtains, but he went to close them anyway and then stopped himself, the search for darkness yet another contrived response. Gerard looked around the room. He saw each item of furniture, remembered how he had researched them, sourced them, how he placed them, the designers' names, the prices he paid. He went to the CD player and scanned the rows of CDs he had arranged in categories and then in alphabetical order according to artist. Jazz, classical, and then modern classical — a category he wasn't sure existed, but he'd called it that anyway. From this, he chose the same CD he'd played the day before yesterday.

He loaded the CD, pressed play, and waited. He watched the timer rise, but there was no sound. And then there was. A single piano chord, soft, tender, lingering, but clashing notes. Then more silence, followed by another chord and then a single note. Stillness settled on the room. Gerard felt he couldn't move, gripped and unnerved, anticipating the warm discords, the patternless pattern.

He listened intently, really, not an act, nothing contrived, no attempt to impress. He heard anonymity. Patternless. Remorseless. Unforgiving but gentle. Insistent but tender. Dissonance. Isolation. Disconnection.

Outside, December dusk had taken over, and lights were shining in the houses below. The green of the fairway grass on the golf course nearby was turning blue-grey, close to the colour of the Mersey, which was snaking past, narrow, unrecognisable from the river which opened out into Liverpool Bay.

He remembered a woman he had once hoped would become his girlfriend, maybe something more. They'd been out on a couple of dates. Dinner, the cinema. Nothing more, nothing further. The last time they met, it was for coffee in the city centre. The café was next door to a commercial gallery, and Gerard suggested they go in. He was genuinely interested but also knew — though he didn't quite admit it to himself — that he was hoping she'd be impressed by his sensitivity and appreciation.

She admired a sculpture — small, abstract, smooth, cool to the touch — and Gerard consequently admired it too. He checked the price, knew he could afford it, and said he might buy it.

To which she said, "There's no need to always have a beautiful thing. Just knowing it exists is enough."

Gerard agreed because he always agreed and knew that this would never develop into a relationship, though he didn't quite admit it to himself there and then, and it took three unanswered texts before he did.

He had arranged his furniture and books and papers and pens and time exactly the way he wanted them, exactly the way that suited him. There were times in the past when he would have compromised, when he would have met someone halfway. More than halfway. But not now. Now he was alone. Despite his best efforts, because of his best efforts, because of who he was, relationships simply hadn't worked out. He accepted that. Love, companionship, family, children, togetherness, all the joys, sadness, moments, opportunities, laughter, and tears, they were not within reach. He could only see others have them.

And that was fine. That was acceptable. Not ideal, but bearable. Not what he thought he'd get, but tolerable, sustainable. But he wondered sometimes. Was it sustainable? Had he lied? To himself? *Yes, and yes.* He had told himself, *This just isn't for me.* When what he should have told himself was, *You have blown your chances. You could have had what others have, but you threw it away.* A character flaw, an inability to be honest, to say, *No, I don't like this, I won't stand for this.* And women saw that weakness, sensed it, despised it, and moved on.

He had never ended a relationship. Each relationship was ended by the woman.

Gerard realised he had been holding his breath. He exhaled and walked through his flat as the CD played, the apparently random notes reaching him wherever he went, surprising him, catching him unawares always, leaving him tense and waiting for the next.

He could understand the music now – its random nature, its soft, kissing clashes, the absence of time – and the understanding reminded him why

he'd bought the CD in the first place: because he thought it would add to

the image he had created for himself, the knowledgeable sophisticate, the man who knew more and understood more. The music told him the truth, confronted him with his artifice. It revealed to him also what lay behind the stage scenery he had constructed instead of a life. What was it Rosalind said? A Potemkin village. As a character in a horror film slowly draws back a curtain, so he looksed beyond the surface to see emptiness, a void, a life wasted, anonymity. Each chord reminded him until he said out loud: "I have no seven legends, no story. I recognise this tension. I now see the anonymity. The sudden, lingering emptiness. I am this."

Chapter Thirty

Then

Jack was a bright boy. He was perceptive, caught on fast. He had emotional intelligence and was quick to grasp situations, moods. He didn't say much necessarily, not about the deep things, the things that matter, but he gathered evidence where he found it, stored it away in the relevant file, and while he didn't use it against anyone, it left him able to build a worldview.

It expanded, of course, as he grew older, right up to the point where he was stabbed and in those couple of days where he lay in hospital dying. That unprovoked, brutal attack was the final piece in his jigsaw. But when he was a boy, this worldview was pretty much confined to his home, his mum and dad, his school, his teachers, his friends.

He knew there was a distance between his parents. He knew that his parents weren't like his friends' parents. He would go to friends' houses and see their mums and dads, see the way they interacted, the way they talked and treated each other, the way they treated their children. It wasn't that his friends came from perfect families. He could tell there were arguments and disagreements, maybe even angry rows. But there was heat. That was the point.

There was no heat in his mum and dad's relationship. There was cordiality, politeness, good manners. There was distance.

There was no laughter, just smiles that didn't really reach the eyes unless it was to signify some loose sense of regret and wrong turning. That changed when his father's business went belly up. Then, there was acrimony, blame, and shame. But when he was eight, there was a mantle of geniality.

Christmas morning followed a set routine. Although Jack went to quite a traditional C of E school that started each day with prayers and hymns and held a carol service every December, they weren't a family of churchgoers, so there was no service to go to first thing. Jack would get up early, of course, to see what was in his stocking. There was no need to wake his parents because his mum was always ready and dressed when Jack showed his face. She'd have the radio on in the kitchen with carols and Christmas songs and messages to loved ones far away and dedications for those at work on Christmas Day.

She would make Jack breakfast and then start giving him his presents before his dad emerged from his lie-in, which was never that long, still in his pyjamas and dressing gown, just as Jack was. His dad would get a cup of coffee and then join the exchange of gifts, catching up on what he'd missed. Jack was always keen to show him what he'd got and make his dad promise to help him build it or paint it or play with it later, and his dad would always readily agree.

His mum would buy his dad one present, and his dad would buy his mum one present. On this occasion, when Jack was eight, his mum bought his dad a jumper with an argyle pattern. His dad gave his mum a matching scarf and gloves. They both said their gifts were lovely, thanked each other, and said they would try them on later or wear them next time they went out. Then Jack's dad produced another present, a small gift, beautifully wrapped.

"I didn't wrap it," his dad said. "I got the shop to do it."

His mum looked nervous as she opened it, a bit taken aback by a second gift.

"I've only got you the one," she said.

"That's fine," his dad said. "I love it. Go on, open it."

Jack's mum peeled away the paper carefully, revealing a box, a rich green with a velvet coating. Jack watched her open the box and saw her face change, a mixture of delight, sadness, surprise, happiness.

"They're beautiful," she said. Her voice was soft. She meant what she said. "Look, Jack." She showed him what was inside, and Jack saw a pair of delicate gold earrings.

"Try them on," Jack said.

"I will," she said. She spoke softly, with wonder, still staring at the earrings in the box, fingertips scared to touch them.

"Merry Christmas, Lindy," said Jack's dad.

And that's when they kissed. Jack's dad stepped towards his mum, put his arms around her and gave her a long, passionate kiss on the lips. At first, his mum struggled with the surprise, struggled to keep hold of the box. Then she took the box securely in one hand, put her arms around his dad's back and kissed him just as passionately.

Later, Jack and his mum were in the kitchen. The radio was still on, still playing carols and Christmas songs and messages to loved ones far away and dedications for those at work on Christmas Day. Jack was examining the pieces of a kit he'd been given.

"You're not going to make that now, are you?" his mum said. "Dinner won't be long."

"No, Mum," Jack said.

His dad came in, having just showered and dressed. He was wearing his new jumper.

"Ooh," he said when he saw what Jack was doing. "Are we going to make that later?" Jack looked up and grinned at his dad, who was now going over to his mum, who was looking carefully into a pan. "Anything I can do?" his dad asked, placing his hands on her shoulders, gently turning her around.

"Careful," his mum said, wriggling free. "This is boiling."

Jack's dad said sorry and went and sat next to Jack. He picked up the box Jack's kit had come in.

"You not wearing those earrings?" he said to Rosalind.

She didn't look over. She just said, "Jeff will be here soon."

Jack's dad stared at the lid of the box without quite seeing the Spitfire painted on it, but the memory was clear in his mind of making a kit just like this when he was Jack's age.

"Dad," Jack said, but his dad, right next to him, didn't hear him.

"Will you lay the table, please, Jack?" his mum said.

"Dad," Jack repeated, and this time, his dad heard Jack and returned to the present.

"Yes, son," his dad said.

"Let's paint it in desert camouflage," Jack said.

His dad nodded. "Nice idea."

"Jack," his mum's voice sterner now. "Table."

"Yes, mum," Jack said. He got up and did as his mum asked.

About the author

Born and raised in Liverpool, Dominic Kearney graduated from the University of Newcastle-upon-Tyne with a degree in English Literature, after which he worked as a staff reporter for the Hexham Courant.

He taught English for twenty-five years, working in a variety of secondary schools and pupil referral units in Manchester. In 2012, he left teaching and moved to Ireland. He works as a freelance writer and journalist, most notably for the Irish News, but also for the Irish Times, Culture NI, The Modernist, and Apollo Magazine. He has appeared on a number of occasions on BBC Radio Ulster and BBC Radio Foyle, reviewing exhibitions and concerts and commentating on current events. He has featured on BBC Radio 4's Listening Project and contributed to The Five-Foot Shelf, also on Radio 4.

He has written a guidebook to Ulster, Ireland's Beautiful North, published by the O'Brien Press. I have had short stories featured in The Honest Ulsterman and on BBC Radio Foyle. He has written short stories for the Education Authority Northern Ireland for use in schools, and his play, The Voyage of the Fellowship, has been performed by three primary schools at the Playhouse Theatre in Derry. His first novel is a press procedural crime thriller, Cast-Iron Men.

He lives in Derry with my wife, daughter, and disabled brother.

X: @KearneyDominic
Bluesky: @djkearney.bsky.social
Facebook: Dominic Kearney
Instagram: kearney49280

Past Titles

Cast-Iron Men
Ireland's Beautiful North

www.ingramcontent.com/pod-product-compliance
Ingram Content Group UK Ltd.
Pitfield, Milton Keynes, MK11 3LW, UK
UKHW022101040925
462599UK00004B/29